EPHESUS
PURE IN HEART

MICHAEL PAWLOWSKI

Order this book online at www.trafford.com
or email orders@trafford.com

Most Trafford titles are also available at major online book retailers.

© Copyright 2016 Michael Pawlowski.

All rights reserved. No part of this publication may be reproduced, stored in a retrieval system, or transmitted, in any form or by any means, electronic, mechanical, photocopying, recording, or otherwise, without the written prior permission of the author.

Print information available on the last page.

ISBN: 978-1-4907-7300-1 (sc)
ISBN: 978-1-4907-7302-5 (hc)
ISBN: 978-1-4907-7301-8 (e)

Library of Congress Control Number: 2016907056

Because of the dynamic nature of the Internet, any web addresses or links contained in this book may have changed since publication and may no longer be valid. The views expressed in this work are solely those of the author and do not necessarily reflect the views of the publisher, and the publisher hereby disclaims any responsibility for them.

Any people depicted in stock imagery provided by Thinkstock are models, and such images are being used for illustrative purposes only.
Certain stock imagery © Thinkstock.

Trafford rev. 04/28/2016

Trafford www.trafford.com
North America & international
toll-free: 1 888 232 4444 (USA & Canada)
fax: 812 355 4082

CONTENTS

Cast of Characters ix
Chronology xiii

Chapter One	The Voyage 1
Chapter Two	Marketplace, Ephesus 11
Chapter Three	Prytaneion Reality 23
Chapter Four	At Home on Bulbul Mountain 31
Chapter Five	Harbour Baths 40
Chapter Six	Sun Rise at the Harbour 46
Chapter Seven	Stadium Plot 51
Chapter Eight	Heaven in the Valley 53
Chapter Nine	Tartarus 62
Chapter Ten	Playing the Artemis Card 65
Chapter Eleven	Counting Coins 68
Chapter Twelve	Fermentation 72
Chapter Thirteen	Peripatetic Roman 78
Chapter Fourteen	Deputy Consuls in Conflict 82
Chapter Fifteen	Desperate Plea 84
Chapter Sixteen	Harbour Farewell 89
Chapter Seventeen	Joy and Trepidation 91
Chapter Eighteen	Confrontation 95
Chapter Nineteen	Non Intelligo 99
Chapter Twenty	News from Distant Shores 101
Chapter Twenty-One	Why is this Night So Special? 103
Chapter Twenty-Two	Ecclesia Asia Minor 105
Chapter Twenty-Three	The Wanderer Finds a Home 110
Chapter Twenty-Four	Pillar of Philadelphos 114
Chapter Twenty-Five	Luke in Troas 117
Chapter Twenty-Six	Temple Turmoil 120
Chapter Twenty-Seven	Saturnalia Festival 123
Chapter Twenty-Eight	Preparing the Foundation 127
Chapter Twenty-Nine	Between Heaven and Hell 133

Chapter Thirty	Paul vs Artemis	137
Chapter Thirty-One	Presence Demanded	140
Chapter Thirty-Two	Blessed are the Merciful	143
Chapter Thirty-Three	Tyranny of Uncertainty	147
Chapter Thirty-Four	Not a Fond Farewell	150
Chapter Thirty-Five	Eternal Rest	157
Chapter Thirty-Six	Reaction and Apprehension	161
Chapter Thirty-Seven	Fate and Determination	163
Chapter Thirty-Eight	Journey to the Interior	167
Chapter Thirty-Nine	Search for a New Home	170
Chapter Forty	Not Just an Inquisition	173
Chapter Forty-One	Searching for Sense	180
Chapter Forty-Two	From Troas to Jerusalem	183
Chapter Forty-Three	Pen to Papyrus	186
Chapter Forty-Four	Be Not Afraid	188
Chapter Forty-Five	Journey to Rome	192
Chapter Forty-Six	Condicio Apis	195
Chapter Forty-Seven	Burning of Rome	201
Chapter Forty-Eight	Flames of Persecution	206
Chapter Forty-Nine	Final Farewell	214
Chapter Fifty	Bishop Timothy	220

Sources ... 227

Special Gratitude

to

Reverend Ralph Villella S.S.C.

for his encouragement

and to

Rt. Reverend Lawrence Sabatini

for valuable information

from his studies at

the Vatican

"Ephesus Pure in Heart" is the fact based account of the evangelical efforts of John and Miriam in Ephesus and Anatolia. With Maryam, the Mother of Christ, they fled Antioch of Syria in 46AD.

That decision followed years of hardship, oppression and tyranny. King Agrippa was determined to eradicate Christ's memory in all of Judaea and Palestine. He beheaded John's brother, James, in Jerusalem. Then he cast his net of oppression into Syria. In the midst of the tyranny the entire region was suffering recurring droughts and famines making it almost impossible to remain in the area. Later Luke joined them in Ephesus; and from there he extended his project of evangelization into northern Anatolia.

Meanwhile Peter was visiting other communities in Anatolia; while Paul was completing his apostolic missions. At the same time: Timothy was in Corinth, Mark in Alexandria, Jude and Simon in Armenia, and Thomas in India.

In spite of grave resistance, significant progress was achieved in numbers and commitment, and in social programs and religious practice. The Risen Christ, forgiveness and Redemption, and the influence of the Holy Spirit were the focus of their preaching. Meanwhile all of their efforts were constantly being challenged by the lecherous Emperor Claudius, the treacherous Emperor Nero, and the murderous Deputy Consul Celer. Christians were also erroneously accused of granary theft and the murder of the Pro Consul. Roman and Greek polytheistic beliefs had been ingrained for more than seven centuries. They would not radically change. Idolatry was everywhere. Morality was an abhorrent standard. Orphans, widows and the infirm were treated worse than third class citizens. Although thwarted on so many occasions the Christians persevered. The positive impact of example steered many into their communities. Becoming the Corporal Works of Mercy in action assured their success. Ultimately Ephesus became one of the most important centers for further expansion in the early Ecclesia.

Their story of teamwork is memorable; and their commitment, in the face of persecution and even death, remains truly inspiring.

CAST OF CHARACTERS

<u>Christian</u>

Maryam	Blessed Virgin Mary
John	Apostle
Miriam	Disciple
Paul	Disciple from Tarsus, Missionary
Luke	Disciple from Antioch, Evangelist, Missionary
Timothy	Disciple from Tarsus, Missionary
Mark	Apostle, Missionary, Evangelist
Anna	Blind girl
Bernardus	Deacon, Convert to Christianity from Roman culture
Aquila	Convert and disciple
Alexa	Spouse of Philemon, Christian convert from Roman culture
Apollos	Convert to Christianity from Jewish Faith in Alexandria
Chiara	Care provider for Orphans
Clement	Farmer
Cybil	Convert to Christianity from Greek culture

Donaldus	Convert to Christianity from Roman culture
Elena	Care Provider, Christian convert from Greek culture
Erastus	Convert and disciple
Luxor	Emissary, Convert to Christianity from Greek culture
Naomi	Convert to Christianity from Jewish faith
Oscirus	Farmer, Convert to Christianity from Roman culture
Philemon	Merchant, Convert to Christianity from Greek culture
Phoenicia	Young Prostitute, later convert
Priscilla	Convert and disciple
Rebecca	Care Provider, Convert to Christianity Jewish faith
Rosea	Convert to Christianity from Roman culture
Sentillus	Contractor, Convert to Christianity from Roman culture
Simon	Emissary, Convert to Christianity from Jewish faith
Susannah	Friend of Miriam

<u>Greek</u>

Aretius	Merchant
Gaius	Merchant
Hemiah	Merchant
Agnete	Servant

<u>Jewish</u>

Sceva	High Priest of Ephesus
Ananias	High Priest of Jerusalem
Gamaliel	Hebrew Philosopher and Teacher
Alexander	Resident of Ephesus
Eitan	Resident of Ephesus
Herod Agrippa	King of Judaea 41 – 44
Cupius Fadus	Procurator of Province of Judaea 44 – 46
Alexander	Procurator of Province of Judaea 46 – 48
Cumanus	Procurator of Province of Judaea 48 - 52

Felix	Procurator of Province of Judaea 52 - 58
Festus	Procurator of Province of Judaea 59 – 62

Roman
Caligula	Emperor 37 – 41
Claudius	Emperor 41 – 54
Nero	Emperor 54 – 68
Agrippina the Younger	Wife of Claudius, Sister of Caligula, Mother of Nero
Seneca	Rome Patrician, Advisor to Nero
Burrus the Senior	Nero's tutor
Marcus Silanus	Pro Consul 47 – 54
Lucis Junius Torquatus	Son of Marcus Silanus
Junia Lepida	Sister-in-Law of Marcus Silanus
Publius Celer	Deputy Consul
Hypatius	Deputy Consul
Antonius	Deputy Consul
Lysias	Roman Legionnaire
Burrus	Roman Legionnaire
Darius	Roman Legionnaire
Muscipula	Jailer, Legionnaire
Helius	Freed Slave, Legionnaire
Gaius Piso	Roman General

Fictional characters include:

Agnete	*Anna*	*Aretius*	*Chiara*	*Clement*
Cybil	*Elena*	*Gaius*	*Hemiah*	*Luxor*
Muscipula	*Naomi*	*Phoenicia*	*Rosea*	*Simon*

CHRONOLOGY

198BC	Syrian occupation of Judaea. Some Jews exiled to Asia.
144BC	Judaean alliance with Rome
138BC	Macabees defeat Syrians. Kingdom of Israel established
129BC	Asia (western Anatolia) becomes Roman Province
89-63BC	Mithridiatic Wars for control of northern Anatolia
70BC	Pharisees become influential members of Sanhedrin
64BC	Cilicia (southern Anatolia) becomes Roman Province
64BC	Syria becomes Roman Province
63BC	Pompey conquers Israel
44BC	Julius Caesar assassinated
37BC	Herod appointed King of the Jews by Pompey
30BC	Egypt becomes a Roman province
27BC	Augustus becomes emperor
27BC	Joseph born about this time
25BC	Galatia becomes Roman Province
23BC	Mary born about this time
20BC	Construction of temple in Jerusalem starts
7BC	Christ's birth

4BC	Herod I dies
4BC	Herod Archelaus rules Judaea to 6AD
1BC	Peter born
0	Hebrew Year #3760
4	John the Evangelist born about this time
6	Mary Magdalene born about this time
6	Romans murder 2,000 Hebrews near Nazareth
8	Saul born in Tarsus, Cilicia about this time
9	August appoints Tiberius as Consul
9	Ambibulus is Procurator of Judaea to 12AD
14	Augustus dies. Tiberius becomes emperor
14	Marcus Silanus born
15	Valerius Gratas is Procurator of Judaea to 26AD
17	Cappadocia becomes Roman Province
23	John the Baptist starts preaching about this time
24	Jesus begins public life about this time
25	Mary Magdalene meets and begins to follow Jesus
26	Pilate is Procurator of Judaea to 36AD
27	Crucifixion & Resurrection
33	St. Stephen stoned to death
35	Saul's conversion on road to Damascus
37	Caligula becomes emperor
37	Herod Agrippa rules Judaea as Governor
38	Anti-Hebrew sentiment in Alexandria
39	Peter and John teach in Samaria
39	Caligula's statue in Jerusalem's temple
40	Caligula's edict against Jews in Asia Minor
40	Church established in Alexandria
40	Church established in Corinth
41	Caligula is murdered. Claudius becomes emperor
41	Herod Agrippa appointed King of Judaea by Claudius
41	Famine starts in Judaea

41	Herod commences tyranny against Christians in Palestine
41	Church established in Antioch
41	Church established in Damascus
42	Conversion of St. Paul
43	James beheaded in Jerusalem
43	John, Mary and Magdalene escape Jerusalem and go to northern Palestine
43	John, Mary and Magdalene meet Luke in Antioch
44	Herod Agrippa dies
44	Famine starts in Egypt
46	Failure of corn harvest in Syria
46	John, Mary and Magdalene journey to Ephesus
46	Paul and Barnabas start first missionary journey
47	Blessed Virgin Mary's Assumption about this time
47	Marcus Silanus Torquatus becomes Pro Consul of Asia Minor
48	Church in Antioch Syria established about this time
49	Jews expelled from Rome due to disturbances caused by Chrestus
49	Claudius' edict against Jews in Asia Minor
49	Paul and Silas start second missionary journey
49	Paul meets Timothy in Tarsus
49	Seneca and Burrus become Nero's tutors
50	Luke is in Ephesus with John and Magdalene
50	Claudius marries his niece, Agrippina
50	Ephesus granted privilege of issuing coins
50	Council of Jerusalem
50	Matthew in Antioch writes his gospel about this time
50	Veneration of Mithras spreads in Roman world
51	Famine starts in Asia Minor
52	Felix is Procurator of Jerusalem to 59AD

52	Paul and Silas take Timothy with them to Macedonia
52	Thomas lands in India
53	Paul starts third missionary journey
53	Paul arrives in Ephesus
53	Paul in Ephesus writes Epistle to Galatians
54	Nero becomes Emperor at age 17
54	Pro Consul Silanus murdered
55	Paul leaves Ephesus after 2 years and 3 months
56	Paul meets Luke in Troas (northern Aegean)
57	Peter leaves Corinth for Rome about this time
58	Paul arrested in Jerusalem
58	Paul, Luke and Aristarchus begin fourth missionary journey
59	Paul and Timothy in Corinth
59	In September, Paul and Luke begin journey to Rome
60	In March, Paul and Luke arrive in Rome
60	Peter considered as the First Pope about this time
60	Mark writes his gospel in Rome about this time
64	Last date in Acts of the Apostles about this time
64	Great Fire in Rome
64	Nero's persecution of Christians starts
64	Suspicion of treason automatically means death
64	John exiled to Patmos
64	Timothy visits Rome to see Paul in jail
64	Peter crucified (October)
65	Paul appoints Timothy as Bishop of Ephesus
65	Paul beheaded
65	Jude Thaddeus martyred in Armenia
65	Simon martyred in Armenia
66	Jews revolt in Jerusalem
66	Christians flee Jerusalem for Pella
68	Nero's Domus Aurea completed

68	Linus selected Pope
68	Nero commits suicide
70	John writes his Gospel about this time
70	Roman conquer Palestine
73	Hebrews defeated at Massada
75	Luke writes his gospel
80	John writes his 1st Epistle
80	Acts of the Apostles completed about this time
90	John completes writing of Revelations
97	Timothy murdered
100	John dies about this time

Chapter One

The Voyage

October, 49

Ceres could not prevent the famine. Once started, it recognized no borders. Even Roman deities had to bend their marble presence to the inevitability of drought. Across the African continent north winds had blown incessantly. Normal seasons became an unrelenting bluster forcing arid temperatures and driving sand storms over fertile lands. Winds from the west across the Mediterranean Sea propelled top soil inland away from the coast, disrupting productive growing seasons. From the north, the Estesian Winds howled crossing the Black Sea ascending the Anatolian Hills and then cascading onto the crumbling soils of Palestine.

Alexandria, in the first year of Caligula's reign, was the initial region to suffer the shortage of grain. From Egypt the drought marched west like Roman Legions ready for the kill. Carthage in 39AD was the next to suffer. Regarding events in Egypt or Palestine, Caligula generally gave no thought. As long as there were no riots, and the conquered masses adored his statues, the Emperor cared little about the territories. However, when famine in the provinces interfered with the city of Rome's daily consumption of grain, action became necessary. In 40AD edicts against the Jews were decreed throughout Egypt and Asia Minor. Who else could Rome blame for the drought?

However edicts did not stop the famine. Symbolic offerings to Roman gods did not end the droughts. The festivals of Cerelia in April and Ambarvalia in May to Ceres and to their many deities for agriculture and harvest proved to be inadequate. Eventually the droughts did abate causing the Emperor and his Senators to praise themselves for their sacrifices to their marble statues and for appropriately blaming the Jews for the travesty.

Then just as suddenly, a couple of years of plenty became ominous famine. Egypt was cursed with the drought once more in 44AD. Then, two years later all of Syria became famine's victim. Noting the prior benefit of blaming the Jews, Claudius repeated his decree focusing it on the city of Rome itself, expelling Jews from the Eternal City. However blaming the Hebrews did not stop the arid conditions. From Palestine and Syria the drought spread north towards Cilicia, only to be stopped by the granite of the Anatolian Hills.

It was that edict by Emperor Claudius in early 49AD that created a situation later emperors were required to address, not by logic or analysis, but by blood and martyrdom. Claudius centered on the Jewish communities as he was expected to do, but in declaring his reason the Emperor referred to the riots and unrest caused by "Chrestus." Suddenly the influence of Christ was recognized by Rome, and His followers in Antioch became known as Christians.

John grabbed the cross beam, holding firm the timber that secured the massive linen mast in place. He knew too well that the latter days of Tishrei, weeks after Rosh Hashanah, were not suitable to tempt fate on the Sea of the Philistines. Many, in that Roman era, called it 'Mare Nostrum', a name too passive for salt water that could in an instant swallow a man's last gasp.

This was his third such trip. So much had happened in Palestine to compel the most resolute disciples to flee. After Stephen was stoned to death, many of Christ's followers immediately left Jerusalem for safety: north to Antioch in Syria, to Phoenicia, to the island of Cyprus, or to the Greek colony of Cyrene in North Africa. There they became active sharing the Saviour's Message of Good News among the Jews and the Gentiles. It was at that time that John accompanied the Lord's Mother and the disciple Miriam to Ephesus. The Roman Province of Asia was known for its tolerance and commerce. That city could provide the security and opportunity they desired.

The first visit was brief before John returned to Jerusalem to be with the disciples. The prospects and progress of evangelization, which at times seemed so positive, radically became a series of horrendous events. James, John's brother, was beheaded. Peter was then imprisoned, although he mysteriously walked out of prison. Herod, who had received his mandate from the Emperor, focussed his tyranny on the followers of Christ. Many fled north to Syria. After Herod transitioned his palace to Caesarea, tyranny became widespread in the regions of Sidon and Tyre. It was those events that forced even more followers of Christ to flee from Palestine. On cargo ships they sailed to Greek communities on the Aegean Sea.

Many joined the bearded man boarding the vessel at Tyre. He never recorded names as such was the captain's duty. John was well aware of designated chores having had to listen endlessly to his brother while they earned a meager living on the Sea of Galilee. Memories were a continuous recollection of the trying times and successful catches, but especially of that day when this preacher told them where to cast their nets. He reflected often on the apparent insanity of that suggestion with a smile, recalling how they had worked many nights and early mornings casting nets, trolling with the prevailing breeze, and then swearing at the catch that avoided their nets. It was this same time of the year that they first met Christ, a month when the incessant winds churned the waves driving schools of fish into deep waters away from the shore. In that respect, the catch was even more miraculous.

John and so many others had for more than a year before that followed another preacher: the Baptist at the River Jordan. The son of Zebedee was during that time amazed at how contrite the residents of Judaea had been in spite of the promising verse that added direction to their lives. Recollections of the irate Pharisees and indignant Scribes tainted those memories. How could people listening to the same message have been so divided?

Then Christ entered their lives with His invitation, "Follow Me." The lame walked, the blind regained their sight, and devils fled.

This man was not the Baptist. His words were calm, inspiring, and promising a dream far beyond the tribulations of this world. Yet at the same time, the message was forceful. The preacher did not patiently suggest. They knew enough of the Aramaic and Hebrew languages to know the difference between the forceful indicative and the passive subjunctive. Yes, he challenged their customs. However, to hear him speak, there was never intent to destroy the past, but to use it as a foundation to build. How could so many be so deaf to the full message of hope?

The captain called to the disciple as the vessel steered north of Sidon. Purposefully the vessel, laden with silks and spice in the hold, hugged the coast. Tides would naturally push the vessel farther north. That route was less prone to sudden massive waves. Without oars and relying only on two masts; the knowledge of tides, currents and winds was essential. Fog in autumn was always a significant factor as high pressure dipped south across the Aegean and Adriatic Seas into the basin from which there was no escape.

John's firm response in Greek shocked the captain, "I'll remain." It would have obviously been preferable to be safe on the deckhouse. However, staying with the men who relied on his leadership was absolutely essential. John accepted the risk to remain on the main deck, and so directed several women to the back of the boat where they could either be secure with adequate railings or be seated upon the stairs. Remnants of a tattered mast covered several of them, especially those women with children, providing shelter from the spray of incessant waves. Belongings were not a luxury for most as they had had to sell nearly everything in Tyre just to eat. They had no other bedding or clothing. Huddled together, pressed against each other, they found some warmth but never enough to dispel the chill on board.

During the many gusts of wind John praised himself for being there, seizing the opportunity for service as the Master had demanded. The disciple was totally committed to that creed: that nothing was to be gained without carrying the burden of others. The famine for two years had been the last straw for nearly everyone in Judaea. Many suffered prolonged agonizing death due to starvation. In some cases, the elderly just walked away into the desert never to be seen again. For the young, education became non-existent as the needs of children were insignificant compared to the necessity of exploring every possible venture to procure food. Those, whom the Romans blamed, were exposed to brutal crucifixion. Others were just slaughtered by sudden rampages of delirious soldiers convinced they would suffer the same fate if they did not enact the imperial decrees. Even though the Roman edicts had been against the Jews, by the time the decrees got to Palestine everyone became susceptible to the infamy of Roman justice. John had seen enough: the Baptist's murder, his Saviour's crucifixion, the stoning of Stephen, the beheading of his brother, citizens being jailed or scourged, and devout followers being blamed for the drought. He was leading them away from starvation and brutality.

Overland through northern Syria and Cilicia was not an option. John and so many others dreaded the prospect of even stepping foot in that land once ruled by the Hittites and dominated by the Assyrians. Bloodshed, beheadings, and daily carnage – any person in Palestine was well aware of that history and the tragic tales of misery and annihilation.

The commercial vessel had two sails: the large square sail across the width of the boat, and the smaller sail at the front of the vessel. Unlike the ships built for troops and war, there were no oars. However, this one had peculiar openings for four rowers to ply their skills in the event the winds died down; but that was not going to happen in October along the western coast of the Mediterranean Sea. This cargo vessel had no rowers, just two masts.

Even in the wind, as the shipped tossed to and from, John could hear the eerie roll of the earthen jugs in the cargo space. When filled with spice, grain or wine, they had to be upright and absolutely immobile. Storing goods properly on board was essential to prevent sudden tipping. He could have said something, but disagreeing with a Greek Captain in a Roman vessel might mean his hasty demise. John knew he couldn't swim that far.

Fears on board were considerable as the sun dipped into the horizon. Silent hopes became fervent prayers. For some this was their first voyage; others were frightened by the threats of strange imaginings. Leaving harbour late in the afternoon forced them to sail past Cyprus during the night. Concerning that portion of the voyage, John was less than enthusiastic. The long high-rolling waves were more severe to the west of the island. Meanwhile the counter-clockwise current propelled the vessel north toward the junction of Syria and

Cilicia and then west along the coasts of Pamphylia and Lycia towards Rhodes. However that could be tempered by winds off the mountains pushing the vessel south toward the island. There were no lights, and the rocky coast was an endless peril. Rains had not yet fallen although the light fog suggested they were inevitable. Although the rainy season was not due for another month, no one was about to instruct any god as to when it should start.

Then at night, there was another hazard, an ominous one for which there was no defense. Pirates continued to patrol, and at times controlled that region of the Mare Nostrum. Piracy had been prevalent for centuries. Augustus had stopped their domination, but did not destroy the threat. From concealed ports on the Adriatic and defended venues in the Aegean, with vessels built in Dalmatia, and storage houses in Cilicia, piracy was a threat not only to ships and cargo, but also to the many refugees fleeing tumult and tyranny.

Crouching and moving slowly to the front of the vessel, John sat with several who found limited shelter behind the linen fore-sail. The comments and questions were as many as their fears. Hope is only as good as it is accepted. Tyre and the region presented perils, but so did that voyage. "Two days", they had been promised; but John knew it would take more than three.

The disciple tried again to ascertain the number on board hoping the vessel was not imperiled by overcrowding. However, the number of passengers on any commercial craft was always dependent on the captain's propensity for greed. There were obviously more than he expected. The hold was intended exclusively for cargo; but events and demands in recent years had compelled modifications to some vessels to accommodate more passengers. When goods were not available to be transported, fee-paying immigrants became a lucrative commerce.

Ephesus was their destination. So much had been said about the city. "Are there really more than two hundred thousand people there?" One of the passengers asked the disciple. Others questioned food and jobs. No one queried about religious practice. Putting food on a table under a roof: that was the common dream. John could only offer what he had heard. Paul would surely have returned to Antioch if everything was not well in Anatolia. This was an age when no news could be golden.

The number of city states on the Aegean provided significant alternatives if the harbour at Ephesus could not accommodate the craft. The captain remained aware of their intent, but he was the captain and ultimately the choice in a Roman vessel on Roman seas was his.

As the sun set, John led the group in a series of prayers he had composed and recited by memory thanking God for the blessings of the day and ending with a petition to see the morning sun. When fears and perils tainted their dreams; destiny, even with all of its uncertainty, glowed above the shadows of Palestine.

****

Between the pillars carved into the face of the cliff, the hag stretched forth her arm through the fog, into the black of night. Toward the vast expanse beyond the Andriake Harbour her finger pierced the realm of Poseidon's Kingdom. Her robes swung wide with each step as she continued toward the precipice, being deliberate in the persuasive manner attributed to her being. This was her realm when all creation bent to the will of the daughter of Erebus.

Like the Hellenist voracious hound with wings, she was not; but at any moment she could become. Atropos was her name, the goddess who made all in the Hellenistic World shudder with fear and dread. Her father was Chaos, the void before creation. Nyx, her kin, was the goddess of darkness. Together Erebus and Nyx ruled that uncertain passage of dread between earth and Hades.

Atropos knew her place. She was ever mindful of her influence, relishing in the apprehension that fear produced. She was the eldest of the Three Moirai, the Three Fates. Each of the sisters had her own role in the lives of every man, woman and child. Where they lived – no Greek could say. Perhaps it was in Athens most assumed, or maybe Delphi, or on Mount Olympus tending to Zeus' bidding, or among the hills with shrilled voices echoing in the icy blasts.

Clotho was the youngest sister. She was revered as the giver of life: spinning the thread and deciding when a person is born.

Lachesis was the middle sister, the one who cherished the task of carrying the rod that measured the length of thread.

Atropos was not revered as most of the Greek gods were. In fact she was deplored with every wish to avoid her interference. She was considered inflexible, the goddess to whom offerings and sacrifice meant nothing. She made the decision when to cut the thread of life determining the time, the place and manner of death. Atropos held the ultimate power to cast any person into the horror of the abyss ruled by Erebus and Nyx. As she pointed her finger toward the waves and water, the spell was cast; and with assurance she turned her back to the sea and moved slowly toward the inner sanctum, her robes sweeping the marble floor. The temple of Myra, in Lycia, was her domain if only for the night. Before the statue of Artemis Eleutheria she stood. That marble goddess was the protector of the town, but Atropos knew best. No one, nowhere would stand in her way.

The Massikytos Mountain Range greeted every sailor between Cyprus and Lycia. The massive granite cliffs were not only inspiring; they compelled every voyageur to dread the uncertainty. It wasn't just the currents or the waves after circling the island. There was a foreboding in a Hellenistic realm ruled by Poseidon. Rumors and fears could suddenly become death. There were few sailors who had not heard of the ominous stories of floating debris, lost cargo, or the desperate pleas of the drowning. Somewhere in those mountains, beyond the temple and acropolis of Myra, across the expanse of the Anatolian Peninsula the Moirai ruled. Regardless of any sailor's belief, their dreaded influence could not be dismissed.

For Clotho there was always time for venture, to explore the visible and discover the unseen. More than a mile from the temple she danced: twirling in the dark at center stage before an empty theatre. Like all such structures in any town, it was impressive. Myra's theatre had thirty rows with eight aisles capable of accommodating more than ten thousand devoted Greeks. Entertainment was the gift of the gods, and the Hellenists knew how to appreciate their endowment. In those hours before dawn, Clotho swung her arms wide, twisting in a lively dance, alluring the many gods who envied the privilege of being so certain in her ability to direct the affairs of men. Then in abrupt instant she stopped. Hands brushed away the veil that had obscured her face. She felt young and every finger tip exploring her features told her so. But young she was not though her agility disguised her age. Since creation, when Chaos ceased to be except in the minds of men, she had been there; and now before the empty theatre she entertained those whom she had chosen to be born.

– Ephesus Pure in Heart –

After ascending the stairs, Clotho looked out toward the harbour. There was always a crescent of light on the horizon. Then as if startled, she cried out, "Shadows waken the night!"

From between the mountains, the valleys echoed, "Dreams fade with the dawn."

Clotho had expected the response in the realm of her kin. "Life quickens." she proclaimed in a shrill voice filling the theatre.

"Shallow thoughts," Atropos reminded her mindful of every thought her sisters could ponder.

"Children hunger," Clotho's words astounded the eldest Moirai.

"They fight men's wars," Atropos crudely reminded her sibling.

Clotho was not about to silenced, caring for what she brought into the world. "Orphans are forgotten."

"Innocence scorned!" Lachesis declared from the acropolis where she had been admiring the statue of Tyche, the goddess of fortune and prosperity.

"Famine!" Clotho lamented.

"Suckles Rome's Glory!" Atropos was quick to add in a quaking echo from the cliff overlooking the harbour.

"Lame walk." The words leaped from Clotho's lips. "Blind see."

"Poor men die," Atropos reminded her sister.

"Dead men rise!" Clotho's retort was instant reminding others of her ability to resurrect the dead.

"In death lies achievement," Lachesis pondered considering the wisdom of Athena.

"Hope spawns life." Clotho's words of encouragement even shocked her.

"To taste the dirt," Lachesis reminded her sister.

"Upon which hallowed walk." Before Clotho could even finish, lightning flashed across the sky. The frustration of Atropos was abundantly clear. So rare was the occasion that the Moirai would incite the discord of one another.

****

On board, refugees huddled together looking up toward those cliffs, dreading the lightning that inflamed the northern sky. Prayers could not obscure their fears.

– Ephesus Pure in Heart –

EPHESUS 50 A.D.

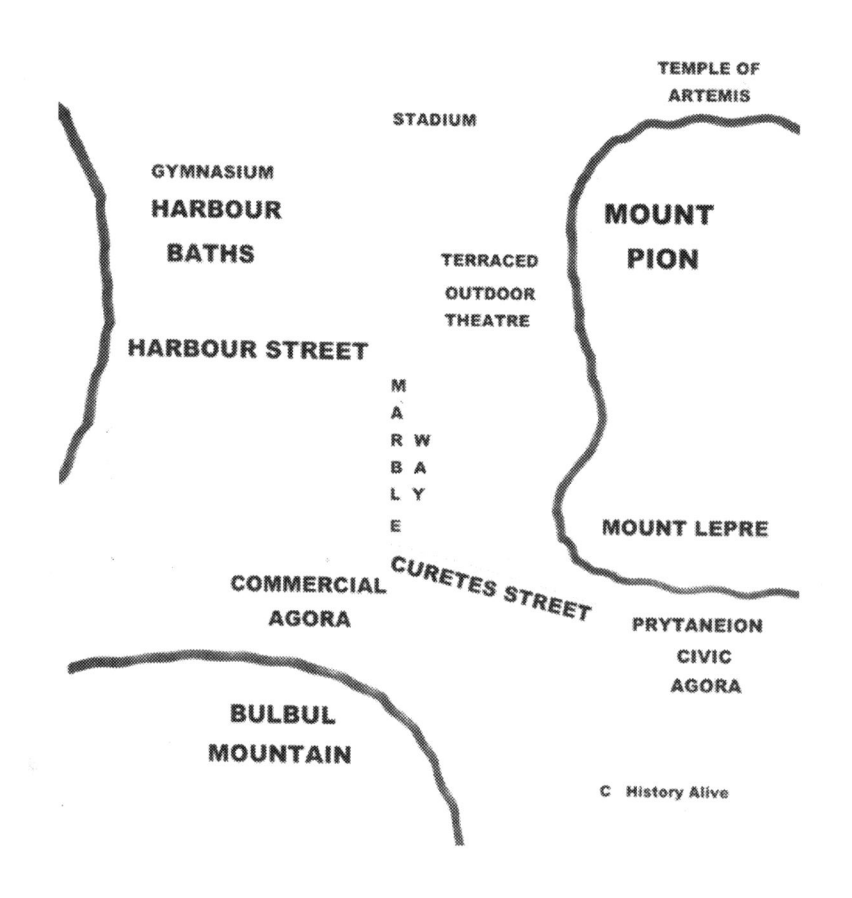

- TEMPLE OF ARTEMIS
- STADIUM
- GYMNASIUM
- HARBOUR BATHS
- MOUNT PION
- TERRACED OUTDOOR THEATRE
- HARBOUR STREET
- MARBLE WAY
- MOUNT LEPRE
- COMMERCIAL AGORA
- CURETES STREET
- PRYTANEION
- CIVIC AGORA
- BULBUL MOUNTAIN

C History Alive

Chapter Two

Marketplace, Ephesus

April, 50

"Silks! Karpion! Gefilte fish!" The woman's normally calm voice resounded above the clamour of the shuffling crowd. Response was not immediate, prompting further exclamation regarding her wares. "Shawls! Fresh catch!" An elderly woman turned for just a second and then moved on.

Miriam stood behind her tables, centered between two marble columns within the Ephesian agora. The marketplace was the focal point of trade and commerce. Like all things Greek it was massive, constructed in the form of a square with each side being one hundred and ten meters in length. Columns surrounded the four sides. There were three gates: from the Marble Way on the north-east, one on the west from the Harbour Street, and the third being the Gate of Mazeus and Mythridates being the entrance/exit to Curetes Street. The south side of the market, that lacked a formal entrance, backed onto the field leading to the forested incline of Bulbul Mountain. Each side provided space for twenty-five merchants. A sundial and water clock occupied the center court, where shoppers met and philosophers talked unceasingly.

The allowable space between two columns provided about three meters for each merchant to display produce. So much was dependent upon quick sales, and having available stock. The need to cart sufficient goods to and from the market elevated the importance of skilled carpenters and tradesmen making the carts, baskets and equipment necessary for the center piece of Ephesian Society.

The route from the harbour to the commercial market was a trek of approximately five hundred meters east on Harbour Street, and then one hundred meters south to the north-east portico of the market. For the residents on the slope of Bulbul Mountain, to the south, the distance would range between three hundred meters and a kilometer. For the Ephesians living in the valley below Mount Pion to the north, the trip to the marketplace was almost a kilometer. The agricultural district near the Cayster River was an expanse at least five kilometers north of the city along the Aegean Coast. So much was absolutely dependent on Roman roads.

Besides the commercial market, vendors could obtain assigned locations along Harbour Street, the Marble Way and on Curetes Street. That avenue extended east toward the civic centre that included a second but smaller marketplace, terraced homes for the influential and the government buildings. This civic agora included a basilica: a center for banking, lending and major transactions involving currency, shipping, and inter-provincial commerce. To the north of the civic market, the Prytaneion, a revered edifice, housed one of the city's most prized possessions: the eternal flame.

The entire length of both sides of the streets was home to public baths, monuments, temples, accommodation for the priests and priestesses, and the customary brothels.

At the junction of Harbour Street and the Marble Way, the Great Theater easily received everyone's attention. It was first built by the Hellenists in the third century BC, and later enlarged by the Romans following their occupation in 129BC when the Province of Asia on the Aegean Sea became part of the Roman Empire.

Miriam was fully aware of the size, importance and cosmopolitan nature of the city. Ephesus was home to approximately two hundred thousand people: predominantly Greeks, Romans, and Jews.

Competition was always intense. Varieties of fresh produce were at times limited. It was always quality that made the difference between sales and having to return home with rejected goods.

"Ivory! Knives!" the merchant to her right declared. Competition was just as important as mutual respect among the vendors. "Ivory!" Hemiah again advertised the rare commodity. Two men turned in his direction.

Miriam busied herself shifting items on her tables. She had earlier altered the display space to allow customers to enter a cove surrounded by her wares. Dried fish and smoked meat were displayed on a portion of one table. Across from these were the silks and material, items with which she had been acquainted nearly all of her life. The table directly in front of her provided baked goods with enticing aroma.

Susannah, Miriam's assistant and at times her best competitor, held up a loaf supported by a wooden tray. "Baklava!" she called to prospective customers.

"Kreplach!" Miriam tried to secure additional attention. After a pause she repeated, "Patties. Meat pies!"

"Silver!" Hemiah expounded on the nature of his wares.

"Aurum! Argentum!" Gaius, a precious metal merchant, yelled from the spot he usurped by the fountain. His presence perpetually annoyed Hemiah who had paid a fee for his tables. Gaius was a rogue, known to many as such. He paid no fee; yet the Romans who patrolled the market would do nothing to stop him from improper transactions at the market's core.

"Libae! Ugiyot!" Susannah raised her voice again to attract customers interested in freshly baked biscuits.

The lull lasted only a moment before Miriam called out to women regarding her seasonal specialty. "Ugentum! Ugentum!" The perfume was her most expensive item.

"Hressos!" Hemiah tried to attract anyone interested in gold. Fluency in Greek and Latin was essential for any merchant.

An elderly woman eventually made her way to Miriam's tables interested in dried fish. They talked quietly. She was a regular customer. Questions regarding the woman's husband and family preceded Miriam's response regarding Anna. Anna was a young girl, age twelve, who suffered a significant permanent disability at birth due to the attempt to abort the child. Her blindness was total. The infant in rags was discarded as was the norm. Every decision regarding any disabled child belonged to the father. However in Anna's case no one claimed to be the father, and many had accused her mother of illicit sex. That was a crime for women; but for men wanting lurid services, it was only natural. After stories regarding a woman from Medjel floated around the community, the child albeit eight at the time was delivered into Miriam's care.

Susannah's mercantile fortune shone that day. By nine in the morning, three hours after the market opened, she was out of available bread having sold the last three loaves to one woman. Then she concentrated on her pastries.

Miriam was pleased with the choice of her location. Being on the south side meant the morning sun was always on their right. For those first few hours, though bright, the sun darted among the peaks and crevices of Mount Pion and Mount Lepre. Once high in the sky, the brightness of the sun did not hinder the potential customers from viewing her items. On the east side, the customers had to confront the sun's rays. On the west side, it was the vendors who were discomforted. Many merchants accordingly wore scarves on their foreheads to shield the rays. Vision was strained everywhere in Ephesus with the brilliance of the bone white columns and stone boulevards. On that April morning, the sun was at its most bothersome. No one was lauding the brilliance of Apollo's journey across the sky.

Aprilis was always a festive month in Ephesus. The Greeks called it Aphro after Aphrodite. Festivities during the month instinctively involved this goddess of love, beauty and procreation. The Romans fed off this tribute to honour their own Diana. Accordingly there were a significant number of merchants selling idols depicting the goddesses. Phallic symbols were equally sought by unscrupulous customers. Although the Jews and Christians opposed such idolatry, very little was said or whispered within the markets. This was a cosmopolitan center and even though there could be opposition to certain instinctive habits and rites, acceptance was above all not only expected, it was mandatory.

Susannah continued with her enthusiastic sales techniques trying to rouse the allurement of the customers for her products. "Perfume to make men lucky! Toys to make children laugh!" Others could only smile. However it wasn't long before their friend Elena arrived.

Susannah's exhortation didn't encourage Elena. The customer would have stopped there eventually. The sale was brisk and the conversation long.

At least two Roman soldiers were commissioned daily to complete the customary patrols. They would start at opposite ends: one at the harbour and the other at the civic agora. Their presence provided a reasonable level of security appreciated by sellers and buyers alike. There were the imps and the urchins, the pick-pockets, and the unsavory youth. Similarly there were the unemployed and the destitute, as well as the maimed who many perceived to be capable of considerable ill. The visual presence of Roman soldiers, if only two, provided assurance; for Roman justice even in Greek culture was to be feared.

"My friend, how are you?" Lysias greeted his cohort by the water clock.

"An Arabian in flight!" Burrus cheerfully responded. "No one corners me on a day like this. Apollo has blessed us."

"Just for Diana," Lysias added, a bit surprised by his comrade's enthusiasm.

"Tell me, my friend, will anyone better you in the javelin?"

"No less than last year," Lysias appreciated the comment on his athletic ability.

"And no more either," Burris added to the light exchange.

"This humility is a fine torture: always right and never wrong," Lysias quipped.

Burrus noted Lysias' fellowship with the people, "You're cultured by your associates."

"To be known as one committed to Rome but appeasing the populace." Lysias was proud of his ability to play the middle road.

"Not good enough for the Asiarchs," Burrus warned. The Asiarchs were the most influential Ephesians: the wealthy who made the important decisions to safeguard their positions. "Has Aretius set sail for Achaia?" Burrus continued.

"Much to my sister's dismay," Lysias advised

The jester, a brightly attired entertainer, commenced his regular routine. A multitude of the market's customers stopped immediately to observe his show. Applause followed with enough coins to keep the busker satisfied.

"And your mistress?" Burrus enquired in derogatory terms.

"Her thoughts challenge my allegiance," Lysias admitted.

"Since when do Roman pleasures become so cultured?" Burrus laughed.

"Her dependence on a Nazarene," Lysias added.

"Then question those there. That woman's from Agrippa's seal." Burrus pointed to Miriam.

"I know her well," Lysias admitted. Just then the jester started his juggling routine with his handmade pins. Shoppers with their children again circled the scene.

A distinguished looking gentleman, who had been a customer at the time of the Saturnalia festivities, returned to Miriam for another vial of perfume. Repeat customers were the goal for all vendors. This middle aged man was distinctive. His toga was spotless white. The sash was a strange green. Most would wear a white or dark cincture. Miriam remembered him, not only for his attire; but because he talked so much about Saturnalia. That was strange for an influential Greek openly celebrating a Roman festival. While Miriam observed the diplomatic attire, Susannah grabbed the coins. "Would rouse Demeter's urge in any woman." Making people laugh was Miriam's usual way of expressing gratitude.

"One day you'll have to show me how to make this." Susannah smiled whispering to Miriam.

As soon as the jester concluded his display, Gaius returned to center court with his sack of precious gems and metals. "Gemmae! Argentum!" He called after unfurling his circular rug. His actions were noticed by many including the two Roman soldiers; but no one stopped him.

Miriam's attention was drawn not to any disturbance in the court, but rather to the solitude of an elderly woman. "Old woman! Yeramenka!" she called. The woman recognized the merchant's voice and attended Miriam's tables. By the time she arrived, Miriam reached under the table top to grab a loaf of bread she had set aside. The elderly woman, someone's grandmother, slipped the packet within her tunic, smiled and continued walking.

Meanwhile Hemiah was haggling with two Romans over a stalk of ivory. Several times they mentioned that they had come to Ephesus having heard of the grandeur of the market; and as visitors they expected a considerable deal. However, these were not foreigners. Miriam recognized them from prior discussions. It was her hand signal that warned Hemiah not to fall prey to their gimmick.

An Arab gentleman, obviously not a resident based on his tongue and his attire, approached Miriam's table. The discussion was fluid. Miriam understood every word having been fluent in many languages while assisting the family business on the Sea of Galilee. He wanted ivory, and perhaps felt he couldn't work a deal with Hemiah. Miriam worked a transaction that benefited both vendors. Hemiah, however felt he could have got more. Miriam then reminded him that the Arab gentleman would return within the week and purchase more once he had completed his other transactions at the harbour.

Lysias, noting the sale, had to admit to his friend, "She could barter Rome away from Caesar."

"We should not be heard to say," Burrus warned.

"Would anyone here disagree?" Lysias had this capacity for occasionally being ultra happy with life, a trait quite rare for a Roman soldier.

****

In the north end of the city, beyond the grand outdoor theatre, John sat with Bernardus on the bank of the athletic stadium. Though it was far from being a major thoroughfare within the city; the stadium area was still robust with passing pilgrims on their way to the Temple of Artemis approximately one kilometer away.

"The Marble Way crawls today," John stated the obvious.

"Everything's their perpetual tribute to Artemis." Bernardus had little patience for foreign customs, which often prompted John to enquire why he was ever in Ephesus. "Just like a serpent swallowing the poor, the rich and the fools." Bernardus was raised in a Jewish family in the town of Zaphon. With the arrival of Roman forces, his father joined their ranks rather than risk losing his family. Then with the tyranny in Palestine, Bernardus chose like others to move to wherever he could live safely. He ultimately intended to settle in Achaia. However those plans went awry when John debated their rabbi on the reality of Christ and Christianity. Bernardus baptism followed.

"They are not the same." John liked making unexpected comments to prompt further discussion. Bernardus enjoyed those exchanges as opportunities to learn and to perhaps one day better John at his skill.

"A constant challenge to our beliefs," Bernardus was concise.

The exchange continued for more than thirty minutes until athletes took to the field. Bernardus thought he won the debate with his final line, "If tolerance ruled your persuasion, you would have never left that upper room. But you did, for a purpose, for more than just other customs."

However, as they sauntered toward the market, John got in the last word, never wishing to lose an argument, "We'll achieve more by expounding on the inadequacies of Rome while living the love of Christ."

"You'd have to say that." Bernardus cherished the opportunity for light banter.

****

Eventually Miriam's friend Alexa arrived. She was a regular customer for jams or dried fruit. "Peach almond," Miriam advised as Alexa sniffed the clay jar.

"Do you have more?" the Roman woman enquired prompting an equally quick response. Miriam handed her a second jar.

Elena re-attended after exploring tables on the Marble Way. Her interest this time was the material. The skein of blue silk drew her attention.

After her decision to purchase the two jars, Alexa reached for a red scarf and placed three silver coins on Miriam's table. The vendor's reply was just as quick rejecting the payment.

"Keep them for your betrothed. Will we see him Sunday?"

"Ask the men. They always make the plans." Alexa smiled. Her response was factual.

Miriam again refused the coins. "Then keep them for your children."

Alexa laughed knowing Miriam's blissful humour. "You know we don't have any. You, you keep them for your children," she urged referring to the orphans that Miriam occasionally tended. With that

Alexa thankfully placed the items in her cloth bag and left. Just as she was doing so, John and Bernardus approached the tables.

Many merchants had already left or were busy packing their wares. From the midst of the remaining shoppers, a young girl with stringy dusty brown hair emerged. Susannah was the first to recognize her. "She's back," she announced. Miriam also recognized the girl particularly the pendant she wore.

Prostitution was a reality in Ephesus even for this girl who might be as old as sixteen. There were very few back alleys where such services could be offered. It was a profession that was front row and center. Special facilities were openly established where women could please their customers. In the baths when women were not allowed to spend time with their husbands, young women offering special services were pleasantly accepted at all hours.

The charm hanging from her neck – the vulva pendant - identified her trade. It was of Roman origin. Greek prostitutes didn't have to declare their occupation. Generally, the pendant was an invitation to Roman gentleman; however when times were tough one man was basically the same as another. Miriam's knowledge of the world caused her to have pity and remorse for such young women. Alone and without family, they really didn't have an alternative in their limited life.

Phoenicia greeted Hemiah with an expressive embrace. Such greetings still shocked Susannah. Phoenicia continued with the precious gems merchant while eyeing his table. Hemiah had no difficulty with her fee for the service she provided.

"She's lacking something," Elena chirped, amused by the camaraderie at the next stall.

The two Romans then appeared. "You do a blissful trade," Lysias remarked.

Miriam's wry character seized the moment. "Who? Them?" Lysias smiled. "All in a day's work," she continued.

"And your young girl?" Burrus was always the more direct.

Miriam's response was a candid accusation. "Blind, saline at birth. Unfortunately she lived."

"You question..." Burris immediately reacted.

"Everything we see and more." Miriam was even hastier in her rebuttal.

– Ephesus Pure in Heart –

"An unjust accusation," Burrus suggested.

"Your term," Miriam reminded him.

"Leave her," Lysias interrupted.

"You're too kind to the offspring of Mezuzah." Burrus referred to the merchant's Hebrew heritage.

"You're a cultured woman, but apparently at times ill advised in patience." Lysias tried again to play the mediator.

Just then an old man passed by. Miriam, recognizing the person in need, called to him. He ignored her at first and kept walking. She called again; and after the third request he stopped and cautiously approached her table.

"They're kind," Miriam told the elderly gentleman in Greek referring to the Roman guards. She took a loaf of bread that she had set aside, and offered to him. Without pause he placed it in his filthy bag and left.

"You challenge our impression." Burrus commented regarding the generosity.

"An opinion's worth vinegar unless it's expressed in the day's sweat." Miriam was abrupt.

"Strange philosophy," Lysias ventured.

"When did kindness become so foreign to Rome?" With Miriam's comment, Burrus turned abruptly to leave. Lysias, though he preferred to stay, left with his fellow soldier. Miriam in the course of their brief exchange never got the chance to mention the sandals she had brought to the market at the Roman soldier's request.

Meanwhile at the next table, Phoenicia had playfully encouraged Hemiah to pack up his wares and leave. Throwing everything into a sack was quicker than taking time to neatly wrap the items.

The two Romans were still in the agora when approached by John. Bernardus was reluctant to engage any Roman soldier in any discussion or to even be seen with them.

"Generosi." John greeted them.

The conversation was pleasant, encouraging each other on a sunny day. Ultimately Lysias begged to speak to John alone about a young lady that had been seen in Miriam's company. Lysias' interest in Naomi was obviously more than just casual.

"Your woman could help," Lysias implored.

"In what respect?" John enquired.

"Will you see her soon?" Lysias' query was considerably aloof.

John grabbed the soldier's arm taking him to the side. "Be direct, my friend."

Bernardus turned aside to spend time at Miriam's table. Burrus had already slipped away from the others on route to the Marble Way.

"The action will be real," Lysias warned continuing to whisper.

"No games," John cautioned.

"So much has been said, words with no direction. It's the uncertainty that beckons my haste."

"What's her involvement?" John had to ask.

"Marcus may again enact the imperial decree."

"My God!" was John's immediate reaction.

"Though she is no longer Hebrew, Claudius pays no respect. Once named, destiny is bound." Lysias warned mindful of the hereditary burden of being born Jewish.

"Then myself and our entire community are in similar peril."

Lysias did not answer John's obvious conclusion.

"The serpent wears the laurel crown dipped in Jewish blood!" The Apostle's voice was not calm.

"Please tell her," Lysias implored.

"She is your woman," John concluded.

Lysias shook his head.

"Who's the real author of such malcontent? Tell me. This is not Marcus. I know him well." John continued referring to the Pro Consul Marcus Silanus Torquatus.

"The Emperor has many cousins, many mistresses, with many daughters and devious sons."

"Say no more," John cautioned the soldier not wanting to be overheard. It was indeed a rare occasion that anyone in the Roman military could or would express him-self in such manner. "Where should she meet you?" John enquired trying to ensure that Lysias remained more than passive after he imparted his warning.

"My part is done. The message must suffice." Suddenly the soldier was realizing his limitations.

John's advice was consoling to the troubled Roman. "Peace my friend. Though we do not share your practice, we appreciate your intent. She will have your message."

Lysias nodded conveying his appreciation, and smiled knowing he had the disciple's assurance; then departed.

John stood there, fearing the consequences of another purge. Prayers were rarely enough to cushion the incessant blows. "Does it profit any man to have all the pleasures of the Roman world, and never look to his soul?"

Chapter Three

Prytaneion Reality

February, 51

From the Prytaneion portico, Marcus Silanus Torquatus peered to the west looking down Curetes Street, proud of the stone white paving bordered by tall ashen columns. The boulevard was an image of luxury, capturing the magnificence of illustrious buildings, terraced homes and temples on route to the majestic intersection of the market place with the Marble Way. Beyond the horizon, Harbour Street was alive with persuasive merchants and enthusiastic traders each trying to benefit from Greek comforts and Roman opportunities. The harbour was busy as it should be under the afternoon sun. To the north of Pryteneion, the imperial gardens were spacious and alive with early spring blossoms: buttercups, violets, tulips and early poppies. The grassy incline of Lepre Mountain provided the visual contrast. The trees would soon bloom. This was just the start of another year of celebrations for the many Greek and Roman deities for which the populace never tired.

This was the quiet world of the Pro Consul of Ephesus. Once outside his government building there was no chance of solitude. Being Roman created no assurance of safety. Being the government of the Roman Province of Asia provided less security. Silanus, who had been assigned his post four years before, was never one for keeping track of days or months or even years. Everything was measured by festivals. Thus longevity was determined by the number of occasions a certain deity was honoured. Marcus Silanus Torquatus owed everything to the Emperor from whom he had received this post. That was Rome in every respect, where positions were assigned not based on any skill but by whom you knew and his proximity to the Emperor.

Once Claudius became Emperor, his supporters and friends were also rewarded. Although many could have disagreed with any appointment, they remained silent simply because everything was such a relief after the debauchery during Caligula's reign. The Senators and people wanted sense, they wanted calm, they required assurances. Silanus, who received his appointment in 47AD, ably fulfilled their initial expectations.

Silanus was born in 14AD, named after his father: Marcus Junius Silanus Torquatus. His mother, Aemilia Lepida, was Caesar Augustus's great grand-daughter. As such he was related to Claudius and could be considered a potential claimant for the position of Emperor. Some Patricians even considered Silanus to be Claudius' brother. Silanus had one son, Lucis Junius Silanus Torquatus.

The Pro Consul's position was onerous. So much was demanded by a class of Romans who were rarely satisfied. His job was truly not defined. There were too many aspects on so many issues pertaining to an incredible number of facets, such that defining these would ultimately hinder Rome's ability to please and control the people. The Pro Consul was basically the face of the Emperor in the Province. He enacted the Emperor's decrees and assured the Emperor of peace, prosperity and continuing Roman rule. In an Empire where Rome sought to secure allegiance by appeasing the interests of the conquered, the Pro Consul's job was to keep the people happy. Expectations may never be met, but rumors of riots could end his career.

In the six hundred years before 51AD, there were thirteen Empires or Kingdoms that ruled the territory. Change was the permanent reality. These rulers included: the Achaemenid Empire, Alexander the Great, Kingdom of Cappadocia, Antigonids, Seleucid Empire, the Ptolomies, Kingdom of Pontus, Bithynia, Pergamon, Gallacia, Parthian Empire, Armenian Empire, and the Roman Republic. The need to control this assembly of provinces required decisive leadership, responding to the masses, while being aware of inescapable vulnerability.

The Roman Empire consolidated its expansion by establishing provinces. Each province had a governor to apply Roman rule. The assimilation process in most venues was successful. Greece had for centuries so much to offer. The Egyptians too were a respected people. As the Empire spread, welcoming arms encircled the many regions offering the benefits of Roman society while generally maintaining the culture that made a specific territory so desirable. The Roman Empire did not spread in one tsunami wave. The process of occupying and ruling territories took place over hundreds of years. Sicily became a province in 240BC. Roman rule in Hispania began in 197BC. Macedonia and the west coast of the Adriatic were assimilated fifty years later. Then in 129BC Rome established the Province of Asia. This was territory on the eastern coast of the Aegean Sea. It included Ephesus. Conflicts in the various regions of Anatolia (present day Turkey) followed with the Roman Army ultimately being successful in the north and securing territory in the east. By 25BC, the entire Anatolian peninsula belonged to Rome except for the region of Cappadocia. As of 17AD, Rome was in complete control of Anatolia. The eastern Mare Nostrum was totally under Rome's domain.

Ephesus was the major asset in Anatolia. It possessed a well-developed harbour with established trade involving Egypt, Alexandria, Cyrene, Libya, Morocco, western Africa, Hispania, Palestine, Arabia, Ethiopia, and India via the Sinai Peninsula. Also Ephesus and Pergamum were depots on the Silk Road from China. Trade with territories on the Black Sea also enhanced the commercial importance of the city. Being located near four rivers provided access from the interior. Although there were significant mountains, there were also productive valleys providing vast crops. Grain was the staple of the Empire, and Ephesus could produce the grain necessary to feed the city of Rome. This was top priority for the Empire. Emperors had long declared that the Patricians in Rome, approximately two hundred thousand influential families, had to receive a daily allowance of grain. After that Ephesus and the provinces could be fed. Maritime commerce involving the transportation of food to the City of Rome itself exceeded four hundred thousand tons per year. Being a key element in the production, procurement and shipment of goods ensured Ephesus would remain essential to both the Roman Empire and the City of Rome.

Assimilation was necessary to ensure peace within the region. Maintaining the cultural integrity of the occupied-peoples required adoption of practices and acceptance of foreign beliefs. Greek Mythology augmented the Roman deities. Names were different; however gods possessed the same powers, authority and demanded the same respect. Jupiter was Zeus. When the Greeks venerated Artemis, Rome did not object. Artemis was the Roman goddess Diana. Together they celebrated festivals enjoying each other's practices.

For all of the benefits that Ephesus brought to the Empire, it was only time before the Province of Asia received due recognition. Caesar Augustus established the position of Pro Consul in Ephesus to govern the communities of Asia, Mysia, Lydia, and Phrygia. This was the entire west and south-west of Anatolia including numerous islands in the Aegean Sea. Other provinces were generally ruled by governors with limited authority.

The immediate response of the Province of Asia was to encourage and ensure Emperor Worship: to build temples and erect statues to the illustrious Emperor. The Greeks had difficulty with that concept, but were not in a position to vociferously disagree. The Roman gods were being replaced with idols and coins of mortal men who chose to declare their immortality.

The Ephesus that Pro Consul Silanus ruled was a city of less than a quarter-million people. This was the second largest urban area in the Empire. The entire Roman Empire included sixty million citizens and slaves. About ten million of these lived in cities. The responsibilities for food production, shipping and consumption rested with the Pro Consul. Silanus was also accountable for commerce, trade and employment. These inherently included care for the markets, maintaining the streets, construction and cleanliness of public buildings, and the maintenance of temples. Although the agricultural areas in the valleys were not his direct responsibility, ensuring that people were fed intrinsically brought farming under his domain.

Mining too provided employment for tens of thousands, not just slaves. Gold, silver, tin, copper, salt, sulphur, flint, and cryptocrystalline quartz only partially satisfied the Empire's need for precious metals, production of hardened metals, quality gems, necessary condiments, and the assurance of fire. Merchants honed their skills in the production of idols, rings, broaches, earrings and necklaces. Bronze was produced from the tin and copper. The network required miners, carpenters, smiths, apprentices, production of tools and mobile equipment, and dependable supervisors. The Pro Consul had to keep himself aware of all facets of the mining industry so as to assure the Emperor and Senators that production, quality and profits were being maximized.

Collegiae were born from this maze of productivity. A Collegia was a Roman guild, comprised of workers in the same trade. A Collegia was not a present-day-union representing the welfare and benefits of workers. Instead the Roman guild was an opportunity and venue to associate with fellow workers both at work and after hours. The ultimate intent was to make each worker feel part of a team. The Collegiae provided training and apprenticeship opportunities, camaraderie and security, assurance and recognition. But for the Pro Consul, guilds also provided another benefit of significant consequence. With the Imperial Cult so much a part of daily life Silanus used the guilds to inject and ensure support for the Emperor. They were very much 'Rah Rah' sessions promoting spirited enthusiasm. The Guilds were then assessed based on the level of their enthusiastic support for the Emperor. The Guild generating the greatest support received the greatest reward. The technique would be copied in political systems for millennia ensuring the devotion of the masses to principles that were at best vague but which sounded so ideal.

The Pro Consul was above all the Roman judge, the pinnacle of justice, deciding cases throughout his jurisdiction. He was the law. Accordingly he had to be concerned with urban conditions because so much in life was the consequence of daily activities. Rome may have tolerated minorities, but at no time did Rome freely accept the consequences inherent with poverty. The destitute, the homeless, the impoverished, the lame, the blind, lepers, prostitutes and orphans: none of these possessed a free pass to violate any letter of the law. There was one set of rules for everyone. Decisions and punishment for these Silanus knew were harsh because no one ever chose to be poor.

Because he was the law in the province, the Pro Consul also had control of the army. There was no separate police force. Citizens could retain body guards; but for the general administration of the law, Silanus relied on the army to control matters. Within Anatolia there were approximately forty Legions. The number would vary with maritime needs or if there were riots in neighbouring provinces. Forty Legions was about twelve percent of the entire Roman Army. This number of Legions included: over two thousand centurions, and over two hundred thousand soldiers. Veterans who returned to the Army constituted another ten thousand legionnaires. Calvary, the elite force, numbered about four thousand. This in reality meant that the size of the available Army in all of Anatolia was almost equivalent in numbers to the entire population of Ephesus. Controlling the Army and keeping the Legionnaires content was essential for the Pro Consul to maintain peace and accord within his realm.

Sanitary concerns, fresh water, mobility and roads: these were also his responsibility.

The importing, the use and the control of the slaves were essential to the economic viability of any province within the Roman Empire. The strenuous work was always performed by slaves. Productivity and profits were based on the capacity and capability of that work force. The entire Roman Empire was based on four classes. The Patricians were the nobles, the elite of Rome. Their rank included Senators. Authority stemmed from the Patricians. An Equestrian was an influential male who could afford a horse and apply those equine skills in the interests of the Empire. The third class was the Plebeians, the common people. They had rights depending on the will of the Emperor, Senators, Pro Consuls and Governors. Nothing was guaranteed. Then there were the slaves. This group included: domestic servants, captured foes who were compelled to work for the Empire, those extracted from conquered territories, the physically challenged, the impoverished, orphans, widowed wives, prostitutes, and the young whose only value was the temporary ability to perform the heavy tasks. Assuring a viable work force of slaves was the Pro Consul's responsibility.

Innovations and necessity also demanded Silanus' attention. Any means to improve productivity was considered to be of significant value throughout the Empire. The steam turbine, the water organ, bellows for blast furnaces, water wheels for grinding, tools for ship building, implements for carpenters, smiths, farming, and mining: all drew the attention of the provincial government. Equally important was the dredging equipment to keep the harbour clear. Anything at any time to improve productivity fell within the parameters of the Pro Consul accountability.

Equally important to any of the other tasks, the Pro Consul had to be a master of the political game. At any moment in time in Ephesus there would have been close to two hundred thousand people who wanted his job or felt they could be doing better. Silanus was well aware of this. Any Roman in any position of authority was certain of the uncertainty of his position.

To maintain consistency in policy and leadership, three deputies were appointed. If the Pro Consul should die, the senior deputy would assume power until the next Pro Consul was appointed. As the selection was made by the Emperor so much depended upon first being the Emperor's favorite, and then maintaining the Emperor's recognition. If the Emperor should die, then the Pro Consul could become vulnerable. Without the Emperor's support, nothing was certain. Moving within the marble-walled offices, Silanus reflected on his fortune: that much was expected, and more was attained. However, he always remained conscious of Claudius' age, infirmity, propensity for immorality, and the many tales of impropriety emanating from Rome.

In 52AD, Claudius was sixty-three years old, having been Emperor for the last decade. There was at least one aspect of Claudius' life that bothered many Patricians. Claudius was born in Gaul. He was not one of them. Physical ailments included: tremors, seizures, and foaming from the mouth. He had been considered an outcast and had been treated as such. His name 'Claudius' had a rank odor. The Latin word meant 'lame'. However, marriages brought him close to the upper echelon of Roman power. He was actually Caligula's uncle. Any relative of Caligula had no right to rule the Empire according to many in the ruling class. Claudius was a drunk, a womanizer, and a gambler. Caligula, almost as a joke, had named Claudius as his Co-Consul. Such a position provided Claudius with ample opportunity to engage in lurid affairs with many women including the wives of his subjects. Claudius was at home in Caligula's realm, and then Caligula was murdered. It was the Praetorian Guard who appointed Claudius as Emperor, a decision not regarded well by many.

In the first ten years of his rule, famine and starvation devastated the Roman Empire on at least five occasions. Claudius had a propensity for lavish displays and at one time held a mock navy battle that destroyed a fleet of Roman ships. Blood baths in the forums and had become a display of brutality. His edicts against the Jews raised the fears of occupied-peoples. Who would be next? Maintaining his affinity for different women, Claudius was married four times. For his last wife, the Emperor in 49AD married his young niece, Agrippina. There candidly wasn't much to like about Claudius. Thus when Marcus Silanus staked his position on Claudius' admiration, he was relying on a dying flame.

His deputies brooded endlessly, looking for opportunities, quietly challenging decisions, and exploring possibilities. Former Centurion Antonius, Equestrian Celer and Patrician Hypatius all had a stake in Silanus' performance and reputation, and they were quite willing to bury the stake when opportunity opened its doors.

Chapter Four

At Home on Bulbul Mountain

May, 51

She was absolutely exhausted by the time she crawled onto her bed. The market had again proven to be very profitable, but tiring, during the festivities devoted to Artemis. She could swear the city almost doubled in size when Greeks from every province arrived to honour their goddess of love and fertility. Miriam wondered more often than not how that culture never ran out of names for its idols. However, as long as the festivities generated profits for her basic needs and many ventures, Miriam dismissed the appropriate condemnation of such idols. She wasn't about to change the world and she knew that. She was in Ephesus simply because they realized they couldn't change Jerusalem. If they crucified Him, what would they do to His followers? That was her forte: being realistic.

Although she refused to sell idols, Miriam sold quality items equally in demand: scarves and silks in a variety of colours. Susannah stretched the truth describing them as being symbolic devotion to Artemis. Remaining true to their own beliefs, they would use the mundane word 'devotion', and never consider 'adoration' or 'honour'. Regardless of how contrary the devotion to Artemis was to the First Commandment, it wasn't difficult to conclude that such festivities provided a significant pacifying influence, encouraging the pilgrims to embrace the sense of a greater community. Miriam envied the Greeks in that regard that they could bring so many together at one location. She had become so convinced that that had to be the future of the Christian community: to celebrate the Lord's Supper in one central permanent location, rather than in small restricted households.

Psalm 23 automatically came to her lips the moment her head rested upon her make-shift pillow. Working with the family business in Mejdel had provided acquired skills with material and stuffing. There wasn't a feather that went to waste. Linen, silks, and wool – even their remnants – were fashioned into durable clothes, bedding and window blinds. Her bed was no more than four narrow boards upon the ground. Soft twigs with an abundance of leaves filled two pieces of linen sewn together. Her sheets were made of quilted pieces. That was her mattress. She had another covering, but rarely used that. Miriam preferred to use two old tunics that she could pull over her whenever she wished. Nights could vary so much in temperature; not just because of the time of year but with the change in winds off the mountains, from the valley or across the harbour.

Her block house was a three room structure. It had been abandoned before they first arrived. In a city that size, it was clearly a case of grab what you could get. Negotiations generated a benevolent deal. The continuing payments were minimal compared to that for the dwellings in the lower city.

Bulbul Mountain was the location, a forested hill on the south side of the city. Many called it a 'hill' simply because it was unlike the other mountains. Bulbul had trees with gardens and top soil. Foliage was abundant with flowers so essential for oils and perfumes. Farm animals – geese, chickens, ducks, pigs – were easy to raise in spite of the limited space afforded to each lot. Its winding road was cumbersome, but not impassable. To the south-east of the hill in a slim valley there was even the potential to grow wheat and other grain crops: commodities cherished throughout the Empire.

The main room provided both dining and additional beds. There was one bedroom divided into two nooks. The only other room was a privy area for hygiene and toiletry functions. Having such a room in any home was indeed a luxury. A small brick fire place occupied one corner. Its main purpose was to bake bread and pastry delicacies. On the rare occasion it might be used to heat the building. By the door Miriam hung a small pouch with a few bronze coins. If anyone was to break in, he'd take what he immediately could grab. Her profits she had buried in the wall by cutting out a piece of timber and replacing it. That corner was also protected by a rusted Roman shield too difficult for most to move. John kept his own the funds. Ultimately they'd be shared with those in need.

Outside the building, Miriam cherished her garden. The double growing season was a significant benefit. Her grinding pit for grain, and her cauldrons were necessary apparatus.

Five years passed quickly since their arrival. There were the three of them: John, Maryam the Master's Mother, and herself. Of course there were others on board that first trip, mainly believers fleeing the hostilities and starvation in Palestine. Before they left Judaea, they had considered alternatives; but those other regions were burdened with various imperial degrees against the Jews. As long as they were still considered Jewish by the Roman Empire, the same fate awaited them. About Ephesus so much had been heard. Having to care for the Master's Mother prompted them to consider that location simply as a haven of safety and tolerance. After reminding herself how quickly they were accepted into a foreign culture, Miriam was always ready to accommodate the intricacies of the multi-ethnic customs that gave them freedom. The number of Christians who were already present in Ephesus was small. The practice of their faith had not been a priority.

Anna lay on her bed already fast asleep. The initial manner in which the youth had just been dumped had irritated Miriam no end. The entire process that lasted no more than a few seconds was based on presumptions: that Miriam would take her, that Miriam could care for her, that Miriam would never bother anyone else about her. However Miriam, though still frustrated, started to conjecture that maybe these women saw something in her that she did not see in herself. Her personal opinions of her troubled self had the tendency sometimes of getting in the way of reality. Then Miriam, realizing the benefit of Anna in her life, started counting her blessings. Anna had made the forty year old a single mother.

Miriam of Mejdel first met the preacher in Naim, a town in a stony valley north of Jerusalem near the River Jordan. She and so many others had heard so much about this man. The stories really seemed too whimsical: that blind men could see and lame persons could suddenly walk. There were the lepers and the diseased, all healed in an instant. How fanciful was that? If the stories were to be believed, nothing could stand in His way; and then she heard that even the devil obeyed this preacher. In Naim, townsfolk directed Him to a family grieving for the deceased mother. Her children would become orphans making them slaves in the Roman Empire. Miriam watched from a distance as did so many wanting to see His magic; and then the unbelievable happened. The woman came back to life! Miriam had no choice. She had seen, she believed and she followed Him. Actually she went one step further: accompanying other women preparing for his arrival in the next town, or cooking meals, or washing clothes or buying supplies – all while He was on His path to Jerusalem. Miriam was well equipped for this role. Working in her parents' business had given her basic skills of being multi talented in any commercial or domestic venture.

Mejdel was a town of moderate size on the western shore of the Sea of Galilee. To Romans this was the Sea of Tiberius. The region was home to many cultures: Greek, Syrian, Assyrian, Samaritan, the predominant Hebrew, and the occupying Romans. Anyone growing up in this region would naturally be conversant in several languages. Mejdel was a center for commerce and trade, even having a branch of the famed Silk Road stemming west from Bagdad. Employment was almost exclusively in family businesses.

Commerce in Roman territory required any merchant to have a total understanding of his product: in terms of accessibility, quantity, quality, durability and marketing. Of these the ability to sell the product, that is to locate and entice buyers, was of prime importance. These skills were not transferrable, nor were they factors that could be delegated. The merchandising of spices was no different. These involved: herbs, salts, perfume, oils and medication. The latter included myrrh, ointments and derivatives of opium.

Her family bartered with Assyria in the east, Jerusalem and the Mediterranean in the west, and with Syria and Anatolia in the north. Her father, like other merchants could never be limited to just one product. Merchants of spices also traded in material and clothing.

Papyrus was very profitable. Silver and precious gems from Achaia, and gold also ivory from the African continent provided additional dimensions that attracted a wealthy clientele.

However the good times did not last forever. Roman taxation, failing crops, and inconsistencies in the flow of trade adversely affected family businesses without warning. Roman law provided little leniency in matters of debt and unfulfilled promises. In any culture at any time, the general interests of a community are directly proportional to the available currency. When funds are limited the propensity to buy goods that might be considered non-essential decreases. The inclination of those with limited income is to purchase only what is necessary. So during the hard times that cyclically pervaded Palestine and the other Mediterranean provinces, people concentrated their spending habits on the necessary items. The non necessities of silks, quality clothes, gold and precious stones suffered. This is the dilemma that Miriam's family and so many family businesses experienced.

Imperial decrees against the Jews blamed them for everything throughout the eastern region of the Mare Nostrum. Ethnic disharmony swept throughout the region: sometimes temporary and other times permanent. The crucifixion of innocent Hebrews in northern Palestine did not abate. Syrian, Egyptian, Greek and of course Roman traders shied away from commercial activity with the Children of Abraham. The consequences were becoming tragic. Roman law had no pity for those who could not pay their debts. Stock and houses could be confiscated, and family members sold into slavery.

The options for Miriam were limited. Even as a sixteen year old, she understood her parents' fears. The threat was very real. Severe was the reality of declining commerce. Inescapable was the prospect of losing everything. A woman's role included management of the business records. She could see the figures. They did not lie.

Men paid a high price for a pure girl, in an age when young meant pure. Funds could be obtained, debts could be paid, and the family business would survive. Miriam regretted ever participating in such a trade. She had no guardian, feeling she didn't need one. Her father had had enough customers who had admired her even in her childhood. Did anyone object then? No, for it was all part of Roman culture to take advantage of available assets. Women were such a commodity. Young women were the prize.

– Ephesus Pure in Heart –

Miriam did not work the brothels as most women engaging in lurid activities would do. If she had, her life would have been totally controlled, basically that of a Roman slave. Years after the fact, she often reminded herself that if she had relied on a brothel she would have caught some disease, and most likely would have died long before her chance to meet the preacher.

There were actually three types of prostitution in the Roman world: the brothels from whom taxes could be collected and syphilis exchanged; the so-called lone does who avoided taxation on part-time employment and a domestic setting where prostitution meant far more than sexual favours. This last situation included all aspects of servitude: caring, cleaning, cooking, farming, crafts, and domestic skills. Prostitution, in such environs, was basically an extension of slavery. Matters of sexual debauchery involving the young could be concealed within domestic walls. Miriam had heard such stories and knew that Caligula was not alone in his fancy. The young could be quickly replaced having lost their attraction. Once used, no trusted man would ever marry such a used commodity.

After a few years, trade flourished once again. Commerce was that cyclical. Although the story of Joseph in Egypt mentioned seven years of plenty and seven years of famine; in Judaea the shifts and cycles never lasted as long as seven years. You could be wealthy one day and destitute within the year. Miriam needed to escape her past. In a world lacking the concept of forgiveness, leaving home was the only alternative. She would have been about nineteen years old when Christ first crossed her path.

Perhaps it was seeing the young John following Christ that prompted some of her attention. Having experienced servitude, she would be responsive to anyone her age with an honest smile. Charity, diligence and hope won her allegiance. In the companionship of His close followers, she carried her five foot three inch stature in style: no one's equal, yet no one's servant. They were individuals, yet all knowing they were part of the team. They had skills and talents, none of which were to be kept to them-selves, but to be shared for the greater good of the many. Being told they had to be servants to one another: this was difficult for her. Servitude, to Miriam, was basically abuse. She did not want to return to that depravity. Pondering the alternatives, as this was a major issue in the preacher's teachings she purposefully dropped the perception of 'servant', and embraced the reality of 'service'. She would be an 'equal' helping people whom she wanted to be her 'equal'; to elevate their lives as Christ had done to hers. Life in Mejdel had done her well in that regard because she fully accepted there would be moments of doubt, and times to embrace the pleasantries of success and enthusiasm.

Friendships included Susanna and Joanna in Herod's Court. These young women performed tasks usual to the Roman domicile within the Jewish echelon. Miriam was rarely questioned about her commitments to any cause. She couldn't recall anyone challenging her with respect to Christ's immediate plans or temporal needs. The wayward villages and struggling towns were always receptive to the popularity and influence of the healing preacher. Then as they approached Jerusalem the crowds were uncontrollable. In spite of the extremes between His followers and the ruling Pharisees, Miriam performed her tasks as if having total immunity. That she never understood.

Miriam also walked without fear among the Roman troops in her capacity as the teacher's companion: into any village, throughout Jerusalem, and moving among the raucous crowd without hesitation to her place beneath the cross. On that Friday evening and Sunday morning she was not stopped by the temple guard or by the Roman tribune. Miriam strangely appeared to have the acceptance of every sector of Judaea.

Famine in Judaea was only one ingredient to inflame the simmering hostility among Christians, Jews, and Romans to a rapid boil. Roman callousness, extreme means, and riotous zealots contributed to the turmoil which compelled many Jews by the year 41AD to seek permanency away from Jerusalem. Many relocated to Syria, some to Alexandria in Egypt, and others to Anatolia. Those heading north beyond Galilee would have included her friends and associates: Susanna, and various members of the Cleophas family. However by 46AD the famine was widespread in Syria, Antioch was in turmoil and Paul had just commenced his first missionary journey. In Jerusalem the Sadducees had achieved an extraordinary degree of support in their disputes with the Christians and Romans. The entire issue of resurrection was vile. Destroying Roman statues was treason. The zealots were no longer silent. Ineffective Pro Consuls, Herod's death, and Rome's inability to control sedition churned the

Judaean province into a sea of volatility that was sweeping the whole of Palestine. For Miriam, it was time to move on.

The cultural background of Mejdel had introduced Miriam to diverse views toward women. To the Hebrews, a woman had little importance except in household chores and the ability to produce another son. In the synagogues, women had no role. The Greeks respected women; however men still had priority in the opportunities of thought and expression. To the Romans, a woman was either a wife or a servant. From Egyptian culture, Miriam learned that a woman was granted more opportunity for thought and leadership. Then there was the Christian approach: a woman could participate. The Christians in Judaea were still very much tied to Hebrew culture. Miriam's effectiveness as one wanting to do more was stultified as long as she remained in Palestine.

Miriam slept well that night as she did nearly every night. Her schedule demanded it as she rarely had free time during day-light hours. She attended her market stall five days each week. This wasn't the result of any progressive labour rule, but rather the custodians of the market wanted to satisfy as many merchants as possible.

In the morning the plan was to take Anna to the Harbour Baths, the time of day reserved for women. Though women were never allowed to attend at times scheduled for men, there were no restrictions on men attending the baths to view the naked women. There were certain aspects of Greek culture that bothered her and this was certainly one of them. However there was nothing out of the ordinary to be seen. Clothes did more to compliment a person than nakedness. With respect to clothing, Miriam was also bothered with the tunics men made for women. They purposefully revealed far more than a woman of class should care to show. For that reason the modifications in the bodice and colour variations that Miriam included in her designs made her tunics a quick seller.

After the baths, Miriam anticipated spending hours at the dock hoping and waiting for her next shipment. There could be clothing material, silks, or perfumes from the traders in Galilee, Syria or Alexandria. Egypt was the main source for the majority of goods to a significant number of merchants. The Pro Consuls of both Egypt and Anatolia knew how to please the Emperor. As a result the Emperor's generosity was bestowed upon these centers. Shipments were essential to ensure that status.

Papyrus was equally important to Miriam because the rolled sheets were becoming a reliable means of spreading Christ's word. Paul wanted many and would later take these with him when he left Antioch. Timothy, also from Tarsus, valued the necessity to record. James too had his supply when he stayed behind in Palestine. And for John and Luke, the need seemed endless. Prior contacts, especially those from Alexandria, remained faithful suppliers.

Miriam came to realize very quickly that the way to capture an Ephesian's respect was sell quality goods. Even though she was viewed as somewhat strange in her beliefs, Miriam was accepted as being very much part of their culture because she was one with them in their commercial environs.

From the harbour to her home, using the available assistance was necessary. The alternative was to bring one's own wooden cart several kilometers among the crowds: through the market, onto the Marble Way and along Harbour Street. It basically couldn't be done by one person, never mind one woman. And for Miriam, it would also mean having to guide the blind girl with her while trying to steer the wooden pull carriage. Miriam objected to slavery. She was so absolutely abhorred by the concept and reality of such being the norm throughout the Empire. However there was also the reality that the entire Roman culture could be divided into two classes: masters and servants. The latter group involved domestic workers, prostitutes and homeless, and all who were employed in any capacity in any trade. Workers were basically slaves, and slaves found their value in work. Tyranny and torment were inescapable for some; but for many in the urban centers slavery had basically become employment. So much could be said, and so much was contemplated about slavery in the many evening discussions with their friends. For Miriam, her task was to be gracious, thankful for any service, and to appropriately tip and reward for the help provided.

Upon returning from the harbour, it would be time to stitch and sew. After supper, baking commenced. Sometime in that schedule John or someone else might show up. Other residents on the winding street just might drop by. There was never a dull moment at any time of any day.

Chapter Five

Harbour Baths

June, 51

Pro Consul Silanus had every reason to be apprehensive; but he wasn't. He sat there waiting on the cedar bench wrapped only in a towel. That would normally make one uncomfortable; but it didn't. The Harbour Baths were an amazing complex providing one massive bath surrounded by several porticos to private rooms, smaller granite tiled baths with flowing water, and massage with exercise facilities overlooking the harbour. All of that luxury did not raise his spirits. The grandeur was all part of the Rome that he deserved and was expected to enjoy.

A prudent man would have realized his perilous situation after having hung his cloak in the Emperor's closet. Nearly all of the Empire had an opinion of Claudius: his drunkenness, licentious living, extravagant spending, and the marriage to his niece. The fact that Claudius was deformed in mind or body mattered a lot. Rumors and stories after being told so many times had become the truth. To many, Claudius was not fit to rule. The fact that he expected Emperor Worship was even more revolting. Silanus was a buggy driver having hitched his cart to an old nag. Marcus, even though he had already completed four years of his rule, could not be considered to be overly wise.

Celer entered the room, totally naked. The Deputy Consul had discarded the towel in the hall way wishing to create the impression of disrespect he had for his superior. Silanus didn't say anything because he basically at all times just wanted to keep the peace. Celer then seated himself across from the Pro Consul in a manner conveying decency was not even a minute priority. The eunuch responded as was his duty providing each Roman with a mug of water. Lysias shortly entered the room being more discreet with his towel in place. Then Darius arrived. He was Celer's shadow: the echo of his thoughts, the perpetrator and the dutiful peon. This was a rare occasion for Darius, for he was rarely sober. In a terse display of disrespect he discarded his towel just as Celer had instructed him. The eunuch reacted immediately almost grabbing the towel before it even hit the floor. Nudity had gained its expected result. Silanus deplored anything homosexual. The baths were the limit of his tolerance for such exposure. Once outside the pool, decency was to rule. However, Marcus seemed to forget that Ephesus was still Roman and everything standard in Rome was allowed elsewhere within the Empire. Regardless, annoying Silanus was Celer's intent and he valued his success in that achievement.

"No matter what we do, the Asiarchs will challenge our decision." Silanus' statement was expected. He was becoming more prone to rambling, and would start conversations leaving those in the room wondering about the topic. "That seems to be their prerogative. Our discussions yesterday, we have to decide."

"This is the glory of your achievements," Lysias stated his support for the Pro Consul.

"Destiny echoes are purpose. Celer, remind Rome that Asia is the pearl in the clear waters of the Roman seas. We are the laurel that adorns our divine Emperor."

Celer then understood that the issue was the Emperor's request for troops. However he had no interest in praising Silanus for any accomplishment. Being good at the political game was his specialty. "There should be no discontent among your people. They will see the merit of your plan."

"Be cautious of Claudius: the political swan is graceful to see, defensive of territory, yet inside the same foul his mother begot," Darius chided without much thought.

Celer immediately jumped in to defend his supporter. "Spoken by one who loves Rome as he does Asia." Silanus could have chastised the legionnaire, but silence ruled.

Lysias muddied the focus of their initial concern. "Must the blood of every Jew in Ephesus stain the harbour? Is this your intent?"

"Do you challenge the Emperor's decree?" Celer demanded wondering if Lysias even understood the issue.

"His rule is just," Darius added.

"And his achievements many." Celer though having no affinity toward Claudius was playing the game to discredit Lysias who was Marcus' friend.

"His means," Lysias retorted.

Silanus reacted trying to quell the dissention, "Fortune cannot be lost in our differences. Though this is not Alexandria, we cannot avoid..."

"What is another Jew to our Grecian friends?" Celer couldn't have been more direct.

"We should..." Lysias was interrupted.

"Caution yourself!" Celer spoke as if he were the Pro Consul.

"When has Rome ever surrendered sense to the day's affairs?" Lysias would not be silent.

"Do you wish Rome to depose every Emperor until one is found who satisfied the whims of every faction?" Celer was not going to let Lysias get the final word.

"Friends," Silanus interjected, "let us not forget the duty we owe to the Senate and People of Rome. In times past, we here persuaded our illustrious Emperor that the Hebrews in particular should be free and have the rights afforded Roman citizens. The fortunes of all Romans in Asia prospered. Now we have unrest, not here but in Judaea, against the benevolence which is Rome. Therefore it now seems appropriate that we must act and do so in good measure. Though Rome is constant, the people it rules do change. That which prompts our action is the unchanging will of Caesar.

"Hail Silanus!" Celer offered mock tribute.

On cue Darius chimed in, "Hail!"

"I am honoured." Silanus smiled at the impression he had achieved agreement.

Following a quick hand signal to the eunuch, Celer was handed a towel to cover himself and was provided with a scroll wrapped in a blanket. He had gained their attention quickly as he started to read, actually pretending to read, from the blank unfurled document in a misty room.

> Our Imperial Emperor, Claudius, tells us he is gravely troubled. He has afforded every opportunity to those he governs. Now he prepares for the conflict upon which the Hebrew faction appears fixed. Procurator Felix is torn by the voice of insurrection. Peace remains uneasy since Palestine was afforded self-rule under the despised Agrippa. This very hour, zealots stir the people. That, which Rome has held sacred, has been desecrated in their marketplace. Their counsel chooses not to control the mob. Rome is spat upon by the poor, and trampled by the rich.

These are the words of Emperor Claudius."

"Hail Caesar!" Darius dutifully saluted grabbing an extra tunic from the side table.

"Felix has requested our assistance. We must respond," Celer continued. There was no immediate response. The Deputy Consul then added, "We must not allow our roads to become the shelter for brigands, our markets a home to criminals, and our outposts burial plots for legionnaires. Felix will march along the coast and inward throughout his territory to guarantee that all villages throughout Palestine and Syria are free from Jewish tyranny. In all towns he will purge unrest. In Jerusalem Claudius will receive the respect he deserves."

"When Celer?" Darius enquired.

The Deputy Consul was direct, "In time Darius. Caesar has graced Ephesus with his request for our assistance in this noble cause. From here our troops will march by way of Derbe, through Tarsus and then to Damascus. Rome will move south to Perea resting there to cast a shadow over the dissention which is now Judaea."

– Ephesus Pure in Heart –

"Is bloodshed inevitable?" Lysias questioned.

"That choice belongs to Judaea. Rome will be ready this time, not asleep."

"And our ships?" Darius queried.

"Setting sail to Caesarea," Celer informed.

Lysias was quite disturbed. "Is all this necessary? Are we to repeat Caligula's folly? Judaea doesn't need more fuel to fire a revolt."

Darius sided with Celer, "You cannot cure leprosy by piercing a boil."

Silanus affirmed the inevitable, "This must be. Celer, tell Caesar that Ephesus will be most pleased to accommodate his need."

"Where will these legionnaires stay?" Lysias conveyed ongoing apprehension.

"Where two live, there shall be a third; wherever Rome requires it." Celer remained decisive.

"Is there benefit if we antagonize our own. Surely with discontent here, Rome's problem will no longer be with Judaea, but with Asia." Lysias was clearly worried.

"A point well spoken," Celer announced rarely agreeing with Lysias. "If we cleanse Judaea with these foreign factions still in Ephesus, much could happen here that would not be to our benefit."

"What are you suggesting?" Lysias demanded an end to the guessing game.

"My friend," Celer started in a condescending tone, "we have to deal with the Jewish problem here. Sending our legionnaires to Judaea, will it weaken our strength at home? We have no choice with Palestine, we will answer the Emperor. We may not agree, but is there a choice?" He paused for further comment and again there was none. "But here? What will happen when our legions depart? Who will safeguard our towns, our harbours, this city?"

"Specifics." Lysias added forcefully.

"Solve the Jewish problem here. Any suspicion of opposition to Rome must be considered tyranny. We cannot and will not tolerate it. We will not be a divided people!" Celer couldn't be more definite.

"You are men of foul persuasion. You hail the Emperor and then challenge the undying support of his people. Leave men of good conscience alone." Lysias looked toward Darius, avoiding Celer's frustration.

"Good conscience! Do you call those Hebrews men of good conscience?" Celer clearly considered the Christians to be Jews. "In the marketplace they challenge our devotion to Diana, and to the Greeks they defy Artemis. We shall never tolerate such sedition."

"Lysias, be assured bloodshed is not our wish. Procurators as well as Pro Consuls always seek peace within their provinces. That is so now and will not change." Silanus' words did nothing to dispel fears.

"This venture will bring security to Rome's eastern empire," Celer concluded.

"We are firm," Silanus agreed. "Tomorrow let us meet at the home of your cousin on the road to Miletus."

"Brothers, we are well resolved," Celer announced. He mastered living off ambiguity.

"Next year we will celebrate with the Artemis games in Jerusalem!" Darius laughed.

With that Lysias abruptly stood, bowed to the Pro Consul, and left.

"He must bear our resolve," Celer was direct.

"I will see him tonight. Leave the day's concerns with me," Silanus added.

"You are a true friend of Claudiuus. He will be reminded many times in our letter of your loyalty and support. But friends' let us return to the baths. There are young ones from Corinth to soothe our worries."

Darius was quick to leave.

Silanus sat alone with Celer. It was an uncomfortable setting. The eunuch had departed to get more towels. Quick glances pierced the thick steam, then eyes looked away no longer able to decipher the other's expression. Silanus was the first to leave being enticed by the prospect of the young women waiting in the central pool.

Celer bent forward looking at the granite tile between his feet. He was a mystic, more than most. The future and course of events were always determined by vague symbols, being interpreted to suit his aim. That tile decreed his purpose for in it he saw the shadow of a warrior raising his weapon and ready to strike. His mind instantly raced with thoughts becoming definitive expressions of his intent. "Now is the die cast. Judaea will be brought back to Rome in chains! As Cumanis washed his hands in Hebrew blood, so shall we here bathe in the afterbirth

– Ephesus Pure in Heart –

Chapter Six

Sun Rise at the Harbour

July, 51

The harbour was unusually quiet that morning. The last vessel had departed the prior afternoon. Laden with wooden cribs supporting timber, terra cotta containers of spice and sacks of grain, the craft was destined for Ostia near Rome. More cargo ships were expected early that morning, but the births remained empty. Worries were not extreme; however dock workers and traders all knew that ships, not in port, nor on the horizon, were never a good omen. Calm winds at shore rarely conveyed the current or waves a mile off port. Howling winds beyond Rhodes could suck any vessel into the depths of Poseidon's Kingdom.

John continued to stare out to sea. The aura continually amazed him. He was similarly fascinated with the harbour's construction techniques. Wooden timbers were somehow secured to a rock base, and then the dock was finished with stripped and levelled beams. Everything had also been constructed to accommodate varying tides and waves. The entire harbour had already been cleansed that morning.

"Where is everyone?" Luke commented eyeing the jester who arrived without an audience. The entertainer paused, stared at the Christian gentlemen, waved his wand in their direction invoking a hex, and then moved on.

"Just a clown," John remarked.

Luke pulled the collar of his garment up around his neck. Tunics never provided enough comfort in the morning breeze. "Attendance is disappointing," he stated.

John didn't disagree. The concept of deacons was accepted quickly in Jerusalem and Antioch, but in Ephesus there was reluctance among the followers. They seemed too satisfied with the status quo. John accepted that he was considered the primate for the metropolitan area, and as such was viewed as having some mysterious ability to be many places at the same moment. The Christians wanted him to be here, there and everywhere, and to lead every ceremony. Because of that he was starting to feel quite uncomfortable. Following Christ was not to be equated with preferring John. This was a significant hurdle. He was pleased with the spiritual enthusiasm for sharing the Body of Christ; but there were human limits to his capacity. More ministers were required.

"Not sure about the idea for the first day of the week." John referred to prior discussions on Sunday worship. "How can we tell the followers that they must honour God on a specific day when we don't have enough ministers or buildings, and when most are compelled to work on the Solis?" That basically concluded that topic, at least for the present.

They watched the jester, as he returned from the far end of the dock. "Don't worry. He'll find his audience," John quipped. The jester slithered away down Harbour Street in the direction of the market. They then followed him at a considerable distance. To their left there was the massive complex of the Harbour Baths. Paving stones were marble. Columns drew the perception of citizens and visitors to the magnificence of Greece. Shops, porticos, and a temple were situated between the columns. Some of the pillars even provided lighting, torches fueled with oil. Beneath the paving stones water ran from the aqueducts. The sewage system also had a conduit under the walkway stretching under the Marble Way and Curetes Street, and ending in the vicinity of the marsh. Whatever might be said concerning the idolatry of the Greeks, everyone still had to marvel at their engineering prowess.

Finding their usual place they sat by a pillar adjacent to a particular merchant's stall. There they continued their discourse.

The Counsel of Jerusalem was the issue that restarted their conversation. The Apostles were definite: Christianity was open to everyone. Basically a person did not have to be Jewish before becoming Christian. John interpreted that decision in the extreme, a view that had at first puzzled Luke. The Apostle viewed it as an attempt to counter the prevailing view of women in all cultures. If Christianity was open to everyone, then it was also open to women as individual persons. They should no longer be viewed as derivatives of their husbands or households. Once the Counsel determined circumcision was not a prerequisite then anyone uncircumcised could be Christian. Many of the converts so far in Ephesus were women: the result of John's efforts, the example of Miriam, and the stories of Christ's mother and women of the Old Testament. It was these women that carried their enthusiasm forth into their homes and neighbourhoods. Luke, based on the Hellenistic heritage, couldn't totally agree with John's conclusion.

"Amazes me how so many care so little about tomorrow, and how they just hang their fate on a trinket." Luke added. Nothing had changed regarding his view toward idolatry. John took the moment to remind Luke of the propensity in the past for citizens in Antioch to adorn themselves with Roman images. Luke was quick to dismiss the comment as that had never been his inclination. "Still," John added, "these cults are now everywhere. Five years ago, they were there but we couldn't say much. Now there seems no limit. When the Romans start adulating this Greek deity they call Mithras, one has to ask, 'When will it stop?' Unfortunately, it seems never. Look at this coin." John held up a silver denarius bearing the image of Claudius. "Now they have two feet in hell worshiping their rulers!"

The increasing influence of the guilds perplexed them. Luke was troubled by their influence and control of so many aspects of society assuring the Imperial Cult. That the Greeks had just followed along was even more puzzling. Few Christians had anything nice to say about Claudius, but they tolerated him doing their basic duty to appease the Romans.

The question was often repeated, "How do we get to the miners?" The Christians had made significant inroads into the agricultural valleys. It was easier relating Christ's stories about seeds and fig trees and shepherds to the farming communities. For the miners, there were no such stories except the pearl of great value. Even so that did not seem relevant. Working to exhaustion in salt pits, chiselling granite beyond all limits of pain, or while suffocating in sulfur mines: Christianity offered little hope. Another inescapable reality confounded attempts to attract miners to follow Christ: they were slaves. Talking to any slave or interrupting his work required the consent of the over lord who saw no need for any religion that didn't generate profits or production.

Slavery was so repugnant. Task masters had no limits to their capacity for oppression. However such servitude ensured the required workforce, a standard generally accepted in the first century. Still John and Luke questioned its need, and how best to end the practice of treating humans worse than animals.

John continued by mentioning his reservations concerning the intentions of Susannah and Miriam to sell Christian symbols in the market. These would be crucifixes and fish or lamb symbols. It eventually had to happen and he was very supportive; but he worried as he always did about anything that might befall Miriam. He admired her more than anyone else. However, he would never impart such words as an expression of personal preference; as doing so could be hazardous to his campaign to spread the Word. Regardless circumstances gave John many opportunities to laud the general efforts of the women in their community. Many of course instinctively understand to whom he was referring.

Luke's comments about the agora involved his persistent fear of Greek or Roman spies. He questioned once more, "Who can we trust?" This was becoming his common refrain.

John then repeated his facetious gratitude to the Emperor for having cited "Chrestus" as being the cause of the unrest in Rome. "We've done well." John continued suggesting they should also convey their appreciation to the authorities in Jerusalem for their decision to purposefully segregate devout Hebrews from the followers of Jesus.

Having done that, the Jews had removed the Christians from the scourge of Roman tyranny following the Emperor's edict against the Jews.

Luke once more, having done so each week, mentioned Christ's Mother and how much she had meant to him, and to so many in Antioch, and at her home on the hill. It was easily discernible that Luke, who had never personally met Christ, knew more about Him and Maryam from the many stories shared among the four of them. Maryam gave Luke details concerning her son's birth, the angels, the temple and the flight to Egypt. Luke enhanced such conversations with his knowledge of recent events. He was very much the pre-eminent historian. Miriam was no less repetitive in her tales concerning miracles, the Passover, His crucifixion and His resurrection. John, not lacking any time for such important matters, added his own recollections that were seemingly endless. For all these, there was never enough papyrus.

Although they could talk for hours more, there came a time each day when Luke would have to end their discussion. Employment demanded his attention in day light hours. As a doctor, philosopher, and alchemist Luke had the respect of the citizens, and worked significant hours each day as his officium.

Luke was born and raised as a Hellenistic Jew in Antioch of Syria. Education provided him with the opportunity to acquire his valuable skills. As a doctor Luke was a valuable asset in the community. Famine and fear in Syria, as it had done for so many residents, compelled Luke to consider new horizons. His friends had already found their home in Ephesus. He followed their direction assured of acceptance, not only because he was skilled, but because he was Greek. Quickly he proved himself to be an adept professional. The medical clinics at the Harbour Baths established his practice at the heart of the city, assuring him influence in the community that was essential to the growth of Christianity. So much was to be achieved by quality example.

That evening, as it was Mercurii, they would share a meal together at Miriam's home. Hosting her ensemble of friends was a weekly event.

Chapter Seven

Stadium Plot

August, 51

The legionnaires grabbed the brief respite afforded them. Such opportunities were rare as they always had to be on guard. Accord in the city was never assured. With famine ravaging the eastern Mediterranean, Ephesus had become home to desperate families. The changing culture became a realm of undefined and unfulfilled expectations. Refugees escaping dire conditions on the islands brought with them acute anxiety. These were all part of the ingredients in the cauldron of Ephesus. Mixing too many flavours did not rid the acidity of discomfort. Frustration could in an instant become violence.

Sitting in the vacant stadium they stretched their limbs feeling for just those few moments relatively pleased with their lives. The Apollo Music Festival was only a week away, an occasion when the entire stadium would be filled to capacity for music and entertainment by performers from regions throughout the Empire. Burrus was assigned the task of managing security on the southern portion of the stadium. That side would accommodate all citizens residing in the central portion of the city including the influential from the terrace houses on Marble and Curetes Streets. Government officials would have the assigned seats nearest the field. Burrus always wondered about that as he realized a preferred view was always attained by being higher up. However that was not for him to challenge or even question. He may have had his moments, but he always remained dutiful: in protocol to Silanus, but in heart to Celer.

Darius, having committed himself to be a trifle sober during the day, had jurisdiction for security in the north end of the stadium. That was more than one legionnaire could handle as many in the lesser class from the valleys would be entering the stadium using that portico. Darius had assembled his entourage to assist the process.

For the protection of the actors, Celer assumed that responsibility. It was a prestigious role and he knew it would be to his benefit.

As they sat there in the stadium, carefully eying anyone who would just stroll in and leave, there remained considerable apprehension. Lysias' opinions and alleged conduct was drawing a knife through the legion separating factions on a multitude of issues. Burrus had no appetite for anyone who questioned Rome's benevolence. The Army had so indoctrinated them to believe that Rome could do no wrong. The Deputy Consul had trained them well.

Darius concluded in a manner that would please Celer, "Here after he'll not be alone with his mistress without our shadows parting their wills."

Burrus agreed quoting the Deputy Consul, "The plan remains ours: one to complete, one to conceal. We should go with the speed of Mercury, the cunning of Hera, and the appearance of Apollo."

After that, there was solitude and peace within the empty stadium.

Chapter Eight

Heaven in the Valley

August, 51

Alexa looked forward to this evening more with special fondness. Other festive occasions were always fretful events with all of the pomp and revelry expected of Greek or Roman culture. This evening there would be no lavishly adorned statues or gaily dressed magicians with their symbolic spells, or barely clad dancers, or the so-called influential trying to convince everyone of their importance. Her husband was with her. She adored him in every respect. That he was Greek allowed him to walk among the Hellenists as their equal. That he had married a Christian made him a respected addition to their community. Philemon was an adept merchant, superior in commerce while surpassing others in the political game. He had that alluring smile that convinced every talker that he was attentively listening. His height and build was such that athletes looked up to him. In his youth the javelin was his skill. Such athletes were always remembered for past feats.

John was obviously proud of these occasions on the Primum Dies Solis of every month. He could accommodate ten persons at the one table. There were six rooms in his home, albeit three were a trifle small. The kitchen was bigger than most having been enlarged in the first year of his occupancy. The lavatory facility was at the far end. John lived by himself but had rooms for two guests. His home was located in the valley between Mount Lepre and Bulbul Mountain,

Curetes Street near the Prytaneon. Passing regularly by the Pro Consul's quarters provided frequent opportunities for colloquial discussions with government officials. Living close to a farming community made him very much one of them: not as their spokesman but as one understanding their difficulties and sympathizing with their troubles. His example, charity and understanding had endeared many to Christian fellowship.

Miriam, Susanna and Anna were busy in the kitchen preparing the meal. They would often jest that they had no problems with such tasks after spending the day at the market showing men how to do their jobs. Miriam always provided the blind girl had a verbal description of their preparations. This meal they had assembled on many occasions – the Feast of the Lord's Supper.

John had already been kicked out of his own kitchen being told to prepare the table. to After assembling the cushions around the table and filling the jugs with water, John positioned the two scrolls, lit the oil lamp, prepared a decanter of wine and set cups and napkins for eight.

Three times that day John had already celebrated the Breaking of Bread in various parts of the city. He came home in the late afternoon quite pleased with the progress both in terms of numbers and sincerity. More deacons were being approved by the congregations. The initial reluctance in the remotest portion of the valley to join the new religion had become new-found enthusiasm causing the numbers to far exceed his expectations. "Absolutely delighted" could barely describe his joy. John was above all pragmatic. The hostility in Judaea had already taught him that evangelization won't happen quickly. Fear of Roman punishment continued to deter participation for many. The Holy Spirit was certainly there to assist, but the Spirit rarely spoke in the tongues of corpses. Preserving life, he felt, would give him more opportunity over time to accomplish more. The Greek fable about being 'slow and steady' was very much the case. That program was now flourishing.

The hosts had previously met Philemon. This occasion was very special for all, especially Alexa, as the gentleman just the week before accepted the new religion as the foundation of his life. John had baptised him and was now celebrating the Lord's Supper with him and their family of friends.

John sat at the center of the table on one side. Alexa and her husband were across from him. Miriam positioned herself closest to the kitchen with Anna on her right. Two places were empty in the event visitors would later arrive.

The Apostle took the unleavened bread from the clay plate. Holding it before him, John prayed silently and then broke the large crust passing a portion to each person present. He ate his first, and the others reverently followed. Miriam then poured wine into one cup and passed it to John. After silent prayer, he took a sip and passed it to each. Alexa's eyes were brilliant with pride when passing the cup to her husband. His conversion was her ultimate dream. Silence followed for personal reflection.

Susannah was the first to speak. "God is good. God is one."

"May His Spirit be with us," John added, and then passed the scroll to Alexa.

"But we are guests," was her instinctive response.

"Appreciation far exceeds…" Miriam spoke for their host.

"Your practice gives much credence to your faith. Alexa, it's their wish that we be honoured." Philemon appreciated the courtesy.

"The Lord is our shepherd," Alexa began to read.

Miriam led the response, "He is our hope and salvation."

"In verdant pastures," Alexa continued.

"He provides rest and comfort."

With phrases describing the bliss of heaven, Alexa read, "In the cool waters of flowing streams."

"He refreshes troubled minds," John and Miriam in unison recited the refrain.

"In the holiness of His Name."

"He guides us in peace."

"Always at our side," Alexa was overwhelmed.

"He gives us courage." Even Anna knew that phrase.

"In the glory of His banquet."

"He anoints us."

"Goodness and kindness."

"He shares all our days." Philemon in his heart was amazed at the simplicity of the endearing verse.

"To dwell in eternity." Alexa's prayerful tears were welling up.

"Ever more."

With that Alexa rolled the scroll and passed it to John. There was a joy that could not be concealed.

"May the Lamb of God pierced for our sins," John concluded the psalm.

"Be merciful to us," Miriam responded.

The meal followed with cheerful discussion. Anna's smile defined the festive nature of the repast.

"About Oscirus, has any more been said?" Philemon enquired.

"No more than yesterday," Susannah added based on discussions at the market.

"How can a family suffer such?" Alexa shared their tribulation.

"It's hard to understand God's love," her husband stated. This echoed Susannah's view until John's admonition that God very rarely causes tribulations that people cannot overcome. He was then challenged about that view with reference to the massive earthquake and resulting death less than twenty-five years before.

"Never judge the extent of God's love," John concluded.

Miriam returned to Philemon's concern. "His family finds shelter with Donaldus. Susannah, you still bring a meal ever second day, don't you?"

Susannah nodded her agreement.

"There are others too; and Rebecca provided clothes. Others have cleared the ashes and debris. There are logs and blocks on site. Sentillius will commence rebuilding the morning after next Sabbath."

"One is amazed." It was easy for Philemon to admit his astonishment.

At that moment, there was a knock at the door. Without pause, Luke entered. The greetings were automatic. Though others may have been surprised, for John this was a regular visitor. The immediate conversation dwelt on Luke's writing and need for more papyrus. More importantly at the time, Luke related what Bernardus had heard concerning Paul and Barnabas, and Paul's plan for a second journey. Luke used the term "missionary work". That for John was enthusiastically inspirational, for he had never thought of Ephesus as a 'mission' or their efforts as being 'missionary'. Both terms to John suggested geographical limitations in their endeavours. This city was not a 'mission'. It was through their lives and example that they could encourage others to become followers. John understood that Paul's attempts to convert the Greek world were slightly diverse with the missionary's intention to establish communities in the diverse regions of the pagan world. That message was abundantly clear in the letter to Thessalonica. Luke had obtained a copy of same from an associate in Troas and shared it with John for the community in Ephesus.

The conversation then turned to the other Christian communities in the northern Aegean with Luke sharing information on the progress and spread of the faith.

> It's the Spirit of Hope that allows faith to grow. The Spirit reminds me every morning that there is more to do than I did yesterday. Then at night, the Spirit in a gentle whisper reassures me that I did do more.

Philemon was incredibly impressed with Luke's narration, needing to add:

> There is much in this faith that is so attractive, yet for many it is so stumbling. Bread becoming the body of Christ is not so easily understood, yet it is something the Greeks could accept because that is the gift they offer Mithras. However, the mean s of attaining this vague eternity just seems too austere. For example, Moses said 'no murder', but you say 'no anger.' 'Must be become God to be His children?' This is what they ask.

John answered immediately. "Mosaic Law was established on a definite set of rules: you must do this, you shall not do that. However, Christ talks of a positive rule of love."

"You mean charity?" Alexa enquired.

"What then for your Hebrews? Can the Jews ever get to heaven?" Philemon was intensely philosophical.

John's advice stressed the Second Great Commandment.

> The Lord said we must love one another. That law was for all, whether Jew, Greek or Roman. We must love one another as God loves us. In fact we are told that at the end of time we will be judged on how charitable we were to one another, how often we fed the hungry, provided shelter to the homeless or visited the sick.

"Then if the same rule applies to all, why choose one religion over another?" Philemon's question was direct.

Luke continued the discussion.

> The Hebrews believe in a life after death. That is what they shall inherit. The Greeks have their gods and the Romans their own. They shall in turn afford themselves the luxuries of their gods, no more and no less. But we respond to Christ who conquered death. We await the promise of His eternal happiness.

Changing the topic, Miriam asked Alexa about the bakery that Alexa's family operated in the north end near the Cayster River. "Still keeping the troops fed?"

"Naomi does. Don't know where she finds the time," Alexa advised.

"Is he still nowhere to be found?" Miriam engaged in woman talk about Lysias.

"She doesn't say. Actually I rarely see her; but when I do, he is never with her."

Miriam's wry personality was taking over. "Men are always at war with women's intentions. They constantly play us as if we're just fantasies."

"Whatever they be?" Luke jested.

"Would you like to know?" Susannah smiled accompanied by light hearted laughter.

"I'm sure they wonder," Miriam mused.

"There must be something inside their heads," Susannah quipped.

Philemon tried to be part of their conversation. "A woman's soul is always script for a man's mind."

"Only if her conscience is open to interpretation." Miriam could switch easily to being serious.

"Come on John. Tell us more." Susannah prompted him to suggest there was at least for one moment a relationship with Miriam.

"You seem to have a reputation," Philemon added directing his comment to Miriam.

"Unjustly so," Miriam smiled.

"She hides many secrets." The humour continued.

"And secrets they'll remain," Miriam responded to Susannah.

"They paint a devilish picture." Philemon appreciated the light humour.

Miriam's comment was brief, "Just ignore them."

The need for banter was grand relief to the many tensions kept inside. Anxiety was rooted in the uncertainties of culture and produce. After Ephesus supplied Rome first, the consumption of quality goods was not guaranteed. While merchants waited for vessels; the temples thrived. Greeks followed like Roman sheep. The cosmopolitan nature of Ephesian commerce was waning. Uncertainty ruled.

"That should give us impetus in spreading the faith. Feed off their insecurity," Luke concluded.

The hospitality continued for another hour, ending just before ten o'clock. In age when sun dials were useless after sun down, it was an inherent instinct to be able to gauge the hour at any time of night. John offered to accompany his guests home, and they politely declined. Susannah then left with Philemon and Alexa. However Miriam stayed behind. With Anna they adjourned to one of the small bedrooms, a venue where they had often slept. Luke stayed awake with John. Only the oil lamp on the table provided light.

They talked further about increasing the number of converts and deacons. John mentioned that he had received word about Thomas beyond Persia. Luke started a personal confession questioning his role and future, concluding his wish to speak with Paul. Regarding the missionary, John couldn't be certain that Paul would even visit Ephesus. The level of superstition was so outrageous that trying to evangelize the area for most disciples would be a lost cause. "So why are we here?" Luke smiled.

They then talked politics, specifically about individuals in the Patricians, Senate, and those still influential in the Greek world. So much success depended on friendships. There had been no recent rumors from Rome; and they viewed that as beneficial. Although they didn't appreciate the threat of Claudius' edicts, silence throughout the Mare Nostrum was a pleasing reality.

Then at long last they returned to the subject that once prompted disagreement: the role of women. John could not say enough about their contribution throughout the city and how much they had led people to Christ by their example. This time, Luke did not disagree.

As if on cue Miriam, wearing her gown, appeared in the doorway. "You were saying?"

The laughter was automatic.

"What are you hearing at the market?" Luke asked. He always valued the intricacies of people's needs. Wells, logs, roads, and even poultry all occupied the conversation. More residents were needing wells, with the rivers tending to have prolonged dry seasons. More people required more housing demanding more logs. Roads that were at best flaky soil became rivers in the rainy season. And with respect to poultry, there was a sizeable portion of the community turning away from just crops for daily sustenance. Chickens were becoming a viable commodity. Accordingly an entire guild had established its role as medians raising, butchering, and transporting fresh meat. Pigs, goats and cattle then received their due during the discussion.

Evangelization was John's topic, an issue in which he knew Miriam had a keen interest. Paul's issue of idolatry was the realistic point to start that conversation. In just a few years, the Cult of the Emperor had consumed Ionia. However the Roman rulers perceiving the benefit of keeping the Hellenists happy allowed Greeks to continue to worship their deities. Thus it became a competition as to who would receive the more worship: Claudius or Artemis. Into that mix, this minute faction of Christians tried to impress the idol worshipers that the Christian way of life and route to eternal bliss was preferable to accepted veneration that had endured for more than seven hundred years.

Preaching 'Christ crucified' was considered repulsive to the Romans as it was the Romans who crucified Him. A Roman, who heard that, wasn't about to embrace the sect that brought such an accusation. Further, the Emperor Cult controlled their lives. The

Greeks were too comfortable with their culture. The fact that even Rome allowed Hellenists to continue with veneration of their deities convinced many that their practices were worth saving. Something had to be done to allow the Christians to display their faith. The symbol 'Chi Rho' became the answer. They agreed with Miriam to have the symbol on rings, broaches, and some attire. Christian symbols of the crucifixion and resurrection could generate enthusiasm for the faith. Murals were already showing companionship, daily events and acts of charity. Going that one step further by adding a Christian symbol of charity to any mural could encourage anyone concerning the Faith. Musical instruments, such as tambourines, cymbals and the lyre, could be used to enhance liturgy. More readings, not just stories, should augment the 'Breaking of the Bread.' Long after midnight, they exhausted the issues.

Eventually they allowed their minds to rest. Luke retired first to the second of the bed enclaves.

"How much more?" John stood in the dark before Miriam. The candle had been extinguished. The only light in the room was her assurance. They hugged as they would do on other occasions, as close friends on the same perilous venture, respecting choices and cherishing the enthusiastic future their companionship guaranteed.

John lay in bed that night once more realizing that he would never be satisfied no matter how much they achieved.

Chapter Nine

Tartarus

September, 51

Celer had only once before descended the stone stairway to the bowels of the Prytaneion. It was a region no one cared to mention, nor even consider, and definitely not visit. Those who had seen it rarely lived to tell the outside world. This was the Roman jail. Tartarus was its name; in Roman mythology a dark adobe from which criminals and sinners could not escape. There was no flaming River Phlegethon, nor Hydra the wild beast with terrifying jaws. Instead there were Romans everywhere on the top floor, and two jailers below. These guards could describe the horror to the outside world but never spoke of the torture. Every morning they would arrive to do their duty for which they were paid pittance. There were two shifts.

It didn't take long for the Deputy Consul to descend to the basement level with its twelve foot high stone walls. Still, he was cautious because of the dampness on the granite stairway. There was no railing, so he had to step carefully. The torch, his only light, was flittering by the time they reached the prison floor. The eerie sensation of the light from the one flame flashing hither and throw onto dank walls made him squirm. As a Centurion he was determined and forceful, but the unseen made him timid and fretful.

The dungeon was cold. Brick walls, damp with cold condensation, ensured the environs would be the most inhospitable. The floor was crusty clay. Every so often there was a patch where an insane inmate had started digging his feet trying to avoid being dragged to inevitable torture. In two areas there were granite slabs upon which prisoners could be secured to the cold floor to ultimately go insane from the frigid conditions or perpetual cramps. Shackles were fixed into the far wall: some high for wrists, and others near the floor for ankles. A large timber stained by blood lay against the wall to his right. Celer knew its purpose. He had seen a crucifixion before. The straw was changed once each month. That was the bedding. To the far left the Deputy Consul could barely make out the stone pillar where inmates were scourged. There was a rack in some enclosure within those depths, but that was not Celer' interest.

He watched as the guard poured mash onto the palms of the two remaining inmates. Celer looked away as the first prisoner grovelled trying to bring the liquid to his mouth before it ran out of his hands onto the floor. The second prisoner barely had the strength to lift his hands to his face, so he had nothing to eat.

The whole scene only for an instant bothered Celer. Ultimately his impression was bolstered with the realization that Rome was so capable of dealing with dissent. While his hand still clutched his sword for personal protection, Celer instructed the legionnaire to bring Burrus to the prison.

Relying on the one torch for light, Celer stood beneath it watching one of the guards. There was an opening in that wall: not to provide air for the prisoners but rather to ensure the flame did not die.

Burrus arrived with the expected expletives regarding the conditions. Celer then called for the one guard, the one wearing the black maniple on his left wrist. The Deputy Consul had been told what to expect. The guard hadn't shaved in weeks and obviously had not washed either. He reeked. His clothes were absolutely tattered. The existence of a second cloak clearly defined him as a guard, and not a prisoner.

– Ephesus Pure in Heart –

The guard had many nicknames over the years. He had no idea how long he had been there. He was not educated so he couldn't count the number of prisoners he had seen arrive or die. Celer had been told that he had once been a prisoner, but no one was sure how he was awarded this position. Perhaps no one else wanted it.

Language too was a major hurdle. Celer started talking to him, but clearly there was little comprehension. Burrus entered the conversation with his limited knowledge of the Thracian dialect.

The jailer was called Muscipula, a name given him based on his initial task – mouse catcher. Celer wanted a spy and nothing more. This guard's job resume was an exact fit. The discussion took almost half-hour to convince Muscipula that the job being offered was real. Burrus would be his go between. Ultimately the guard smiled affirming his agreement. He lacked many teeth, but that didn't bother Celer. The rat catcher was clearly decrepit in nature, a walking corpse who wanted out of the jail and would do anything he was asked to do.

Upstairs he was bathed by maids from the Temple of Julius. He ate well and slept better. Muscipula was a calf being fed for the slaughter; but not his.

Chapter Ten

Playing the Artemis Card

September, 51

He had very little time for any cult or devotion, unless it was to his benefit. Celer, one of the three Deputy Consuls, was adept at reading the mind of the people. He took every opportunity possible to assure the citizens that he was one of them. In reality, he was. Celer was Roman raised in the environs of a Greek community. His family were Patricians, with close friends in the Senate. Such connections with corresponding wealth assured his family's influence. He was never committed to the inner workings of any urban area. Celer was above all a wealthy land owner with sufficient acreage to raise, feed and sell cattle. The husbandry ultimately included horses, wild uncontrollable steeds that calmed themselves in the luxury of his green pastures and sheltered stalls. With these he developed and improved riding skills. With wealth, influence and horses Celer became an Equestrian, an essential component in any Roman Army. He progressed to leadership of his cavalry unit achieving military success with participation in celebratory events. Accordingly he was rewarded for his commitment to Rome.

Celer conveyed only polite respect for Antonius and Hypatius, the other Deputy Consuls. Antonius received his post solely because he was rich, not because of any skill. Regarding Celer, Antonius had no trust. Celer was clearly a master at intrigue and conniving. His reputation like a shadow followed him. Antonius would continuously observe those who followed Celer's every whim, while wondering why Silanus chose not to curtail the ambition.

Eventually it was instinct that caused Hypatius to react in a manner he chose. He knew enough about politics to realize nothing could be accomplished without the support of the people. While Celer sought the admiration of the Roman population, Hypatius chose to pursue the support of the Greek residents. Actually the Greeks comprised more than just residents, they included so many pilgrims and refugees from so many regions: Achaia, Thrace, Bithynia, Macedonia, Lycia, Pamphylia, Cilicia, Cappadocia, Galatia, Syria, Cyprus, Crete, Alexandria, Sicily, Cyrene, and Numidia. Ensuring the veneration of their goddess was his means.

Hypatius established a network of dockworkers alerting him regarding the Greek occupants of any vessel. He had endeared himself to the priests and priestesses at nearly every temple. His associates worked the markets and avenues. Once every week, on the Dies Saturni, he would lead a procession, from the Marble Way into the valley north-east of the stadium, to the Temple of Artemis. There the offerings would be made – normally valuables. The priests revered this custom as those gifts then filled the pockets of the clergy. Relating Saturn to the Goddess of New Moon captured the imagination of the Greeks who embraced the mysticism and aura of the heavens. This was especially the occasion on the Dies Quintus Septembris when the Saturday coincided with the new moon on the fifth day of the month.

Artemis too was the Fertility Goddess, an attractive inspiration to young men and women who rarely shared the same motive. Artemis was a nymph. Her image was embellished with numerous breasts, and that pleased Hypatius no end. Although he was married, there was little in his culture that forbad him from promiscuity. He took advantage of that setting engaging in relations with any young woman or maid who might be so inclined to explore her fertility.

The Temple of Artemis was indeed a magnificent structure. One hundred and twenty-seven columns surrounded the venue. Each was sixty feet high. The temple itself was built into the side of a mountain. The elevated Roman Aqueduct descended from the mountains between the stadium and the temple to the north of the city's center core. Velvet curtains hit the inner shrine and the statue of the goddess. Behind the altar there was another partition that sheltered a banking area where the rich and wealthy could deposit their cherished items. The male clergy were eunuchs. These Megabyzi were assisted by hundreds of Melissae, female priestesses. Slaves completed sweeping and maintenance. The process of adoration included shouts and common pleas, music and dancing. Incense filled the air. Devotees became revellers and worship turned into a frenzy. Morality on most occasions suffered. What else was expected before the over-endowed goddess of fertility?

The Temple also became a marketplace to avail the superstitious and those convinced charms could predetermine their future. Precious and semi-precious stones were traded for mundane necklaces having common gemstones. So much exchanged hands. Commerce flourished. Hypatius was convinced he was doing the ultimate service to Ephesus by assisting the veneration of Artemis. For the Romans he was quick to call the goddess by its comparable name 'Diana'. Everyone was satisfied, and he delighted in the revelry that had no limits to the immorality.

The month before, Hypatius had received news that the Roman Governor of Syria had died. He was hoping to receive that appointment. However, weeks later he had heard nothing more. Hypatius was also the ear-piece for all news from Rome. He had heard about a man named Burrus being appointed the teacher of teenage Nero. With relief he discovered that that Burrus was not the soldier in Ephesus who was committed to Celer.

As long as he remained true to Pro Consul Silanus, Hypatius knew his interests were adverse to those of Celer. He could have said more and even did more; but like everyone else he was vulnerable to accusatory lies and deception. If he proclaimed the truth to Silanus, he could easily be accused by Celer of treason. Every act begot consequences. In that respect, Hypatius was very much a pragmatist. Ultimately it was silence that became his choice – a decision to sit, watch, benefit from his own game, and live a diplomatic life of observing and remaining silent.

– Ephesus Pure in Heart –

Chapter Eleven

Counting Coins

October, 51

Miriam was absolutely exhausted after five years of struggle. She felt threatened by events over which she no longer had control. The disciple sat there alone at her table. The Libra Sun had long disappeared behind the mountain peaks. The candle wick was barely alive floating on the melted wax.

So much she had seen in life: so many superlatives with so much enthusiasm and then ubiquitous decadence. Every opportunity that would normally open doors to any other woman her age seemed to have been slammed shut by the life she chose, leaving her standing cold and shivering on the porch. Miriam was very aware that life was a perpetual series of crests and troughs, and in that respect she was no different from any other person. However, extremes can cost any person dearly.

Her fingers flipped through the coins on the table. She had done well at the market that day and had achieved similar results for months on end. However she realized success at the market would be difficult to sustain. More had to be done: her material, clothes, pastries, breads, and jams: and then prices had to be competitive. It was no longer quality that sold; the price had become the key attraction. That bothered her as she was not about to let herself make or sell second quality goods. If other merchants dropped their prices to ridiculous levels, Miriam would naturally be burdened with carting more goods up the hill every afternoon.

She didn't so much care about her own needs, but it was her concern for others that prompted her frustration. The Christians who arrived in Ephesus in the first phase were able to establish themselves at a reasonable cost. Those just arriving were confounded by inflated prices. The cost of food too was escalating significantly to the extent grains and corn meal had become for many families the only daily meal. Demand was deciding the amount people would pay.

Miriam checked the coins closely. Her eyes strained to determine the images in the dim light. One coin in particular struck her attention. It was the tiny bronze Ephesian coin with the bee on one side and a stag's head on the other. "Surely they could have thought of something more regal," she mused about the four hundred year old token. However the imprint on the coin was not the issue that puzzled her. Miriam was concerned that such a coin would even be used at the market. It certainly had a value far greater than the actual cost of the baked goods. Miriam, as a young girl at the family's stall in Mejdel, had developed an interest in currency from the many regions. The images, size and metal of the coins were intriguing. They each told a story. That interest was revived in Ephesus after the Emperor afforded the Province of Asia the privilege of issuing its own coins. That decision was very much spawned by the Cult of Emperor Worship. Accordingly the coins on one side pictured Claudius and usually on the other side Artemis. That was shrewd because it kept both the Romans and Greeks compatible in commerce. The Christians and Jews had to go along with the currency. There was no choice.

Was it only Miriam who recognized the ominous shift? Roman coins included the silver denarius, the larger bronze sesterius and so many from other provinces bearing the images of the Roman Republic or more recent emperors. And what did the Greeks have to offer? Only the drachma that some merchants wouldn't accept! Even currency from Achaia and Corinth had become small bronze coins with the bust of Roman gods. Did this mean that everything Greek was subordinate to Rome even in commerce? The answer was resoundingly, "Yes."

As she blew out the candle, Miriam was convinced that that reality had to be seriously considered in her discussions. Should the emphasis of their evangelization be more focussed on the Greeks? Miriam was convinced it should.

After sealing the door, she retired for the evening. Anna was already fast asleep. Silver coins found her pouch. A few bronze coins she left on the table for anyone to take. That was a purposeful decision. As much as they were important, they did not decide her life. Closing her eyes was difficult. Sleep did not come easy. Too much churned within her active mind. So much had been achieved, and so much more was still demanded. Prayers did not quieten that anxiety.

Miriam was a follower, not a leader. She never pretended to be more than that. Becoming a team player was thrilling. New passions were aroused that spawned greater effort. Being able to measure progress by the number of converts was providential. Being able to perceive the visible result gave meaning to every moment in the entire process.

"Why me?" she asked herself in bed. "Why was I allowed to see a woman brought back to life? Why did I have a chance to witness blind men regaining their sight? How is it I saw Lazarus walk out of his tomb?" Her mind would not rest.

Getting out of bed Miriam tried to take control of her midnight games. Pausing briefly she checked on Anna. The cane was resting against the foot of her covers; Miriam smiled to herself. "There, for her you should be thankful." Then her mind flipped to the four orphans who received comfort and support from other families. That pleased her. When housing was problematic, the community shared accommodation. That too was a blessing for many. When some of the farmers encountered restrictions getting their produce to market, other vendors were asked to cart and sell excess goods. Miriam knew that she had every reason to be pleased with her life and their accomplishments, but there was still hesitancy to accept the joy that those moments created.

Her thoughts once again pondered coins, this time the token she held in her palm when she first met John: the Prutah of Herod

Archelus with the stem of grapes on one side and the cup of wine on the other. It was almost as if the Lord was reading her mind just then when He started talking about vines and the vinedresser.

"Have to get the papyrus to Luke. What about Paul? His letters?" With those thoughts she summarized tomorrow's priorities. In a world without paper notes, midnight thoughts were the usual means of scheduling events.

"Sleep in." She told herself. Her mind was delighted with that plan. Finally her eyes closed with a glow of satisfaction soothing her heart.

– Ephesus Pure in Heart –

Chapter Twelve

Fermentation

March, 52

The grey block buildings intimated the residential area. Brick homes were miniscule compared to the endless rows of stone elongated buildings. Walls towered up to forty feet. Some were crested with peaked roofs so uncommon to the age and region. Toward the Cayster River north of the city near the sea, such buildings were rounded, at least sixty feet in diameter like large ominous forts protecting a valuable commodity. To the south of the city near the Meander River, stone block silos loomed more than eighty feet toward the heavens. These were the silos feeding the people and allowing Rome to be satisfied.

Because of their importance, each venue was protected by legionnaires. To accommodate their presence additional buildings were constructed as barracks. Dogs ruled the area and perimeters as well – hungry canines keeping the rats away. Having employment at a granary was considered a pristine position: being respected as well as being the recipient of considerable salary.

Slaves were rarely employed or even allowed near the premises. Their role if any was to grind the goods into useable commodities for bread or other foods. These grinding facilities were situated near the silos and storage buildings to reduce the hazard of exposure to the elements.

Wooden stairways and maintenance of roofs and floors were essential. Having available carts and equipment to transport the goods was equally important.

Accountants performed an indispensible function recording the shipments, the size of remaining stock and its age. The stock was just not grain. It included rice, barley, and various kinds of wheat from throughout the Empire.

Celer and Darius found privacy in an office within the barracks after completing their inspection. Those facilities, beyond the Temple of Artemis, were in an isolated region susceptible to thievery. They were older buildings, not overly high, situated near the back slope of Mount Pion. Not being ones to abstain, both Romans took advantage of their positions and engaged into the late afternoon indulging in excessive brew. Regardless of his intake, Celer was always ready to take advantage of any situation. To his liking he thought alcohol aided his ability to sway others.

"Token rituals mean nothing to them," Celer stated intending to be his most persuasive. "What we decide…must be…has to be quick. Sever the mind from all reason. Silanus is still respected by Caesar. Lysias walks free among the people, while we sit like beggars' dogs waiting for scraps. We should be the guests invited to the feast. My friend, we've been silent too long: deaf swimmers hearing no splash, drowning without a murmur. If we act, more can become ours."

Greed attracted Darius. "Your plan?"

"There can be no sense without blood. Rumours crawl through the dark streets of the Ephesian night. Famine is challenging their love for Rome. Christians eat plenty while they question our tribute to Diana. Jews live free because our Emperor does not act. Must we be forced to follow Silanus' shadow?"

"No!" Darius' response was automatic.

"Are we certain of the garrison support?" Celer questioned.

"You already have my answer," Darius assured him.

"Nicanor made such a pledge. Do I have your oath?"

"You know you do," Darius affirmed his support.

"What now of Lysias?" Celer asked knowing in advance what Darius would say.

"Seen with his Christian woman at least twice last week."

"Treason?" Celer expected the affirmative reply.

"We can presume." Darius was not direct enough.

Celer warned him, "No superstition. We leave that to these Christians. No hearsay, that's for philosophers. Just facts. But, wait my friend; have Rome's presumptions ever been wrong? We need only a story to stir the anger of many."

"And Silanus?" Darius asked pouring each more ale.

"If Silanus should die before Lysias, sympathy may compel Lysias to assume his position. But if Lysias is weakened first, then Silanus may fall quickly."

"And how?" Darius had to enquire to rid his mind of any ambiguity.

"We must separate the Christians from the Jews. Without Silanus, Claudius decree against the Jews is final." Celer wished to perpetually revitalize old decrees to his benefit. "That leaves us to consider only these Christians."

"And the Greeks?" Darius' comment didn't make much sense in light of Celer's intention.

"Dwell on the issue. Lysias must be our first goal. Yet, you raise a point. The Greeks prospered before this famine." No one had yet decreed there to have been a famine, although reports from elsewhere in the Empire suggested that possibility. They will favour us when we cure the famine's cause. Therefore, if Lysias be our goal, he must also be our cause."

"His woman?"

"Precisely." Celer was pleased with the simpleton's attention.

"How?"

"Which is the hardest crime to disprove?" Celer's query tested intuition.

"Murder?" Darius suggested.

"Seriously."

"Adultery?"

"You speak from the heart." Celer was accurate in his summation of his cohort.

"Theft?" Darius continued.

"Exactly. Let us enjoy the evening's air," Celer suggested while troops elsewhere in the barracks were eating supper. In March, the sun was already setting behind the slopes.

They sat upon the most accessible boulders. Their mugs were left inside, an issue that Darius regretted.

"The sabinae are returning to the baths," Darius offered concerning the Numidian virgins expected at the Harbour Baths that week. Celer offered no reaction except to note in his mind that Darius was quite consistent on that one topic.

"Tell me what you know about his Christian woman?" Celer returned to his issue.

"Many in the garrison pass her daily."

"What reason?" the Deputy Consul enquired.

"She's a baker, makes the finest honey cake we are told, just apparently right for soldiers on the march. Must be her ingredients."

"How did we come upon her?"

"She could feed a hundred legionnaires," Darius replied in a tone suggesting his amazement.

"And her profits?" Celer enquired further.

"She pays her tribute. I've collected it myself." Darius' advice didn't help the Deputy Consul.

"And the rest?"

"Orphans, Christian needs, and a woman from Mejdel."

"What influence?" Celer asked.

"A Christian." Darius was a trifle nonchalant.

Celer spoke from his heart. "We must attack the weaker link. Your Mejdel must not be hurt now, but maybe later. This woman, Lysias' friend, must draw our attention. She is the link to the Christians and our means to Lysias."

"How?" Darius' question was simple.

"Right before us," Celer stated candidly.

"I am not fit for games."

"How does this woman get her grain?" Celer questioned further to develop their plot.

"I don't know."

"She feeds herself and her Christians and still has enough for our troops. How is that possible?" Celer continued verbalizing the basis of his plan. "You say Lysias attends their needs at least twice each week?"

"Without exception."

"But Darius, they say there is a famine. There is one, isn't there?" Celer was profoundly direct.

"Yes," Darius replied to the Deputy Counsel's argumentative tone.

"Tell me, why do Lysias' troops eat well while others go hungry? Why do Romans and Greeks starve? Do Christians hunger? I don't hear their cries!" Celer's eyes could pierce the listener whenever he chose. "Could it be?"

"What?" Darius started questioning his need to be there, as the Deputy Consul was already reaching for his conclusion.

"That sacks of grain are missing from our granary!"

"You mean Lysias?" Darius replied, his chest heavy with the weight of Celer's allegation.

"Lysias takes the grain to feed his Christian woman and her friends, and then to prevent suspicion food is given to our troops." Celer concluded.

"Are you sure?" Darius rarely, if ever before, questioned his superior.

"Are you with me?"

"I am," Darius' answer was the only one acceptable to the Deputy Consul.

"Be sure!" Celer admonished.

"What if..."

"There are no exceptions. How does she get the grain?"

"Possibly from the hills, or maybe the valleys."

"Darius, be certain where you stand. No one has ever said they have seen her carry grain from the hills or through the valleys. Or perhaps, Lysias orders his troops to do this in the black of night."

"I don't know." Darius rather quickly had become significantly timid.

"This is treason!" Celer voice echoed among the boulders." Whether the grain be stolen from the granary or taken before it is stored, it is treason! Be with me on this, I will have no opposition!" The Deputy Consul stared at the soldier; but there was no reply from the stunned cohort. "Go inside, rest my friend."

Before Darius could even move, Celer stood quickly, and returned to the barracks. From there it was just minutes before he was in the corral mounting his horse. As he rode, the words came quickly in a habit that of late he was finding hard to avoid. Mumbling out loud to oneself was never considered a virtue, but then Celer never claimed to be virtuous.

Be patient. Darius will prove his worth. Sacks of grain I will place in this woman's room. She will be accused and Lysias too. They will beg for mercy. Christians will cry foul. Silanus' decision will prove costly. Like a fool he will demand his cousin's intervention, but Claudius will not lend an ear to Nero's kin. Peace Rome, for this is the last time you will see it in Ephesus.

Chapter Thirteen

Peripatetic Roman

March, 52

His arrival was totally unexpected. There had been many stories, some at times rather unbelievable. This was the man from Tarsus in Cilicia: from his father's birth-right a Roman citizen, but also a practicing Jew and member of the Pharisees. This was the villain who encouraged elders in Jerusalem to stone Stephen to death, and then vowed the death of Christians everywhere. He was the instrument of Herod Agrippa entrusted with the task of eradicating the memory of Christ from history. Saul's conversion was itself miraculous. The Roman-Jew was convinced that Christ himself appeared from heaven, demanding an answer from the Pharisee to the basic question, "Why do you persecute me?" Within a few years, Paul had committed himself not to his own conversion, but to the conversion of the Greek world.

His first missionary journey commenced from Antioch in Syria in 46AD as the Holy Spirit had directed them. The famine had raised the ire of the Jews against the Followers of Christ. With him, Paul took Barnabas who had provided support following his conversion on the road to Damascus. They sailed to Cyprus stopping at Salamis and Pathos. From there the voyage took them to Perge, then on land to Pisidia, Lystra, Iconium and Debre. Two years later they were back in Antioch. Conversions were inspiring. Reception was not always positive, and at times violent. Still they persevered. Paul was committed to the Greeks, while Peter concentrated on the conversion of the Jews.

Throughout his process of preaching and evangelization he built on the aspects of Greek culture that could attract them to Jesus Christ. The concept that one man should die to benefit the entire community was very pertinent to Greek philosophy in terms of defining sacrifice and nobility. Paul repeatedly called Jesus "the Christ", or the "Son of God." These terms could be ambiguous although 'christ' was readily interpreted as being the 'anointed one'. That was not difficult to understand. The phrase 'Son of God' was not entirely foreign considering all of the Greek deities. Identifying Jesus Christ as the Messiah, as the one who redeems and who forgives and who is the Lord of eternal bliss: these again were understandable to the Greek communities because they too believed firmly in the afterlife and sought the means that would best achieve that goal.

The fact that Paul spoke Hebrew, Latin, and Greek dialects greatly assisted his propensity to express the attractiveness of the new religion. However, he still had to overcome the ingrained culture that believed in deities that had never died over the course of at least seven hundred years. It wasn't just the deities that created the obstacles. The entire Greek culture, with Roman dominance, was embracing superstitions bordering on witchcraft. Veneration in their temples frequently became robust orgies. Charms determined the future more than commitment or hard work. Sorcery, polytheism, lechery, immorality, slavery, and citizens everywhere unwilling to relinquish any of their rights: these appeared to be impenetrable brick walls. So much of it was so foreign to the rigid rules that governed the Jewish nation. Paul relied on the Ten Commandments as a guide for morality. He employed the Mosaic Law to remind the Jews that he revered their laws and the Hebrew Code of Ethics. Paul also had to overcome the phenomenon of 'Pax Romana' throughout the Empire in which relative peace and accord afforded mutual agreement. Why change what works? Even the Jews had by the edict of Claudius been given the privilege to practice their religion.

During that first missionary expedition: a sorcerer was blinded because of his witchcraft; the Pro Consul of Cyprus supported the preachers; Paul declared the Good News in synagogues in Pisidia; there was violent division among the Jews in Iconium; a lame man was cured in Lystra; presbyters were appointed in Derbe, Pisidia and all of the communities that accepted Christ Jesus as their Lord and Saviour.

For less than one year Paul remained in Antioch. When Barnabas departed with Mark for Cyprus, Silas committed himself to accompanying Paul on the second mission.

At Tarsus on the route to Achaia, Paul met Timothy a well respected citizen and son of a Greek merchant. Timothy's mother was Jewish, as was her mother. Timothy was attracted to Paul's zeal and his message concerning the Son of God. This was not an austere religion but instead a faith that offered hope. Timothy was soon baptised. His mother Eunice and his grandmother Lois also embraced the new faith. When Paul left Tarsus for Pisidia, Timothy accompanied him. Troas, a city on the Aegean Sea, received the visitors although with some reservation. The concept of the Resurrection of the Body was a stumbling-block. Greeks could accept the soul continuing to live, however to them the body decayed.

They sailed south along the Aegean coast to Neapolis, and then to Achaia stopping at Thessalonica, Athens, and then Corinth. Timothy journeyed farther to Macedonia. In each city, town or village, more were baptised; and with the increase in converts, enthusiasm blossomed. In Corinth Paul stayed for more than one year in the company of many Greek and Jewish converts.

After leaving Corinth and before returning to Antioch Paul stopped at Ephesus. He had been acquainted with Ephesus in his youth having been raised in Cilicia. Ephesus had a reputation as a commercial center, an attraction for many merchants. However, Ephesus was also known as the home of witchcraft and superstition, a situation Paul had encountered often on his first journey. When the Holy Spirit forbad Paul from preaching in Asia, was the Holy Spirit directing Paul away from the world of idolatry in which no one could be saved? However, Paul had heard there were followers there, and had been made aware of John's efforts and leadership. Was there something to be learned, some inspiration to acquire, or some more souls to convert?

Paul's visit was short. He met John, and they greeted one another enthusiastically sharing their successes. John was introduced to Aquila and Priscilla whom Paul had brought from Corinth. They were converts from Judaism.

Paul's message to the synagogue was precise. He preached about the necessity of Christ's death as a means of redemption. He declared the reality of the resurrection, that Christ Jesus had conquered death. The term 'Messiah' described the Lord's Kingship. Repeatedly he mentioned the promise of salvation to believers focussing on the reality that Jesus was the fulfillment of the Messianic Promise.

Paul's vessel then left days later with necessary supplies and unlimited encouragement.

Chapter Fourteen

Deputy Consuls in Conflict

April, 52

The two black steeds shuffled their fore hooves losing patience in the mid-day heat. Their driver too wondered, but he was astute enough to maintain his tolerance. These were important men inside that building. They paid him a wage, and on the extremely rare occasions even tipped him for his service. The chariot was adorned with silver trim, bearing the Roman Eagle on each side. It had been Silanus direction to avoid any gold on chariots as that privilege rested with the Emperor.

Inside Celer and Hypatius were meeting. These occasions were at best once per month. Silanus had already left for the Harbour Baths. Hypatius attempted to control the initial discussion. His first comment riled Celer. "They have done us well," he said concerning the Christians. That raised a brick wall between the compatriots. After that Hypatius interrupted as much as possible to affirm his opinions on: the Hellenistic cult of Mithras being adopted by the Roman population, the fears of an expanding famine, feeding the army and the necessity for more legions to control the rivers, harbour, crops and valleys.

Celer easily agreed with the last item. That was his only acknowledgement in the first hour of discussion. The next hour belonged to him. He immediately countered anything positive

Hypatius had said about the Christians by repeating his aversion to the Chi-Rho emblem and to the many "trinkets of vile persuasion" including medals, rings, broaches, and cloth patches. These, Celer eventually called, "Sedition." That comment raised the temperature in the room significantly because the Deputy Consuls were clearly trying either to attract or accuse the various minorities. Celer added fuel to the fire by challenging once again the Cult of Mithras suggesting it detracted from the honour that should be afforded to the Emperor. He loved the game of conflicting views of the Emperor. He could either accuse opponents of sedition or use the opinions to bolster his view against Silanus.

Celer purposefully did not respond to Hypatius' comments about the prospect of famine or the feeding of troops. He had his own agenda.

Hypatius' concern with the propensity of spies ubiquitously throughout the city was never mentioned as he was already convinced that Celer was the director of such a program. A few other comments begot silence that affirmed Hypatius' opinion. With that, he had had enough of Celer. Everything was diplomatic as it had to be; but when they parted company it was only seconds before he was aboard the chariot. Just as quickly Hypatius was on his way to the harbour with plans to attend the silos near the Cayster River.

Celer sat there in the Prytaneion: alone, pensive and knowing he had taken too long to act. "Say Good-bye Lysias."

Chapter Fifteen

Desperate Plea

May, 52

Six years after their arrival, the Christian community had increased significantly. Deacons and presbyters constantly reported to John on the growth and enthusiasm of the believers. However for some of the new followers, Christianity was just another guild. Guilds prevalent in Ephesus, although tied to specific trades, were basically social organizations. In that respect Christianity for those believers was comparable to a guild in that it was an assembly of persons with commitment to mutual tenets of service to one another. The care of the needy, the unemployed, the hungry, orphans, widows, the aged and the infirm became Faith in action. John preached endlessly about Christ's instruction concerning the Day of Judgement using that analogy to stress the importance of the Second Greatest Commandment. He was achieving abundant success with that approach.

However, the Romans were not impressed. Guilds were the Romans the means of ensuring the Cult of the Emperor. That deflated the Greek deities and assured Rome of its dominant respect. But when the Christians assembled themselves into a setting similar to a guild and did not worship the Emperor, Roman response was feared. Still, as long as Claudius' decree providing religious liberty to the Jews was intact, the Christians seemed to have little cause for worry. How the Emperor treated the Jews would determine how the Prytaneion in Ephesus considered the Christians.

Miriam sat at her table late in the evening once more counting her coins. The market that day was again a profitable venture. This time she arranged three pouches: one for her home, another for orphans and their clothes, and the final one for the purchase of her market supplies. Allowing herself to conjecture, Miriam was convinced that troubles were not just brewing they were boiling over. Her impression was created by the realization that the only silver coins came from Rome, and the coins minted in the provinces were all bronze. Was silver restricted to the Patricians? It appeared so. Yet, the people were satisfied. How easily they were being duped!

The terra cotta oil lamp provided the light she needed to read once again from St. Paul's letter to the Galatians. She had retained John's copy for safekeeping.

> A person will reap what he sows. If he sows in the field of worldly desire from it he will reap the harvest of death. If he sows his seeds in the field of the Spirit, from the Spirit he will reap eternal life.

Anna was with Alexa and Philemon that week giving Miriam the opportunity for the luxury of extra sleep. However, having to be at the harbour early in the morning for her shipment would alter that expectation. Doing more than that expected of her was her reality.

To accommodate those demands, Miriam trained herself to set aside moments at the end of the day for meditation. For her the quick recitation of a memorized prayer was no longer sufficient. If more with and through the Spirit was to be accomplished, then prayer and devotion had to change. Private thoughts became an exercise trying to identify the Spirit, and to give a face to the Spirit of God. That alone seemed impossible for no one had actually ever seen the Spirit. Did the Spirit even exist as a physical being, or was He an Exalted Creature similar to the angels? Was it even a He? Embracing all that was beautiful around her, Miriam became one with the Spirit in addressing the needs of others. However, it wasn't only the measure of service that determined her oneness with God, it was the entire concept of Redemption that included all of the ramifications of sin, the benefit of salvation, and the goal of eternal life. Her mind was always active, even though at times fatigue caused her to doubt. For these quiet moments she was thankful.

Pounding at the door interrupted her private thoughts. Before she could even turn to address the annoyance, the banging was repeated. Finally the door opened.

"Please?" the bearded gentleman in a dark cloak begged.

Miriam recognized him and without pause bade him, "Enter." Nathan stood there. Miriam knew only his first name. She tried to recollect the surname, thinking it may have been something Greek. More importantly she knew he was a rabbinical student, and so extended courtesy respecting his position.

"Do you know any more?" Nathan pled.

Miriam had long ago passed the threshold of tolerance for ambiguity. "What's this about?" She tried to be patient.

Nathan mumbled through his litany of fears stressing the rumours concerning the intention of the Romans in Ephesus to send legions to Judaea to quell any unrest.

"You know more than I. Your numbers surprise me. We understood they were to be far less. Will they even go? Rome called it sedition. We pray that prudent minds will rule, that riots cease, and that Rome accepts that the unrest has ended." Miriam responded.

"And what will happen here?" Nathan was extremely worried.

"That we earnestly tried to determine. If your figure is correct and the Pro Consul sends twenty thousand soldiers to Jerusalem, who will be here among the Romans to impart any rule? It is only when those legions return from Jerusalem that we should fear Roman tyranny."

"Is all this inevitable?" Nathan continued hoping for a ray of hope.

"If I were a Senator, I would say yes."

"Such simplicity profits no one. They've burned our Torah."

"I was not aware," Miriam confessed.

"What would you do if you were still Hebrew?" Nathan asked.

"Tell me about Simon and Luxor. Have you heard?" Miriam continued.

"What will they accomplish?" Nathan demanded, forgetting he was the one seeking assistance.

"Caesar will do only what is recommended to him. He respects Silanus. You should have no fears in Ephesus. But in Jerusalem, should unrest flourish, if the zealots cannot be controlled by the Pharisees, then the Roman response is predictable. You must plot a course aware of Rome's intention. Knowledge is therefore necessary."

"Shall we raise an army?" Nathan was facetious.

"What we mentioned before. Are your merchants willing to freely donate any greater portion of their profits to the interests of Rome?" Miriam was referring to the privileges afforded the Jews in Asia that limited taxation on their profits. "Rome won't disagree with your generosity. Caligula oppressed the Hebrews in Alexandria and even here. Claudius followed that course in Rome; then he chose to define your liberty. Why? It is simply this: he correctly sees something positive in Christians and Jews working together with Romans and Greeks. If Procurator Felix should also perceive such cooperation with the Hebrews, then the prospect of Roman violence in Jerusalem is nil. Felix will not call on Caesar for aid if he doesn't need it. Felix too, we are told, is a proud man. All governors are. He won't admit to any weakness by calling on Rome for more troops unless it is absolutely necessary."

"Claudius is not Pompey," Nathan referred to the liberties granted by the latter.

"And Aristobulous was not Felix," Miriam referred to the incompetent Roman official.

"You are well versed in politics," Nathan admitted.

"Is support for the governor out of the question?" Miriam looked for a desperate answer.

"Your efforts are lost in the innocence of the times," Nathan opined.

"And the Saducees, are they still in charge?"

Nathan was surprised Miriam did not have that relevant information. "The Pharisees are still much disgraced. Your Jesuah can be thanked for that. Caesar's statue stood in the center of our temple. The ashes of our Torah cannot be read. The simpletons run to the hills. The Romans won't follow. They're too afraid to turn their backs to the mob inside Jerusalem."

"Couldn't they support the governor?" Miriam searched for any possibility.

Nathan had lost his patience which seemed strange as he was the one begging for reason. "Rome! Famine! Your Christ! What's left? People look to the Saducees to challenge the governor to his face; while zealots prepare to stab his back."

"There's no purpose then." Miriam abruptly concluded.

"We have spoken honestly. Israel has no control of the zealots. They raise Rome's anger daily. The Saducees stir hatred against you as well. Denial of your resurrection has the Hebrews convinced. About your friends, you should pray."

"We've secured safe passage." Miriam advised.

"Don't be so sure," Nathan cautioned. "May the God of Abraham protect them."

Miriam had no more to add. Other ideas had already been dismissed. There were more than twenty thousand Jews in Ephesus, about eight percent of the population. These had been afforded the right of assembly and religion. They were even entitled to collect their own taxes and then send those funds to Jerusalem. Jews even had the privilege of refusing to serve in the Roman Army. Although the Greek community objected to the special treatment of the Hebrews, Rome was not about to alter the Emperor's decree; but in Judaea the Romans were not about to entertain Jewish rebellion.

"Remember this: Ephesian dreams do not readily become Judaean reality." With that, Nathan departed into the black of night.

Chapter Sixteen

Harbour Farewell

May, 52

Beyond the stadium musicians lured the festive throng north toward the Temple where all would display their raucous veneration to the stone idol of Artemis. The annual festivities for those few weeks tripled the population with the arrival of visitors from all regions of the Empire: buying charms to secure the future, making lavish donations to display one's importance, being there to convey respect for antiquity, or to engage in the drunkenness and orgies that society allowed without any concern for morality.

At the harbour sentiments were profoundly different. There was no joy, nor celebrations. Roman soldiers were boarding a series of vessels. They had no choice. The request had been made, and Silanus obeyed. Wives bid their husbands farewell. Many women were convinced they would not see them again. They would either die in action, or just choose to remain with the army in some foreign land. Such was the commitment of so many soldiers. The army was their life. Family was just a part time experience.

Naomi was not his wife, yet he was very dear to her. She hugged Lysias devotedly. In the legionnaire she had seen a man truly committed to the common good, always willing to assist those in need, and wanting perpetually to do what was best for the community. He cherished her, and her commitment to her faith. She was Hebrew when they first met. Actually, he was the one guarding the synagogue. When she first mentioned that she would embrace the new religion, Lysias was supportive even to the extent that on one occasion he said he too would consider Christianity. However, he knew as a soldier that would not be possible. So often he argued against sending troops to Judaea, but knew that would come to nought. Eventually it would happen, the ships would dock, and the troops would board. The last farewell was bitter for Naomi; but that was not the least of her problems.

The silo was locked except for the rear door which Darius left open. Taking a bag of grain, he dropped granules along the pathway into a wooded area. Beyond that area, clay thatched homes were residence to many citizens, among these was Naomi. Within her home, two soldiers ransacked the premises leaving a bag of grain below a padded cushion. Muscipula was absolutely delighted in the military uniform.

Celer stood on the dock watching the tearful departures. He should have opposed such displays of frailty; but he afforded them these opportunities, knowing many would not see each other again. His written instructions were abundantly clear. They were to fight on the front line against the zealots who had nothing to lose.

Chapter Seventeen

Joy and Trepidation

June, 52

The bliss of family life can be easily shared by close friends. Smiling, they embraced life together with all of its disappointments forgotten in the moments of unexpected success. "I can just imagine!" Miriam gleefully exclaimed in response to John's commentary on Paul's debate in the synagogue. The impact of Paul's dissertation was starling. Five new converts from the very staunch congregation that had forcefully fought the intrusion of Christianity.

John dutifully cradled the bowl of beans and berries as they gingerly followed the path through Miriam's garden among crops of cabbage, beets and tomatoes, under the shade of an oak tree, curving amid flower beds to her front door. Just seeing John that pleased, made her even more so.

Laughter continued once inside even while they were mentioning the apostolic efforts of Timothy and Luke. It wasn't out of disrespect at all. Whether it was their age, or varying aspirations, or just a feeling of accomplishment; the need for comedy was at times of prime importance. Needless to say, if humour was involved John was sure to take a stab at the role of women. That usually set Miriam off with even more rebuttals and prolonged diatribes about the ineffectual nature of men. Ultimately John had to admit that women have had a significant impact.

"How is Timothy?" Miriam returned to a moment of sincerity.

"Leaving shortly for Macedonia; had much success there. They still want him. Much like Philadelphos and Smyrna: sure they were at first ready to drag us out of town, but others let us speak."

"Women," Miriam smiled. "You needed women," she continued.

"No. You're not going." John added with an expression that their light hearted conversation could instantly initiate.

"One day you'll see the light," she quipped.

Anna was attempting to set the table and Miriam allowed her to continue, concluding with a compliment even though everything may not have been perfect. Miriam's heart was moved by Anna's perseverance, wondering often how she or any blind person could continue to function.

"We hear many stories," Miriam mentioned.

John sat on the cushions by their table complimenting Anna while listening to the hostess. He paused trying to grasp her topic; then realized it must be about Luke as they had already mentioned Timothy. "Was trouble expected?"

"Always concerned," she admitted.

John reported on what he had heard from Luke on his journey beyond Pergamum with the conclusion, "You shouldn't be worried." While Miriam returned to the fireplace for the chicken patties, John mentioned Luke's compliment, "You have much thanks for your parchment."

Miriam continued with her meal preparations eventually bringing the food to the table and assisting Anna to the cushions upon the floor. Then taking her normal place, she sat between the two loves of her life. John commenced their prayer in Hebrew ending same in Greek with, "Kyrie Eleison."

The meal was always a delightful repast for Miriam as she had a marvellous way of embellishing the taste with garden herbs. Salt was not always available and at other times its cost was rather exorbitant. That was unfortunately the case for most food products. For that reason, having a well situated garden producing more than one annual crop was an absolute blessing.

"A wayward soul finds much comfort here." John was searching for the unique way of being polite. He always tried to include new and previously unheard compliments as such always seem to be more meaningful.

"Not too many wayward souls here; just regular customers," Miriam quipped.

"Paul is planning a letter to Corinth." John advised.

"Have you heard from him?"

John's advice was repetitious about their network of disciples, friends and contacts. The inescapable conclusion was that the information was only as good as its author.

"He'll be back." Miriam was confident.

"Nothing planned to my knowledge. I'm not about to stand in his way or suggest his schedule."

Her admiration was easily discernible.

"Do you ever rest?" he asked her noting the parchment, and papyrus stems she had picked from the marsh.

Miriam dismissed that as a daily chore and then politely paid tribute to others living on the hill who contributed to the needs of the community. There were many and her list seemed endless.

"Couldn't have done this without you." John admitted and leaned over to express his gratitude with a hug. Miriam reached around Anna's shoulder so the three were mutually sharing their appreciation. The embrace concluded with John gently kissing Miriam's forehead, a confident expression of gratitude for efforts and achievement. "I miss your smile," he whispered.

The dessert was equally succulent, sliced fruit with a couple of grains of sugar.

"Does Cybil still direct the sharing of food?" John enquired in a manner knowing the answer so as to compliment the one who made those arrangements.

"With Rosea, he takes bread into the hills. We feared difficulties last winter. Providing warm clothes is not always possible." Miriam regretted her inability to be totally successful in the provision of clothes.

John then asked about agora sales. It was his way of enquiring about other issues at the market.

"I should mention the young girl, Phoenicia..." she started.

"The one who fancies merchants?"

"Among others, yes, that's her. We may have another convert." Miriam looked him in the eyes expecting a snide response. "Don't be so surprised. It's Susannah's efforts again. Just after Saturnalia she was found beaten and discarded in the garbage pit. Susannah took her in, cleaned her up, and waited for the bruises to heal. Then days later the girl is helping bake bread for the needy. She professes to be truly repentant. Will you see her?"

John's answer was immediate, "God's face has many expressions, even the battered and the homeless. Please make the arrangements. I'll baptise her."

At that moment, Susannah rushed in. There was no knock, no pause just her desperate plea for attention. "Miriam!"

She stood immediately responding to the urgency.

"Naomi, she's been accused!" Susannah declared.

"What?" Miriam demanded.

"Treason!" Susannah was about to burst.

"It can't be!" Miriam exclaimed.

"Where?" John enquired, with no calm in his voice.

"To Prion Hill," Susannah advised in the midst of tears.

"With murderers!" John was absolutely horrified.

"What has she done?" Miriam was suddenly on the verge of tears herself. John did not wait, he rushed out immediately.

"Wait for us." Miriam begged wanting to accompany him. However John was already at the bottom of the hill by the time Anna was in her room and the two women were rushing out of the house. There was so little time to do so much.

Chapter Eighteen

Confrontation

June, 52

Celer slouched in the Pro Consul's chair, determined that one day it would be rightfully his. He gloated as he peered around the room. Murals on the four walls perfected the portrait of daily life. Silanus was away and would be for at least five weeks, travelling the province as its magistrate. That chair represented everything Celer envied, a display of grandeur in a room embellished for the gods – only Roman ones.

Everyone had to wait for him. Senators were nowhere to be found, too worried about their estates in Rome. Darius and Burrus attended every so often to provide news, bring the daily wench, or ensure that the food was not poisoned.

In an outer room far from the Primum Officium, John had waited for nearly a day. His only comfort was a fireplace without wood. The chair was ready to collapse. The couch, a discard from grander days, was not fit for government buildings. John had been in other rooms on other occasions, and had always been treated respectfully. Long after others had consumed the noon meal, John was escorted into the Pro Consul's room; but Silanus was not there.

"You may go," Celer instructed Darius who had led the disciple into the lavish hall. Celer watched the legionnaire leave rather than pay attention to the petitioner. After seating himself in the elevated chair, much like a throne on a dais, Celer scornfully directed his comment to the older gentleman standing twenty feet before him. "I am told you require Rome's assistance. Your business?"

"A woman you have imprisoned." John's voice echoed.

"There are many," Celer snorted in derision.

"Naomi, the Christian," John announced.

"Her…" Celer paused, "a matter of treason."

"Specifics are the Roman custom." John was expecting Silanus' style of justice.

"Thievery from our granary!" Celer declared stressing the importance of 'our'. "You know what we do with thieves, don't you?"

"Totally unjustified!" The echo proclaimed the message.

Celer sneered, "Not an appropriate comment for one seeking Rome's mercy."

"Mercy is not the issue. You have falsely charged this woman!"

"Your words border on sedition." Celer acted like the child with a ball who disliked others winning the game.

"Be serious!" The shouting match continued.

"We are. Very much so." Celer gloated at his superior position.

"With what evidence?" John continued.

"A sack of grain from the granary found in her room." His plan had gone to perfection.

"That's impossible. She suffers palsy in her hands. She couldn't lift more than a quarter-stone." This was approximately three pounds.

Celer laughed cynically, "She wasn't too weak to fight off three guards."

"You swine!"

Celer reacted immediately, "Guard your tongue." He was delighted that his statement had generated the expected response.

"Where is Silanus? I implore his attendance," John enquired.

"Not in Ephesus," Celer announced.

"He was returning from Miletus six days ago," John advised. The town of Miletus was about sixty miles from Ephesus.

"Who are you that you should choose to know the comings and goings of our governor?" Celer demanded, while using the word 'governor' to demean Silanus' title.

"Silanus is a civil gentleman. We have his trust and assurance."

"He's not here!" Celer was getting more than a trifle infuriated.

John remained determined. "Then where? Your crime of rape is worse than your false accusation of thievery."

"Don't you tell me..."

John interrupted the Quaestor, "Better I than Christ!"

"Now you declare treason!"

"Custom compels you to state your evidence." John returned immediately to the process of the law.

"Your accusations alone confirm rebellion." Celer had nothing else to say; but whining like an angry child had done him well in the past.

"What specifics, Celer?" John wasn't about to relax his position.

The Quaestor was more than a touch uncomfortable. "You Christians eat well while Rome starves! Why? You answer that!"

"Your gluttony is not starvation." John referred to the opinion of Seneca in Rome concerning the overindulgence of the Patricians.

Celer rose from his chair with a vile expression threatening to call the guards.

"Since when has Rome raised arms against poverty and obedience?" John continued. "Why do you accuse her when she more than any other person provided food for your troops? At no cost! Yet, you hold her with murderers!"

"Watch your tongue, sorcerer!" Celer pointed his finger at John.

"We speak no evil and do no wrong," John replied.

"You do so now in your own deceit," Celer accused him.

"Is it against the will of Rome to feed your army?"

"That is not the issue!" Celer shouted.

"We come to you with trust for Rome's mercy," John declared.

"Your mercy belongs to your God. Rome's mercy is favoured for those Roman." Celer delighted himself with suddenly presenting a calm argument.

John was determined not to stop, "How does a woman not capable of carrying anymore than a pouch of coins handle a sack of grain?"

"We have no doubt that there was another. However we are very certain that your Christian woman was involved. We will find him. You can be certain of that."

"Then set her free!" John's logic escaped the Quaestor.

"Get him out of here!" Celer ordered Darius.

John boldly asserted, "Why are you so afraid of her?"

Celer's leer pierced the air between them. "Seize him!"

John just stepped back instructing Darius, "Don't bother sir." With that he turned and walked toward the far door. "Your prisons are already filled with the innocent. You don't need another."

The door was barely shut before Celer instructed Darius, "Spread the rumour that it was her lover, Lysias. Don't worry, my friend. He's not coming back."

Chapter Nineteen

Non Intelligo

July, 52

Panic swept through the inner-city flooding beyond Smyrna and south to the Province of Lycia. Closer to home, the valley between Pion and Bulbul was wrought with fear. Rumours were tainted by their origin, simply declaring that there was a granary theft and that Christians were responsible. Few disputed the story as it provided weak logic for the general shortage of rice, wheat and barley. Christians radically objected to the falsified evidence. As difficult as it was to believe, it was just another example of Roman injustice.

Those who had so deeply committed themselves to the new religion were deeply challenged by the dire events. Some posed the obvious question, "Where was their God?" Others blamed John for letting it happen. Most never knew Naomi, nor had any information on her faith.

To some in the Jewish community, she was a renegade having abandoned the Mosaic Law. For the Rabbi, there was gratitude that

Naomi was no longer one of them. Although they still held John in high esteem there was nothing they could do to assist his cause.

Miriam was horrified, and stunned as she stood behind her market tables. Customers were apprehensive. A few asked Miriam about the incident. She asserted throughout that Naomi was innocent, and that the Romans had criminally planted the evidence to falsely accuse her. Such accusations themselves were treason.

Susannah did not attend the market for the entire week, as she was strenuously occupied in exploring every avenue to acquit the Christian girl. Her trip to the silo itself and then to Naomi's residence were barred. By the second week, Naomi's abode was being rented to others.

Her belongings were discarded.

John tried to visit the victim but any access to Naomi was prevented. The prospect of bargaining with the Romans confronted a brick wall. Silanus had not returned to Ephesus. Celer had locked himself in private quarters near the Cayster. His usual entourage was nowhere to be found.

Doors were secured. Miriam placed a pot on a chair and moved it against her door to hinder access and warn her of any attempt to enter at night.

Within her cell, Naomi lay shrivelled on the floor having been divested of all humanity. Raped and barely clothed she shivered and whimpered among the flood of tears crying to a God that had abandoned her.

Chapter Twenty

News from Distant Shores

February, 53

The north winds howled across the entire Anatolian Peninsula. In the second week of the wintery blast, starvation became rampant. The sleep of death was welcomed by those who were alone, hungry and freezing to death. Only a few of the impoverished were able to escape to the inner city hoping to find shelter. Slaves had no refuge. For those not able to flee from their homes, where open windows invited the freezing temperatures, they huddled together hoping that Roman officials would ease the mandated restriction on firewood. Meanwhile the elite comforted themselves within their pristine establishments with shutters, blankets and blazing logs in their fireplaces.

Within the warm confines of his private quarters, Celer sat at his table awaiting the anticipated arrival of news from the harbour. He was content, as much as he had ever been. He had shown the Christians the capability of Roman justice. The leaders of the Jewish Temple he had once more embarrassed in the latter days of Saturnalia. That situation he confounded with threats of reversing Claudius' decree concerning freedoms and taxation. For the Greeks, more and more of their culture was disappearing. The Temple of Artemis was still there; but the arrest of one Greek citizen for not performing appropriate tribute to Diana caused a significant group to worry. That any vessel would have attempted any voyage at that time was never expected. However one did complete the trip. Its supplies were limited: less than fifty bags of grain. There were no spices, and no salt. Only one Roman legionnaire completed the voyage. His pouch contained one scroll – the only purpose for his visit.

That legionnaire was overly grateful as he welcomed into the foyer of Celer's dwelling. Then further inside, he almost melted. Upon handing the scroll to the Deputy Consul, the messenger was greeted with Celer's endless smile. The news had been long expected.

The continuing grin could not be hidden as Celer read the document. The news met his every expectation. Lysias was dead!

The entire cohort had been slaughtered in the desert of Palestine. Almost three thousand soldiers were slain, ill equipped to confront the determined zealots, becoming rotting corpses suitable only for the vultures. He felt no remorse. Lysias challenged him. That soldier even embraced the Christian faith; so Lysias deserved to die. As for others, there was no regret. Their deaths gave Rome even more reason to send more troops to annihilate the Jewish menace. In fact another fifteen thousand legionnaires from Ephesus were already stationed there ready for action. As for the Province of Asia, that even gave Rome more reason to restrict the freedoms previously afforded the Jews. Everything he wanted had happened. Celer was so delirious with joy he even allowed the messenger the privilege of feasting and then enjoying the waiting maids. Success knew no bounds.

Chapter Twenty-One

Why is this Night So Special?

April, 53

The Christian community still held true to the celebration of Passover. The Seder Meal preceded the Breaking of Bread to celebrate the Jewish tradition with devout commitment to fulfillment in Christ. It was a reverend occasion, with all of the solemnity possible. John viewed the entire sequence of those three days as the culmination of the Promise God the Father made to humanity in the Garden of Eden. Christ was the Messiah and He proved it by His resurrection.

Everyone in the Christian community cherished his messages of hope and life. His stories about Christ continuously had the followers spell bound. The Holy Spirit had given them the gift of tongues not just to hear but also to focus.

Miriam with Anna spent that evening at John's residence in quiet reflection. After Luke completed his visits he too arrived. Their worries about this life abated with stories recounting the day of the Lord's death. Luke was particularly interested in the thieves. Their presence, being crucified at the same time, conveyed that the Romans considered Christ as just another criminal. Luke was even more attentive to John's advice concerning the scorn one levelled at Christ, and how the other in rebuttal declared Christ to be innocent. Their discussion as they did after every Passover Meal dwelt on the issue of Christ opening the doors to Heaven. As to what happened to all who died believing in God prior to that, they devoutly offered their views. The concept, that Abraham, Isaac, Jacob, Moses and all the prophets were not in heaven right after their passing, had them perplexed. It was a good time for discussion and they took every liberty to enjoy the opportunity.

****

From Corinth to Sparta then to Crete she was taken, bound with ropes to eventually be forced into active employment as the amusement of the rich who had no interest in morality. After being raped in the prison and surviving forced abortion, Naomi was provided with temporary warmth and comfort to develop the lurid skills of satisfying the nobility of society. She so wanted to flee but eunuchs, themselves fearing for their lives, safeguarded the wench. After being herded with others north to Smyrna, then across the Aegean, they sailed past Athens to Corinth. There she was physically enhanced and psychologically altered to agree with their vision of 'desirable'. Often Naomi was warned that at her age there would be very few men who would be interested, and as such she might be better off dead. Naomi wished for that. However the Greeks, who now controlled her lost innocence, would not allow any such opportunity. Naomi, in her mid twenties, was considered to have other values: primarily as a guardian of the younger girls. Naomi was also forced to be there for the pregnant prostitutes knowing what pain or death awaited them in the abortion process.

Alone she grovelled remembering her younger brother's prayer at the Seder meal, "Father, why is this night so special?"

Chapter Twenty-Two

Ecclesia Asia Minor

June, 53

By the summer of 53AD, the Church in Asia Minor had grown profoundly. Although there were Christians in the Roman Province of Asia prior to their arrival in 46AD, John's evangelical enthusiasm and Miriam's commitment to corporal works spawned a significant commitment to the Lord Jesus. Christianity was no longer just a social guild; it had become a meaningful lifestyle. Celebrating the Breaking of Bread was not the only highlight. Support and encouragement among the followers became just as important. Short term interest became long term commitment.

The world that John and Miriam tried to convert was: Greek by nature, ruled by Romans, with a Jewish culture being about ten percent of the population. Prior to Paul's second journey in 49AD, it was determined that Paul's mission was the Greek towns and cities, whereas Peter would concentrate initially on the Jewish communities in Palestine and Syria. As for John, he was left with the task of evangelizing the Jews, Greeks and Romans in the Asia Minor.

Luke, Paul, Timothy, Aquila, Priscilla and Apollos were just some of the influential motivators. Paul became acquainted with twelve disciples who were deacons. However the number of deacons and elders throughout Asia Minor far exceeded this number. The position was not awarded nor based on wealth or affluence as the Romans would have done; but it was determined by honour, respect, knowledge and commitment to service. This was intriguing to the Greeks and Romans as Plebeian could have an input beyond their temporal restrictions. Even the concept that the body would reunite with the soul after death was attractive to many who had known misery and servitude all of their lives. Asia Minor, prior to Christianity, provided no opportunity to the Hoi Polloi to be anything other than mundane servants to the Patricians, Senators, Equestrians and Roman Officials. Christianity gave them an opportunity to be themselves, to be involved in the present, not just at some undefined time in the future.

John focussed his efforts on Ephesus, in addition to preaching in Smyrna, Pergamum, Thyatira, Sardis, Philadelphos, Laodicea and Miletus. Historians have spent significant effort analysing excavations, remains and artifacts. There is no document telling us the exact number of Christians in Ephesus or throughout Asia Minor. John, Paul, Luke and Timothy did not keep count. They were not accountants. They were preachers who on a daily basis witnessed the growth of Christianity in the communities.

Regarding Ephesus, there remain considerable variations in the estimate of its population during the first century. Figures range between 20,000 and 250,000. The difference is significant; however we have this reality. Within the city core besides the land devoted to buildings, temples, and monuments, there were approximately 550 acres of available land for habitation. If each acre could be home to 400 persons, then the inner city could have housed 22,000 people. From the Cayster River in the north to the Meander River in the south, in the valleys and on the slopes of the mountains the massive expanse of available land could easily have provided homes to a predominantly agricultural population of close to 200,000 persons. Also, Ephesus was not defined by city limits. The Roman roads from Smyrna, Miletus, Hierapolis and Colossae were home to many other thousands who completed business transactions in Ephesus, and travelled frequently to Ephesus relying on its harbour for trade and commerce. When they paid taxes, it was to the Romans in Ephesus.

The exact numbers might be preferable, but for Ephesus John never recorded these. The entire picture was more important with so much to accomplish in so many venues. John and Miriam preferred to hear expressions of gratitude, the news of growth, and witness the incidents of charity and commitment. This was how they measured success.

If there was conjecture to suggest an approximate figure of converts by 53AD, that figure would include these potential assessments:

5% of the Jewish congregation being	about 1,000
1% in the inner city	about 2,000
2% in the rural agrarian areas	about 4,000

This figure of approximately seven thousand Christians in Ephesus was still less than the entire Jewish population. For that reason, in those first years, Christianity wasn't a major worry. To most Romans, 'Chrestus' was still a sect of Judaism. This gave the Christians the liberties afforded to the Hebrew Faith by Emperor Claudius and the protection of Marcus Silanus.

Luke journeyed from Ephesus to Troas, Pergamum, Mytilene, Cyzicus, Nicaea, and the villages of Bithynia and Pontus. Although he was away from idolatry and the Temple of Artemis he was still confronted by communities who deplored the Romans, and the dominance of the Province of Asia in the region. Besides the dramatic fatalists, the gods of the Hellenists, and the Greek lore and myths, Luke had to overcome the growing stoic philosophy which gave little concern to the future and regretfully accepted the present without any plan for an alternative. A satisfied culture was not going to be overly receptive to change. However Luke reported some success in every venue he visited.

Paul in his journeys visited Tarsus, Derbe, Lystra, Iconium, Antioch of Pisidia, Perge, and across the Aegean to Athens, Corinth, Thessalonica, Berea, Neapolis and Phillipi. The expanse of his influence was not limited to the major centres but included small towns, villas, and insignificant innumerable communities. It was this enthusiasm and commitment for Christ that eventually swept Asia Minor so that by the time of Constantine's conversion, Christianity was the predominant influence in the area.

By 53AD, in Asia Minor excluding Ephesus, there were approximately seven thousand Christians. This assessment is based on 200 to 300 in every city where they established communities; and about fifty Christians in every town, having a population of at least two thousand persons, through which they passed.

The approximate number of total converts throughout Asia Minor by 53AD was approximately 14,000 men and women.

The term Greek 'Ekklesia' in Ephesus had referred to the assembly of ruling officials. In Christianity, the term was used to describe the Church as an assembly of believers. John, though still so important in the stability and growth of Christianity, had surrounded himself with devoted and capable leaders. He had delegated so much authority and responsibility to these elders that by the time Paul wrote to the Christians of Ephesus from Miletus he was addressing the letter, not to John, but to these elders.

Christianity influenced the economics and commercial vitality of Ephesus in numerous ways. Except for the production and sale of idols, and the obvious immoral activities; the followers were actively involved in production, trading, and selling. They paid taxes. Specific industries developed because of their needs. More bread had to be baked, and so the number of baker's increased. Refugees needed basic amenities. People were feeling better about themselves, thus production of non-necessities grew. Orphans and widows, protected within Christian settlements, required guardians. Transportation spawned further industries. Traders who professed the Christian faith spread the Word across the seas. When followers passed to eternity, land was there for their burial.

In all of this growth, with its joys and tribulations, there remained an enigma. Who was the Spirit of God?

The Spirit guided their efforts. They put faith in the Spirit; and they relied on the Spirit. The Spirit told them what to say and when to say it. The Spirit gave them strength, knowledge and endurance. The Spirit opened the ears of non-believers allowing them to hear and appreciate the teaching. The Spirit blessed the followers with renewed faith in their personal efforts. Who was this Spirit? Many in each community wanted a definition. Everything in the Greek and Roman cultures had a definition. Each deity and every aspect of life had parameters describing the existence, role and authority. John was clearly aware of that need and requirement when he preached and wrote. For that very reason, in his letters he described God as being Love itself. That truth became the foundation of his writings and teachings, embracing the Spirit as the most wondrous example of God in action among humanity. Luke too referred constantly to the power and influence of the Spirit in his teachings. Paul was relentless about the Spirit's role in all aspects of conversion and the daily life of any Christian.

Late that night, John began writing once more regarding the nature of God. With stylus in hand, and enough ink to keep him occupied for hours, and sufficient papyrus for endless pages of praise, he started composing the verse.

> In the beginning was the Word, the Word was with God, and the Word was God.

Chapter Twenty-Three

The Wanderer Finds a Home

Summer, 53

The vessel broke the final white cap as it drifted with the current into the harbour. The seafarer arrived unannounced, early in the morning of that Dies Mars, two weeks before Shauvot. He timed events using Hebrew feasts; but no longer had interest in such celebrations. Workers remained busy on other docks while the ship bounced against the pier. Eventually two labourers attended to tie the craft and assist the foreigner. He was by no means well dressed. Shaven he wasn't. Two others left the vessel. Both seemed far less enthusiastic.

Paul greeted the workers with salutations affirming his faith in Christ and devotion to the Spirit. He had prepared himself to do whatever was required to build the Faith in the Province known for its idolatry. It wasn't just Artemis that he viewed as an obstacle. Rome and Diana had to be equally considered.

Paul's meeting with John that same afternoon conveyed their mutual enthusiasm for the entire mission. However, there was still unease between the two disciples, the same that was evident during

Paul's prior visit. Paul was persistent and easily dissatisfied. John was very much the contrast, trying to exact as much as possible from the few alternatives he had. Paul advised he was there to convert Asia, knowing it was still predominantly and inherently Greek. The efforts of many others were mentioned stressing the number of conversions already achieved. Paul had already been made aware of Luke's work in the north. Appolos was there to provide more information on the Church in and around Ephesus. John let those at the meeting speak freely. The more that was said affirmed that his success had already been significant. The Lord's Supper was then celebrated before they departed to their respective abodes.

Instead of trekking home, John chose to visit Miriam. Regarding Paul, her enthusiasm was tempered. They didn't need anyone telling them they have not done enough. However, they and so many elders within the community confessed they'd like to do more. Understanding the governing factors was so essential. Naomi's fate and the falsified evidence regarding the granary theft confirmed that the Romans, no matter how acquiescent, could not be trusted. The silence of the Greeks on that issue was deafening. They agreed they did not yet have the political influence to effect a decision on any major issue.

Wanting to discuss other matters, John summarized their discussion concerning Paul's anticipated influence.

> Paul will be good for us. We can't count the number he has healed. The sick even reach for a fragment of his clothing just to be cured. He speaks with the Spirit; I have no doubt. He is direct and forceful. For many that's what we need. Consider this: with him here, they won't focus on us, or on any of our elders. He'll draw their attention away from everything else we do. I'll again be able to visit the other churches.

Miriam then advised him about everything she had accomplished with respect to the orphans. They hadn't talked for almost two weeks so it was beneficial to get caught up on each others' work. "There are now eight children, actually really seven and one young women. Chiara, helps now." John's puzzled look prompted Miriam for further explanation. "One night she came to the door. I had never seen her before. The woman wanted to help. She said her husband had left her and that she had some funds. I don't know how, as no man ever leaves anything for any woman he abandons. Things then just happened that fast. We moved onto that lot at the bottom of the hill, across the street from the fountains. We cleared the rubble. Actually Chiara asked some soldiers to help us. We keep the children occupied. There is food, lots of it, from many wanting to help. Even Silanus dropped by two days ago."

"Amazing!" John was truly impressed. "And your market?"

"Down to four days, earning the same." Miriam's advice reflected the economy with the shortage of some grain crops.

They talked for the next thirty minutes about the progress of evangelization, eventually mentioning the respective efforts of Luke, Timothy and Apollos. "Get ready," was John's conclusion. They closed their eyes that night pleased with their success while in their minds being prepared for more.

Paul did not delay returning to the same synagogue at which he debated with the Jewish Elders on his first visit. The greeting reflected an appreciation of their differences, while acknowledging the monotheistic belief that united them against the current of polytheism. Greek was used as freely as Hebrew in this Hellenistic culture. This meeting like the prior occurred at the synagogue just north of the Harbour Gymnasium. Paul had heard of four other temples: one somewhere within the inner city, one near the Cayster River to the north, one near the Meander River to the south, and the other somewhere near the junction of the western edge of Bulbul Mountain and the Aegean Coast. These he did not visit, preferring to keep company with those whom he had previously met and with whom he felt he could best communicate.

He had their attention when narrating on recent events in Syria and Judaea. The Jewish Community in Ephesus had constantly questioned the reliability of Greek messengers on Roman vessels. How truthful were the reports? Interest was also expressed regarding the range and effect of the recurring famines. Paul found himself in that first meeting being more of a story teller rather than an evangelist. As much as he wanted to dwell exclusively on the Spirit, the interests of the Hebrew congregation were decidedly elsewhere.

Within that congregation Paul recognized several who in their prior meeting had disclosed that they had been baptised by John the Baptist and had been attentive to his preaching. One had even asked Paul then, "Was your Christ really the Messiah?" After Paul left the synagogue and while he was still three blocks away, a member of the Hebrew Community caught up with him. He was that same gentleman, the one baptised by John in the River Jordan.

"Wait," he panted.

Paul turned responding to the out-of-breath invitation. The same question was repeated. To this Paul basically repeated his prior answer dwelling on Christ Jesus as the Saviour. The follower of the Jewish faith was not disheartened. Paul elaborated while they stood close together in the shadows between buildings. The inquisitiveness became a look of inspiration and the desire for more knowledge. The sun was setting by the time Paul had recounted his own conversion concluding that, "All is possible in the Spirit."

The next day, before even meeting with Timothy or Apollos, Paul met with the twelve. Many of the questions and answers were repeated. They shared fears of the temple elders if it was ever discovered that they were meeting and asking such questions. Accordingly there was mutual consent to be discreet. In accord with that wish, Paul turned the instruction into a discourse on the Second Greatest Commandment. His message regarding charity as being the Spirit in action was quickly appreciated.

When one challenged Paul on the need to be baptised again, Paul responded accordingly:

> John's baptism was for those who turned from their sins. He told Israel to believe in the one who was coming after him, that is in Christ Jesus. (Acts 19:4)

There were two more meetings each conveying progressive appreciation and knowledge of basic Christian principles. Following their profession of faith, Paul baptised the twelve. He then laid his hands on them and the Holy Spirit descended giving each the gifts of knowledge, understanding and fervent respect for the Lord.

For the next three months, Paul met often with Pharisees and Elders at their temple hoping to persuade them with enthusiastic dissertation about the Holy Spirit and the Resurrected Christ.

Chapter Twenty-Four

Pillar of Philadelphos

August, 53

Attempting a successful trek to Philadelphos was a challenge for any person. Even though the city's name meant 'a person who loves his brother'; accepting Christ Crucified was not within that city the accepted norm. Professing such faith could trigger considerable harm.

Philadelphos was established in 189BC by King Eumenes II of Pergamum. More than five decades later, due the lack of a rightful heir, the area was bequeathed to the Romans. Thereafter in 129BC Philadelphos became an integral part of the Roman Province of Asia.

The city was sixty-five miles from Ephesus. Valleys constituted the route east towards Sardis, then south hugging the mountains to the right. A small stream appeared every so often providing fresh water. In the rainy season, the valley could flood with the torrents off the mountains or rising water from the lakes in the interior. Ultimately all of the water flowing from the mountains was destined by nature for the Aegean.

Vandals and thieves hid among the boulders, in the caves or on the hills. Safety and security were abandoned once the journeyman left Ephesus. Rome provided legions for the interior; but these were not always positioned for quick response. At best they would be stationed in Sardis to quell unrest in a center known for regular disturbances.

Philadelphos was constructed on a mesa above the Cogamus Valley about nine hundred, fifty feet above sea level. This site provided a definite military defense position. To the west of the city, the steep incline of Mount Tmolus assured protection from rebel forces. Tmolus belonged to the same mountain range that accompanied the traveller once he entered the valley east of Ephesus.

Industries were not of any great size. Jobs were never assured for any degree of longevity. Commerce was mainly farming with emphasis on grains, figs, olives and pitted fruit, with the processing of oils for cooking, and lamps.

Philadelphos and all communities in the valleys among the Anatolian mountain ranges suffered from 'Reality Anxiety'. It was not a question of 'if' or the presumption of 'maybe'. The question most often asked was, "When?" Earthquakes were a regular occurrence in the Province of Asia. Several would appear in quick succession, and then not happen for several decades. In the case of Philadelphos, it was almost destroyed in 17AD by a massive quake. The damage was so severe that the Emperor Tiberius lifted the obligation on the city to collect taxes. Funds instead went to the rebuilding of the city. Then just six years later a subsequent quake again levelled most of the city. To understand the severity of that damage, only pillars remained where there were once monuments. Even Caligula recognized the deplorable state of the city and allowed Philadelphos to raise more funds by issuing its own coins. Caligula then commissioned the establishment of an outdoor theatre backing onto the mountain. That ensured employment.

Before Roman rule, the community and the entire Anatolian interior were predominantly Greek. There was also a sizeable Hebrew community: Hellenistic Jews who survived the Hittite purge. Indebtedness to the Romans was unavoidable with all of the rebuilding projects, and the taxation benefits afforded to the city. It was this Hebrew group and these Hellenist factions that became the initial focus of John's attention.

The Jewish community despised his presence and vehemently disputed his teaching and the authority he claimed. There was no capacity for the Spirit to enter their lives. Ultimately he referred to their community as the "synagogue of the devil."

The Greek community was far more receptive. The Christian assembly was not a large, and the believers were generally impoverished. Resources for many were almost non-existent, with funds being committed to the major projects commissioned by emperors. The realm of poverty prompted many Greeks to embrace a social ethos committed to sharing. Examples of charity strengthened their faith. Believing in Christ Jesus gave purpose to their lives. Leaders stepped forward willing to risk everything. Even though the believers were a visible minority in the Greco-Roman culture; they met on regular occasions choosing not hide their faith. As they didn't have a building in which to meet, they congregated at a pillar that had been left standing when the temple collapsed.

John was inspired by the commitment of these followers. In spite of attacks from the Jewish community and followers being rejected by their former Greek friends; they held true to their faith. Keeping his promise, John prompted Philemon to accompany him on this particular journey. Just seeing and experiencing the stories of a Greek gentlemen from Ephesus could enhance their enthusiasm for the Faith. With the support of three other followers they completed the trek: safely and in timely fashion. This was John's fifth journey to the community; and he vowed it would not be his last. Such visits gave John a further understanding of the Faith and the potential for its meaning to so many different individuals. John was compelled later to write about Philadelphos praising its devotion to Christ.

Chapter Twenty-Five

Luke in Troas

September, 53

Luke had only one expectation on his return to Troas. Three years prior, the Spirit directed Paul to the city of approximately one hundred thousand residents. The area clearly offered a higher prospect for successful conversion of the Greek population. Other communities in that area were more entrenched in their polytheistic beliefs.

The city of Alexandria Troas (Troas) was located on the northern coast of the Aegean Sea across from Thrace. Nine hundred and ninety acres were home to a multi-ethnic population reflecting its proximity to the many cultures in Eastern Europe and Asia Minor. The ancient Greek culture still flourished even under the administration of the Roman Governor. The city provided two major harbours within the one city. The buildings as would be expected included: government structures, temples, monuments, baths, public latrines, a large outdoor theatre, an enclosed theatre, a gymnasium complex, the essential stadium, and of course the market.

Mining for gold, silver and precious gems was the major industry contributing to additional production and refining facilities. The agrarian economy also flourished in the multitude of valleys irrigated with streams and rain water flowing from the mountains. Above all else, Troas was a shipping center with vessels sailing to and from all ports on the Mediterranean Sea.

Luke's first visit to Troas was part of his excursion to several cities in the northern expanse of Anatolia. He discovered, as did Paul, that the residents of Troas were culturally committed to the Hellenistic traditions. Luke expected that to be a hurdle. However some in the Greek community were not alarmed by Christian teachings. The more that Rome forced its rules on the Greeks, the more the Greeks were prone to reject the Divine Emperor and steer their devotion to the Resurrected Christ. It was the Cult of the Emperor, or as some called it 'Emperor Worship', that was driving the wedge between the Greek inhabitants and the Roman occupiers. If they had to amend their culture, Rome was not their preference. Christianity waited in the middle to accept all of the Greeks dissatisfied with Rome's dominance.

The community of Hellenistic Jews was significant, but less than ten percent of the population. As Jews they opposed the idolatry of the metal images and stone deities. As Greeks they opposed the Roman deities. Luke discovered they were amiable to discuss the many facets of religion, culture, their differences, and the ultimate goal: eternal life.

However, as Paul discovered, there was no reception by the Romans to anything Christian.

Because Troas was a center for heavy industry, and bearing in mind its proximity to the established communities on the Black Sea, slavery was an inescapable phenomenon. Luke was absolutely opposed to its existence, but in a city of one hundred thousand persons and so many dependent on the profits of heavy labour, Roman slavery in a Roman world was unfortunately there to stay. Taking into account that reality, Luke in his lessons stressed the importance of the human, concluding that all life is sacred. The parables of the sick being healed, the blind being cured, the devout destitute man praying in the synagogue, the Good Samaritan and the declaration of the thief on the Cross: all conveyed the 'open-arms' perception of Christianity that was available to all persons.

Having witnessed the progress achieved by the women in Ephesus, Luke brought that message to Troas. The women in many households embraced the prospect of being important to their community. The concept, that women did not have to be just submissive to their husbands, was an entirely new teaching. It challenged nearly every aspect of ancient Greek and Roman culture. The idea for women was attractive, and then for believers it became a way of life.

The elders and congregation were enthused with Luke's presence and were receptive to his instruction. Unlike communities of believers in the Anatolian interior, the faithful in Troas was not predominantly the poor and needy. This was a thriving community: prepared to accept new ideas, responsive to unfamiliar logic, and ready to achieve the utmost in every quest. It was an industrial, goal oriented society. Luke accordingly molded his style to interact with as many as possible, realizing he had almost no prospect with the Romans. He was a debater to the influential, an attentive ear to the underprivileged, a hand to the needy. Luke was employing every element of Greek culture that he knew from his youth, realizing the acceptance of indisputable sense was the most effective means of evangelizing the Hellenistic community.

Chapter Twenty-Six

Temple Turmoil

October, 53

"He casts out devils. I tell you. I saw it myself." Alexander unequivocally declared to his friends as they rushed toward the temple.

Eitan was convinced otherwise. He was a profound Jew who professed every aspect of the Mosaic Law. Eitan's only interest in hearing Paul was the disciple's total opposition to the sale and existence of idols. In that sense Eitan had something to share with the Christians, but definitely no more. It wasn't this Christ, according to Eitan, that cast out devils through the intervention of any Roman from Tarsus. To him and others in the Hebrew community, God the Creator alone had the power to dispel the satanic influence.

Inside the temple, they listened for those first moments. Many came expecting to see another miracle. Instead Paul addressed them with expressions of praise for the Lord Jesus. The rumbling started immediately, and soon became a rabble response. Raucous shouts objecting to his message stopped short of violence. For months, this scene had been repeated. Opposition to the foreigner's message was consistent.

Sceva, the High Priest, was not about to tear his garments, though he had every right to do so and simultaneously declare Paul to be a blasphemer. Even though Sceva held a double edged sword: to rule and to keep the peace; he was determined to prevent his congregation from being decimated by any man who no longer professed God's Promise to the Children of Abraham. However as a Jew and a Pharisee, Paul had the right to speak in the temple. They heard his message repeatedly about the Word, the influence of the Spirit, and the salvation offered to them in Christ Jesus. The foundation of his teaching was simple: Jesus Christ is the fulfillment of the Messianic Promise. That many in the congregation freely debated with him provided Paul with a continuing audience especially when he condemned the pagan influence of Artemis and the fictitious idols. On that subject, they had mutual interest.

Pride and arrogance were as much a part of life in Ephesus as anywhere. Having themselves witnessed Paul casting out devils in the name of the Lord Jesus, the sons of the High Priest attempted to do the same. However invoking Jesus' name did not achieve the desired result. In fact the devil inside the possessed man rebuked them, asking in whose name they were intending to dispel the devil. When they hesitated, the devil angrily revolted and chased Sceva's sons throughout the city. Delirious and unclothed, they escaped. However the story of the inability of the High Priest's sons to cast out devils spread everywhere. Respect for Paul, his authority and his message grew progressively. Some Roman officials befriended him. The Jewish community became increasingly cautious and adversarial.

On his return from Philadelphos and Laodicea, John met with Paul and Timothy. The meeting at Miriam's abode provided the inconspicuous venue they preferred.

Amulets, rings, figurines and bracelets were askew on Miriam's table. These were mainly bronze and silver. Similar items were also made of gold, but those were the cherished belongings of the devotees committed to the false gods. From a small pouch Miriam also removed various gems of brilliant colours and hues. "We're not just talking about one deity," Miriam stated the obvious.

Their task had suddenly become extremely universal, because any decision they would make would pit themselves against too many in the community whose lives were involved in the mining, production and sales of these items. There was a sense of reluctance to challenge each and every image bearing in mind the consequences, and the reality that so few within the community would ever support them if it meant losing their employment. Yet, there was agreement that something had to be done.

John was the most insightful when he raised the issue he had discussed with Luke on several occasions,

> If the Romans and Greeks agree with us, what then? They will still need images on their coins, or do you suggest blank slugs for imperial currency? That won't happen. So what do we do? I suggest leave the currency. These tokens could mean anything to anyone. Are you going to tell me this warn bronze still means Apollo?

His dissertation was precise leaving the others to address solely those charms, gems and amulets used exclusively for Artemis.

After hours of flowing discussion the meeting concluded with the intention to first attack Artemis realizing all could not be possibly achieved at once. Paul was slightly dismayed because his message had been basically an 'all or nothing' approach.

Paul's final advice that evening shocked John and Miriam. Paul was dispatching Timothy and his associate Erastus to revisit the Christians in Macedonia. Timothy had already been alerted, and was fully prepared to depart that week. Words of respect and appreciation accompanied salutations regarding the progress and achievement to date in Ephesus. Timothy vowed to return but had no definite plan.

Throughout the next year, Paul continued to meet with his Jewish friends engaging in lively debate while preaching the Word and opening their hearts to the Spirit.

Chapter Twenty-Seven

Saturnalia Festival

December, 53

Before the Temple of Dea Roma just after sunrise, Pro Consul Marcus Silanus, in full military attire, stood in profound respect silently adoring the newly created statue of their god Saturnus. He was the deity of peace and agriculture who ruled the world of magnanimous bounty in an age of innocence without labour. The world before original sin: this best described this god's realm. The image stole the imagination with its detail: the deity seated on his throne. To its right lost among the multitude of columns, the Temple of the Divine Julius Caesar awaited worshippers' devout attention. However that would not happen on this the first day of the Saturnalia Festival.

From that temple, the Pro Consul turned his attention to the gathering of philosophers in the State Agora. Assembled near the Temple of Isis, they awaited Silanus for the customary opportunity to debate at length their philosophical opinions and differences. Plato was for this group the most influential person in Greece, almost a god himself. No one disagreed with Plato's view that virtue was necessary to achieve the ultimate state. Similarly they all agreed education was necessary to acquire virtue. The corollary followed that education was dependent upon the state. There really wasn't much to argue as they all agreed with the insight that citizens could best be governed by educated leaders sincerely committed to assuring the truth. The number of City States within the former Greek Empire affirmed the general commitment to leadership by learned officials representing the hoi polloi in all matters of truth. Debate followed with the question, "What is truth?" There was no agreement, which gave purpose for their need to meet again next year. "Unless philosophers become rulers and rulers become true, there will be no end to the troubles of states and of humanity," one of the elders concluded quoting Plato from 'The Republic'.

The Pro Consul turned his attention then to the multitude and festivities along Curetes Street. From the fountain near the Prytaneion he peered once more down the avenue as it descended toward the commercial market. The mass of humanity, brightly attired with shawls, masks, painted faces and plumes, greeted their governor. With only six body guards, he had little protection among the revelers. Cymbals and drums greeted him as he approached the Portico of Hercules marking the approximate mid-point of the street between the commoners with their market and the elite with their government building. Beyond this the marble paving stones, were still an issue having been raised and tilted more than two decades before with the last earthquake. Rubble to his left affirmed the extent of that damage. However the enthusiasm of the raucous gathering buried all prior woes in the dust of Ephesian glory.

Silanus was greeted at the commercial market with many of the wealthy traders dressed as slaves waiting on their servants at prepared tables in the core of the plaza. Changing places and assuming roles was an essential aspect of the Saturnalia festivities. The tradition confirmed the significance of slaves and classes within the Roman world. Though they were slaves, they were not all mistreated, and Saturnalia was the opportunity for the wealthy to convey their appreciation if only temporarily to those who assured their comforts.

Jesters, buskers and clowns filled the market, with the crowd pressed together celebrating with laughter. In the midst of that enthusiasm, Miriam guided Anna. The joyous sounds were so exhilarating to one so keenly aware of every sound.

John had been with them for a short while, but decided to leave the city's inner core to visit believers in the valley. There were many who were denied access or were financially unable to attend. As a youth he would have grabbed the opportunity to watch the games in the stadium; but the rites and adoration of a marble statue prevented him from attending the spectacle.

At the far end of the market, an orchestral group played their lyres greeting the governor as he passed by. His path in that direction was predetermined as a second group of philosophers awaited him. These seven gentlemen, each bedecked in their impression of their hero, discussed the attributes and teachings of Socrates. Truth also was a major issue in their philosophical exchanges. There was no adverse opinion on Socrates' view concerning humility, understanding, appreciation, ignorance, and necessity. "Knowledge exists in knowing that you know nothing," a gentleman quoted the Greek philosopher. Not being able to define 'truth', the ultimate knowledge, compelled a person to appreciate his limitations with an acknowledgement that more could be learned, and that in those attempts to learn. the 'truth' was discovered. Silanus abundantly appreciated these opportunities to discuss philosophy with such elders as it affirmed Rome's appreciation of Greek antiquity and the accepted perception that education, leadership and truth march hand in hand toward assuring good governance.

Darius and Burrus joined the guards as Silanus greeted the multitude on the Marble Way. Ultimately he stopped before the throng that were seated in the Theatre. A second statue of Saturnus had been erected at the base of the Theatre. Almost fifty years before at the decree of Caesar Augustus the practice of offering a human sacrifice had ceased. Priests and priestesses filled the air with incense from swinging thuribles. The scent was intoxicating not by the burning of exotic grains, but from the charring of perfumed petals including those taken from the plenteous poppies. After a short speech praising the god once more, dancing and music took over the celebration. The festivities were never limited to just the Romans. This occasion was equivalent to the Greek festivities of Kronia.

A late afternoon meal was already prepared in the harbour facilities. There, the Pro Consul and his entourage removed their uniforms allowing the servants to wear the illustrious garments. Barely attired, the Roman officials served meals to the Greek slaves. Those servants who did not have the chance to don Roman military garb were given the colourful 'synthesis' clothing for the occasion. Only later after the servants had dined, did Silanus and his cohort eat and then redress for further rites. Throughout the city, servants were treated like land owners: a truly special occasion with unlimited definition.

Gambling and games of chance were also part of the celebrations, but these would wait for the evening hours. Several slaves could also be awarded their rights as freemen. The celebrations also provided the opportunity to designate a Roman woman as being a 'freewoman'. Gift giving was an appealing event in households throughout the Empire. At the Temple of Artemis, everything Greek became Roman. Morality was no obstacle.

Silanus eventually made his way to the stadium where races, competitions, challenges, and chariots ruled. In the evening the festivities became a celebration of light with candles generating an encompassing glow in every venue. Candles themselves symbolized truth and knowledge and the light conveyed the quest for those attributes.

Other cultures would relate these celebrations to the winter solstice. The Roman world transformed the event to the adoration of a god, not just nature. In that way the festivities became important to humans because the festivities were about humans for humanity. Saturnalia started on the morning December 17th and lasted seven days until the evening of the twenty-third. Saturnus was the seventh of the celestial orbs, the honour being extended to the world where peace and harmony ruled.

Two days later on December 25th, the Dies Natalis de Sol Invictus was celebrated as the Birthday of the Invincible Sun. For the Christians, the concept of celebrating the Birth of Christ that day would not happen for more than two hundred and fifty years.

Chapter Twenty-Eight

Preparing the Foundation

January, 54

Miriam wrapped herself in the shawl, a garment she considered almost sacred. On cold mornings she donned the thick scarf the same one that the Lord's Mother wore when they abandoned Antioch for safety. The bluish cloth had faded in colour over the more than six years since her passing. Miriam refrained from saying much about the miraculous occurrence. She understood why, as she had seen it before with the Lord's Resurrection when she discovered the blood stained cloth without the body. Maryam was slightly different though: she went to sleep, there were some clothes in the room the next morning. Then to her and John there appeared an angelic vision reassurance them, "She is with her son."

The shawl was frilled as was expected with age, no different from her usually dishevelled hair. Miriam tried to keep aptly groomed, for hygiene and appearance were always important. However, the occasional gray hairs were becoming the majority. Most times she thanked her mirror for being opaque.

Philemon and Alexa sat on the cushions near the table having brought Anna with them. The blind girl never lost her sense of the furnishings within Miriam's house, a characteristic that truly amazed everyone. Anna cherished being with the woman she still considered to be her mother. Philemon was all prepared with so many thoughts scurrying through his mind. The purpose of the meeting was significant. He revered the idea that some people thought his opinions were important.

John had already returned from his pilgrimage to Miletus, having become quite accustomed to that sixty mile trek. Wishing to involve others whom he deemed to be equally important he left Miriam's abode to personally invite the others.

Luke had already made his way up the mountain to Miriam's residence. He too was enthused about the prospects of this meeting. They had met before, just the three of them, on these topics; but now others were invited who could convey the common perceptions of the general population. Luke's last trip to the villages in Mysia and Bithynia would probably be his last. He had become more concerned with the Christians in Troas in light of the progress already achieved there.

Bernardus greeted John warmly and then excitedly conveyed the latest news. "More converts," was the message repeated several times when referring to the various portions of the city and surrounding districts. Even when Bernardus mentioned the difficulties encountered in Iconium, Lystra, Derbe and Antioch of Galatia; John was ready to express that based on Paul's reports he had no other expectation. John was well aware that many of the Jews who stoned Stephen to death were from Cilicia and Galatia; and therefore his anticipation for those regions was never that significant.

Apollos, the convert from Judaism who came to Ephesus with Paul, was equally delighted in being invited to such a gathering. Respect among all present was mutual which assured that the honest discussion would be coherent and achieve the desired goal.

Even before the Saturnalia Festival, the leaders of the Christian community realized that something had to be done to address the issues that were hindrances to the process of conversion. Idolatry, superstition, witchcraft, charms and immorality were everywhere. In November, John and Miriam had met with Paul and Luke. Paul's opinions were consistent with those he was expressing to the people in debates and lectures. John too had been consistent in his approach for preserving the peace, and through the example of that peace he could entice the multitude to become followers. Saturnalia and all polytheistic celebrations were obstacles to Christianity. Just preaching about Christ Crucified and events in some foreign land was not enough. More had to be done. When questions were asked, definite answers had to be provided.

"It's now clearly an absolute situation." John declared after more than half an hour exchanging opinions on the issue of idols.

"And what will we say about their coins?" Miriam wanted to be sure that matter was not dismissed.

"If we say idolatry is wrong, and we must; then it we have to consider it is wrong in every respect. The issue of the coins is somewhat different from the metallic charms made exclusively for their fabricated deities. Yet these coins insult the Lord just as much. If we oppose the observance of all rites relative to the Imperial Cult, we cannot allow ourselves to accept the image of Claudius on our coins. For someone who in his life was honourable and achieved much for the common good, there is sense in coins bearing the impression of such leaders after their deaths; but when a man demands his image on coins solely to satisfy his own self worth, that is idolatry. It is no different than a golden calf being made while Moses was on Mount Sinai. This must be our emphasis, as God said to Moses: I am the Lord your God. You cannot have any false gods before me."

Bernardus readily agreed. Apollos felt it was necessary to be firm on this issue but wondered how Christians should react when receiving or using the coins bearing the current emperor's impression. Philemon went one step further asking if someone was going to instruct the Pro Consul to stop issuing currency in Ephesus bearing Claudius' image. The conversation continued exploring all factors. Finally John concluded,

> We must and I will definitely state my opposition to all charms, precious metals, gems, amulets or trinkets of any nature that depict any image of Artemis. Second, we will oppose all offerings to Artemis, Diana or any Roman and Greek god. Third, we will continue to

use Roman and Greek currency as issued, but if ever asked we will state our opposition to the issuance of new currency bearing the impression of the current emperor.

They broke for lunch that Miriam had already prepared. John approached her while outside by the garden and asked about the issue she felt had been important two months prior. This was the same point that Luke had mentioned on more than one occasion. The meeting resumed with Miriam's query on that point, "If we tell our Greek brothers and sisters that they cannot offer veneration to their gods, and if we say the same to the Romans about their deities; should we not be prepared with alternatives? Will words about Christ Crucified be enough to convince them to turn from their idolatry?"

Luke was impressed and immediately expressed his opinion on that point. "Very true. John, as you have said the Lord told you the parable of that man who was cleansed of many devils. Afterwards, he did nothing and then became worse than he was before. We must avoid that happening."

Miriam continued, "All images are not idolatry; just those of false gods. A coin with the impression of Christ could almost be considered sacred for it portrays the semblance of one who is the definition of sacred. Should we consider, should Christians produce their own charms, rings, insignia, and images for reflection that bring us closer to the Lord?"

The others in the room were enthused realizing the consequences of such a plan. "Far reaching," Alexa declared.

"John, do we have silversmiths among our converts?" Miriam continued with her questions believing she had total agreement in response to her first query.

Philemon and Luke answered for John both declaring that they believed there were sufficient numbers of silversmiths in all communities that would be willing to produce and sell these Christian items.

"We must make it very certain that we are not adoring the ring or any item displaying the image of Our Lord. We use them solely as a reminder of God's goodness, His promise and His importance in our lives. We cannot honor any coin of any nature, but we are urged to honour the Lord when viewing the image." John established the basis on which any religious could be used.

Luke's reaction was automatic, concluding that such religious items would fill the void created by the Christian opposition to the stone and metal images worshipping false gods.

"And about our statues?" Alexa enquired. "We have masons and artists too."

"Ultimately that should be our goal. But as for now, start with this." Luke was committed to the step by step approach having witnessed the rejection of being too abrupt in some towns and villages.

When they rested briefly in the early afternoon sun, Miriam removed her shawl and passed it to John. "We must declare our belief with respect to His Mother. Too many ask questions which we are loath to answer."

"His Mother. Bernardus and Apollos, the rest here have met her. We have imparted to you what we know and what we saw. This here, this was her shawl. That jar there, it contains the myrrh we took from Jerusalem, still sealed, ready for her anointing, which we never had to use." John slowly provided additional information.

"She was taken directly to heaven," Bernardus wished to confirm.

Miriam agreed. John added, "By the power and authority of Christ, so that His Mother, pure as she was without sin, could be with Him."

Realizing the significance of the event, the room was hushed.

"I still think of her each day." Miriam reverently continued. "Incredible person in every sense." Miriam then continued recalling those hours with Maryam after the crucifixion and burial, and the fears and trepidation experienced prior to discovering the resurrection.

After John blessed himself, Luke added, "That must be our symbol more than any metal object." There was quick agreement.

The ceremony of celebrating the Lord's Supper was then discussed at length with particular attention spent on the use of scriptural readings and the format of prayers. Consensus was almost immediate that readings from the Old Testament were an essential element in the rite. However just as quickly, they had to address the scarcity of such scrolls. The resulting resolution was unanimous: that somehow, somewhere, by someone, more parchments had to be rewritten, and that more importantly the narratives on the life of Jesus Christ must be completed so as to encourage the believers and be consistent in the retelling of the extraordinary events.

Equally important they agreed that Die Solis was their Sabbath Day and that the celebration of the Lord's Supper must take place on that day for as many believers as possible at several locations and times throughout Ephesus and Anatolia. "We cannot have one rule for the believers here; and another for congregations elsewhere." John was firm in his conclusion.

Following that it was time for supper. The logs in the fireplace were lit and soup in a pot was brought to a boil. While a loaf of bread was being cut, and some cooked meat sliced for the meal, Alexa and Apollos were in the garden searching for any green leaves to augment the meal. By the time they sat on the cushions around the table, several neighbours had joined the gathering, each bringing a separate bowl to supplement Miriam's preparations. The quiet meal quickly turned into a festive celebration, with games blind-folding the participants, word challenges, or just humour. Such impromptu events assured the lively nature of the Christian community. Although many perceived the end of the century to be the end of time, preparations were clearly being made for the Ecclesia to last beyond the millennium.

Chapter Twenty-Nine

Between Heaven and Hell

March, 54

"They won't stop." Closing his eyes tight, John lamented that he could no longer rid his mind of heinous discord. His expression painted the image of a terrified old man, too frail to thwart any limitation. Miriam looked at him caringly as he lay there on her cushions. She had seen him in such a trance twice before, but this time he was ever so fragile. John gripped his fists crossing his arms tightly over his chest; then swung his arms wide with a foreboding expression. His words were Aramaic, a language he so rarely used. Then suddenly his whispered refrains embraced angelic images and his voice became calm once more.

In these moments, Miriam felt so absolutely helpless trying to care for the person who had always stood by her side. Anna sitting in the corner was overly troubled by such disturbances, and repeatedly begged Miriam for some sense. However, reason was not to be had while the devil roamed, capturing his mind if only for a moment and then hurling it into the abyss between heaven and hell.

Miriam, on seeing John in that pitiful state, recalled how on more than one occasion the Master ordered the devil to leave a person. John too on had several times cast out devils. Now here he was, so absolutely not himself, in a near delirious state, with no remedy. Prayers had not been their solution.

She soothed him wiping his brow again with a cold face cloth while repeating her gentle encouragement, "May the Lord bless us with peace, and heal us in His mercy."

He smiled clutching her hand. She kissed his forehead, and hugged him dearly.

It was following his last visits to Miletus, Colossae and Laodicea that the apparitions started. She had no other word for them. After the first bout when prayers didn't work, with every image so incredibly vague; it was John who suggested the origin might be divine. That was beyond Miriam's comprehension. If any of these phenomena had a heavenly origin surely the Good Lord would grant peace of mind.

Once more, she prayed reciting her paraphrased version of the Amidah. John clenched her hand holding it over his heart for comfort, knowing Miriam and the entire community would not abandon him.

Was there some mystic relationship to the papyrus hanging on the line by her fireplace? What suddenly prompted her to return to that skill? There was so much more to do. She viewed them and looked around the room knowing she had so many other chores to complete. She had little to sell at the market and knew time was not her companion.

Rising from the cushioned floor, she assisted Anna to her bed. This young lady was very much a woman now, attractive in personality, and lovely upon first impression; except she was blind and as such she would be considered less desirable than a prostitute. Miriam cursed the Romans for that. Instead of helping such persons in need, they condemned them to a life of misery.

Returning to John, Miriam continued to wipe his brow until he closed his eyes. Was he asleep? She didn't know; because John had this incredible ability of closing his eyes to rest while still being completely aware of discussions and events around him. Choosing to do what she did after the second bout, Miriam read from a parchment that they had received from Mark being the start of his description of the Lord's life:

> Jesus went to the synagogue and began to teach. Those who heard him were amazed at his teaching. He was unlike the other teachers of the Law. He taught with authority. At that time a man, possessed by a devil, entered the synagogue and screamed, "What do you want of us, Jesus of Nazareth? Do you wish to destroy us? I know who you are. You are God's anointed messenger!" Jesus ordered the evil spirit, "Be still. Leave this man." The man shook hard, and gave a loud cry and the devil left him. People were so amazed they asked one another, "Is this a new teaching? He has the power to order evil spirits, and they obey him."

Miriam then continued to wipe his brow. The muscles in his face became relaxed. The torment was over. Still he needed rest. She cuddled him close providing whatever assurance he required. Still uncertain of the origin or cause, she whispered her private prayers. His eyes remained closed but his ears embraced the litany.

In the morning he spoke about his visions: dragons with seven heads, sweeping tails, destruction, torment, oppression. He spoke directly in concise verse about the need to confront Rome. He called the empire "Babylon", cursing every element of its government, its oppression, and the concealed moments of tyranny known to only the victims.

Miriam begged him to stay with her for several days wanting to be sure that the nightmares had stopped. John ultimately agreed for that short time hoping to acquire full understanding to their meaning. In his mind he knew he had to create a picture for all the faithful from the dire revelations.

Before the conclusion of the Saturnalia Games, another bout occurred. This time it was more sudden yet shorter. Based on his description the following day, the aura was more inspiring. John told Miriam that he had seen Maryam arrayed in heaven. He talked of a New Jerusalem, and eternal bliss. John mentioned Alpha and Omega as if the Greek letters were an actual person. It was so astonishingly insightful. Images of the devil's realm had ceased, and now he was painting a portrait of heaven.

"He must write his thoughts." Miriam started telling herself. Others were already doing it. His imaginings, though bewildering, were beyond the realm of current wisdom. She would encourage him; and he would agree. She knew that.

During their supper, Miriam looked up at the drying papyrus and understood why she had been so suddenly possessed with the urge to prepare and press so many sheets.

Chapter Thirty

Paul vs Artemis

April, 54

Throughout the city, in the gymnasium complex, in the markets, at the baths, in the stadium, or on the main floor of the theatre, Paul engaged many citizens and visitors in lively debates. Greeks, Jews and Romans equally exchanged opinions each with their own litany of supposed facts and suppositions. For months Paul remained steadfast. He never backed down on the idolatry issue. The multitude continuously heard the message of Christ Crucified and the Spirit but shied away from commitment. Conceding ingrained cultural habits for a new way of life that generated no greater profits seemed to be illogical to the philosophers. Finding peace and life's ambitions in an entity contrary to the Imperial Cult was out of the question for the Romans. Paul's miracles remained the main attraction. The message of peace and hope were for a select few the promise of a better life.

It was in the stadium precincts that Paul first met the Greek silversmith. Paul's denunciation of idolatry, particularly regarding Artemis, raised the ire of that rotund gentleman. The confrontation had to eventually happen. The merchant's comments were not debate, rather an expression of infuriation against that Christian whose ideals would radically interfere with his profits. It was the month of April, a month before the Artemis Celebrations, a time when he could lose a substantial amount if more Greeks and Ephesians accepted Paul's teaching. Sales prior to and during the Saturnalia celebration at year's end could also be adversely affected. With so much to lose, Demetrius chose this occasion to silence the missionary.

Paul's enquiries provided him with further understanding of Demetrius' interest. The Greek merchant operated two stores between the stadium and the temple. One of those locations was so close to the temple that sales of amulets, rings and charms was inevitable. Merchants generally had only one store, usually the front of their residence. The two stores explained the added reason for Demetrius' determination to confront the missionary. Understanding the interests of his foe made Paul even more resolute. His commitment was total: every charm, amulet or broach honoring Artemis must be stopped.

The devotion to Artemis took place as scheduled. It was always a delightful time for the Greeks and Romans with the revelry and forgotten code of morality. Throughout the summer months and into the fall, Paul continued his lectures and debates moving these inside the halls and gymnasium during inclement weather. After the Saturnalia Games, the entire issue again exploded. Whether his profits had fallen substantially, or perhaps he was just being coaxed to action by other merchants; Demetrius acted abruptly.

One on one against Paul, Demetrius came to realize he would not be successful. Roman officials were distant in their support. There were few factions in Ephesus on which he could rely. Accordingly he decided, after listening to Paul for the final time, that to gain the support of others who shared his interest for profits, a general meeting was essential. He addressed that group.

> You all know that our prosperity is the result of our work. Now, we can see what this man, Paul, is doing. He tells the people that our images are not gods at all. He has so far convinced many people in Ephesus and throughout the Province of Asia. There is a danger that our business will suffer. Not only that there is the risk

> that the Temple of the Great Goddess Artemis will cease to be, and that her greatness will be destroyed. Our goddess worshipped by everyone in Asia and in the entire world! (Acts 19:25)

The infuriated assembly quickly became a raucous mob: screaming and chanting; and moved to the theatre to accommodate all of the Ephesians that supported their cause. Paul attempted to enter the theatre but was prevented from doing so. Alexander, the Hebrew elder, stepped forward from the angry horde wishing to address the gathering and beg them for sense. When he was recognized and known to be Jewish, the mass of Greek merchants had Alexander removed from their presence.

Ultimately the civic clerk stepped forward to quell the uproar.

> Everyone knows the city of Ephesus is the keeper of the temple of the great Artemis, and of the sacred stone that fell down from heaven. Nobody can deny these things. So you must silence your uproar. Do nothing reckless. You have challenged these men even though they have not robbed the temple or said evil things about our goddess. If you accuse anyone;we have authorities and days for court. charges can be made there. But if there is something more that you want, it will have to be settled in a legal meeting of the citizens. (Acts 19:35)

Paul escaped the area of theatre unharmed and hid himself from the mob. It wasn't just out of fear that he decided to immediately leave, although apprehension was very real. After meeting for the final time with John, Paul departed the Province of Asia. Macedonia and Timothy's work there were his destination.

The twenty-seven months in Ephesus had passed quickly for Paul: the instruction, lectures, debates, as well as the infuriated mobs, and ultimately a positive impact on the number of committed believers. Much had been accomplished in the name of Christ Jesus with the inspiration and direction of the Holy Spirit.

– Ephesus Pure in Heart –

Chapter Thirty-One

Presence Demanded

July, 54

A sealed scroll demanded his immediate presence. A trieme anchored near the harbour awaited the Deputy Consul's compliance. Within the hour Celer gathered his attire, placing clothes and the opened-scroll in a leather bag. His instructions to Darius were precise, that he was expecting to be away for some time. Silanus was to be dutifully advised upon his return. In the meantime, Ephesus wasn't going anywhere; but Celer was.

Agrippina the Younger was the name most feared by everyone of any sense anywhere in the Empire. She was ambitious, ruthless, violent and capable of murder. At the same time she was sly and absolutely controlling. She had her place in the Senate and in the bedroom of the Empire. Agrippina was masterful at the game of intrigue. Being able to assign blame elsewhere was her forte. Licentious and arrogant: she was the best at her trade.

Agrippina was born into nobility and as such she was destined to be more than someone's harlot. On January 1 of 49AD at age thirty-four, she became the fourth wife of Emperor Claudius. Claudius was also her fourth husband. Matrimonial commitment was not a virtue in imperial Rome. Marriages were arranged among the elite to benefit both families by means of dowries or political ties.

Agrippina's ambition was resolute, demanding her place among the most elite in the Empire. She was the great grand-daughter of Emperor Augustus, the niece of Tiberius, the sister of Caligula, and above all Claudius' niece. Incest had become an inherent standard in the imperial family. Although many deplored such relationships, acceptance among the elite was the norm. The Empire had learned that lesson when those who questioned Caligula's marriage to his sister were permanently silenced.

Agrippina had a son, Lucius Domitius Ahenobarbus, from her first marriage. History would know him as the infamous Nero. She controlled his education, those within his inner circle and planned his marriage to Nero's step-sister from Claudius' third marriage.

She was determined that Nero would become emperor and everything she did was destined to fulfil her wish. By the time Claudius became Emperor, four of Agrippina's close relatives were dead. These included her two brothers: Nero Caesar, Drusus Caesar and her first two husbands: her cousin Gnaeus Ahenorbarbus and Gaius Crispus Passienus. Her third husband suddenly left the scene prior to her marriage to Claudius. Prior to the Praetorian Guard completing the task, Agrippina had even plotted to kill her brother, Caligula.

Celer was very much aware of her involvement in Ephesus. To understand the dynamics and treachery, Pro Consul Marcus Silanus throughout Rome was very much considered to be Claudius' brother. That would make Lucius Junius Silanus Torquatus, the only son of Marcus Silanus, a potential heir to the position of Emperor. Further, Pro Consul Marcus Silanus was Agrippina's second cousin.

With much celebration, Lucius became betrothed to Claudia Octavia, Claudius's daughter whom Agrippina wanted as Nero's first wife. To destroy that relationship she falsely accused Lucius of incest with his aunt Junia Lepida. That charge became diabolical with the accusation of witchcraft. The rumour spread that Lucius committed suicide; however silence ruled the general perception that he had been murdered. That was the reality but not the designated account provided to the Patricians. Lucius was exiled to Bari where he was ordered to commit suicide. After refusing, Lucius was beaten to death on the day Agrippina married Claudius.

Agrippina had every reason to feel uncomfortable with Marcus Silanus, her husband's friend and a member of the imperial family, being Pro Consul of Asia. As long as Marcus Silanus was alive, he could accuse Agrippina of murdering his son.

Rumours circulating from knowledgeable sources in Rome were suggesting that Claudius was having second thoughts about declaring Nero his heir apparent. The Emperor was reverting to his own flesh and blood, Britannicus. At the same time there were only two persons preventing her son, Nero, from being the Emperor: her husband and his son.

Celer was primly attired in military dress as the vessel left port destined for Rome. He pondered the urgency of her request. Was it his military prowess, his renown for philosophical debates, his linguistic skills, or his knowledge of medicine, alchemy or botany?

Chapter Thirty-Two

Blessed are the Merciful

August, 54

Miriam pondered the lyrics while leaning back against her cushions. Papyrus, she found, was not the best median for composing if it was ever the writer's intent to scratch and correct. Regardless of any difficulty, Miriam was far beyond getting frustrated at such mundane challenges. Humming the verse once more, she tried to elevate the simple lyrics into an inspiring hymn.

> Rest sweet my child
> Let peace like jasmine petals ease your mind
> Rest sweet my child
> Let love of your mother's soul warm your heart.
> Rest sweet my child
> Till morning shines and you rise to sunny smiles
> Rest sweet my child
> Sleep with Him who rose for Thee.

Music was not her forte; however it was becoming such an essential part of their liturgical celebrations. She smiled to herself at the end of the day knowing she had tried.

The terra cotta lamp had been extinguished when the pounding at the door started. Her first impulse was to conclude that she definitely required stronger hinges as everyone who ever attended seemed to delight in pounding the wooden door. How the door frame held, she didn't know.

The pounding continued until Miriam opened the door. The instant she saw the woman she exclaimed her horror. Chiara stood there with blood dripping from her right cheek. The gash was serious enough that pressure was not stopping the bleeding. It was only moments after discovering the severity that Miriam applied gentiane, commonly used for deep cuts to prevent infection. Then taking her needle with fine silk thread she applied three stitches to the cheek of the sobbing woman. More pressure and aloe ointment later stopped the blood seeping. Only then was it time to ask questions.

Chiara's story was not uncommon: a situation the Christians had brought to the attention of the Roman officials. Her former husband was to blame, who in a fit of rage exacted upon his ex-spouse his version of punishment that would make her appearance so deplorable that remarriage to anyone of any respect would be most remote.

In Roman society, marriage was basically an agreement between two families. They celebrated the betrothal they arranged with the giving of gifts and a verbal or agreement. If a sizeable dowry was involved, the accord was always signed. The marriage agreement was then sealed with an iron ring and a kiss. The day of the wedding was not a formal occasion. Usually the groom arrived at their residence first to await his bride. They exchanged gifts. On occasion the bride would bring a torch lit from her family's hearth. The custom of sacrificing an animal had long been abandoned. For Chiara, her own wedding was simple just as she expected: a formality without endearing love.

Divorce was similarly uncomplicated. Just an expression was sufficient to dissolve a marriage. If the divorce was caused by the woman's adultery, the formality was decided in the Quaestio, family court. This was Celer's jurisdiction that paid him well for the gratitude he received from the men who once more had their freedom while retaining a considerable portion of the woman's dowry.

With the confirmation that Chiara's former husband slashed her face, Miriam committed herself to informing the authorities. There wasn't much she could do about Chiara's face, but there was no intention to let his behaviour harm another woman. Chiara agreed only if she could find another place to stay.

This event extremely bothered Miriam, not solely because of the injury to the woman, but because John, Miriam and their friends had already discussed an issue Miriam called, "the sanctity of marriage." A difficulty encountered in those discussions was the attitude of so many in their society who didn't think the simplicity of marriage and divorce was such a problem. Unfortunately that attitude permeated the Mediterranean.

The next morning the cut was washed. A neighbour had some iodine, indeed a rare commodity. When Chiara begged Miriam to not involve the authorities, she complied. An alternative was Chiara's wish: visiting Clement.

Clement was a farmer, with a sizeable plot of land between the eastern slope of Bulbul Mountain and the marsh. He acquired the land because being so close to the swamp, no one wanted it. Miriam knew the acreage well as she had passed it often when getting her papyrus stems from that marshland. Clement's expertise was crops: mainly grain and green vegetables. Carrots onions and beets were also plentiful. Goats roamed the exterior of the lot, ultimately providing milk, meat and skin for clothing. Clement received the support of the army as he always had excess crops available. In fact, most of his produce was sold at his farm making the trip to the agora unnecessary. His barn provided the venue for his own personalized market. Behind that building, a small silo only one storey in height, provided ears of dried corn to cattle owners in the region.

It was that barn that captivated Miriam's attention. It could comfortably accommodate about thirty livestock, or one hundred persons. Her perception however was not the priority.

Chiara had to show herself to the diligent gentleman she wished to marry. That she was now disfigured, she wanted to be upfront with him. His anger was immediate with his vow to revenge the assault. Chiara finally quietened him, and forthrightly asked

Clement if he would marry her. He didn't pause and declared his affirmation immediately. The wine flowed celebrating their betrothal. Neighbouring farmers attended in the evening for the festivities. Miriam's heart melted realizing it was the little things in life that were so important. Such simplicity always meant so much to someone. Clement and Chiara, beyond life's physical scars, obviously saw the goodness in each other.

Days turned into weeks with each day providing new information, additional aspirations, and incredible conclusions. The formal marriage would take place in September, the month of Chiara's birth. Miriam simply envied her for that, not so much the marriage, but knowing when she was born. The betrothed couple then announced Clement's intention to be baptised. Equally important the barn could be used to accommodate orphans or widows. By October, that plan was adopted. For the next planting season, those widows and orphans receiving assistance were in the fields being gainfully employed. The disadvantaged had an opportunity to feel good.

Ultimately the suggestion was made to use the barn on the Dies Solis to celebrate the Lord's Supper. Miriam was ecstatic. They awaited John's foregone concurrence on that proposal.

Chapter Thirty-Three

Tyranny of Uncertainty

October, 54

A mushroom decided the fate of the Roman Empire. Agrippina the Younger, the Emperor's fourth wife, had a definite interest in its consumption. Tiny insignificant spores had never become so important to her devious intentions. Claudius was a glutton. His Roman festivals were extravagant. Every mundane event became his reason to celebrate. Each deity provided another opportunity to satiate his whims. Morality was totally non-existent. His marriage with his niece, Agrippina, confirmed that perception. She was there. Britannicus, Claudius' first son who Agrippina deplored, was present. Sixteen year old Lucius Domitius Ahenobarbus, better known as Nero, dined while his adopted father choked. Emperor Claudius died with his family surrounding him, to make sure it happened.

Britannicus was dead within the first year of Nero's reign. Britannicus was Claudius' son from an earlier marriage. Once Claudius adopted Agrippina's own child, Nero being older than Britannicus became Consul and heir apparent. Even though Claudius had second thoughts about that situation, he couldn't do much; he was already dead. Agrippina's control of the city and the Senate veiled the entire Empire with a cloak of intrigue. Ambition, revenge, murder: all had no limits. Nero, above all else, was trained well to never let family get in his way.

Family actually included nearly every prominent Senator and the elite in the ruling class. Inter marriage had been so predominant for generations that scarcely there was any individual in any position of authority who was not somehow related to Julius, Augustus or Tiberius. Thus to rule the Empire, successfully, the Emperor had to pay at least equal attention to the aspirations of his relations more than the combatant activities of foreign factions.

Agrippina was profoundly groomed to excel in the many aspects of imperial life that assured her authority and success. Pleasantries and common courtesy were replaced by ruthlessness and ambition. Commitment had no definition. Rome, especially those families who thought they were so secure, had reason to fear.

Military prowess was prominent in Nero's family. He was the great-grand-nephew of Caesar Augustus. His grandfather had been a Consul decades before. Thus military confrontation was not just the norm, it was zealously anticipated. In Britain, Gaul and Armenia, Nero's Roman forces achieved decisive victories. When the Jews revolted in Palestine, he had no qualms about the manner in which the riot was quelled. Pride was returning to the Roman ranks.

There had become a new reality in the military. Victorious generals and legions were hailed as conquerors. Parades and celebrations greeted them on their return to Rome; but not all victories were celebrated in Rome. Many generals stayed, maintaining control the sects, minorities, and factions that they had just defeated. There was a mystique about these generals, centurions, legions and cohorts: the numerous tales, countless stories of epic battles, and spreading rumours of grand conquests. Rome was expanding, but so were the number of those who had become so influential away from Rome. With more than one million soldiers outside of the City of Rome, who was to be trusted and for how long?

For the Plebeians, after the lecherous Caligula and the equally immoral Claudius, Nero was at first refreshing. Enhancing the cultural life of the Empire was the focus of his initial campaign. Theatres and stadiums were constructed in all provinces. Here was an Emperor who played the lyre, wrote and read poetry, was well educated and loved to perform in public. Almshouses to feed the impoverished were opened. He was the image of Plebeian dreams. Trade, commerce and diplomacy were equally important guaranteeing that Rome was respected outside the Empire just as much as it was within the provinces. Even trade with India for silks and spices was enhanced. It clearly appeared that Nero wanted to make Rome proud again.

Regardless of any accomplishment, his fears would not dissipate. Nero invoked decrees as his reaction to suggestions of disagreement. The edicts were strong enough to end any debate on most subjects. Criticising Rome was out of the question. Voicing an opinion against the Emperor meant death. He had become the Three Fates all rolled into one divine god. Statues and busts of Nero were erected throughout the Empire. Before long, his initial edicts became: any suspicion of any dissention was an act of treason.

Nero's impact on Ephesus was the construction of the Stoa of Nero, a covered walkway supported by columns outside of the commercial market along Marble Street, This would be easily viewed by all coming from the harbour, or in the theatre or from the agora. The out-door theatre itself was enhanced. Buildings and projects that had collapsed a quarter-century earlier due to earthquakes were cleared of the rubble, and some were rebuilt.

The most important aspect of Nero's influence was the uncertainty his divine presence caused existing Roman Governors and two Pro Consuls. To Nero, it was preferable to rid his realm of all of Claudius appointees; however he couldn't trust his family in those positions.

Religious sects were apprehensive, but they were free to celebrate their rites as long as respect and devotion to the Emperor were maintained. However, acceptance of minorities was becoming more of a regional issue. If a Governor or Senator or Centurion wished to avoid Rome's direct intervention, then he made his own decision on how best to keep the Roman peace. Depending on the persuasion of the person in charge, religious and cultural freedoms could either flourish or be trampled out completely.

Chapter Thirty-Four

Not a Fond Farewell

December 54

Celer was determined that the festive occasion would fulfil Agrippina's resolute dream. Twenty of society's elite were gathered in the Prytaneion Hall for the illustrious rite of endless feasting. Contoured cushioned couches comforted the Asiarchs. Marcus Silanus had returned to Ephesus that week from his four month trek throughout the province with additional visits to eastern Anatolia and Cyprus. The guests included Patricians, Senators, the other Deputy Consuls, several benefactors, the Equestrian General, and legionnaires Darius and Burrus who were both well known to those in attendance.

Servers were naturally also present, among these Muscipula and Helius. The latter had only in the last month been awarded his freeman status. Both were greatly indebted to the Deputy Consul for this opportunity and other occasions to escape the world of dire servitude.

Celer reclined surrounded within his mound of cushions. He was absolutely delighted with the event following weeks of planning.

The suggestion had been freely offered to him when he was in Rome. Within minutes of it first being mentioned, the idea became an order. In Rome, Agrippina had already been assured of the evening's end result.

The residue of the poppies had already eased Celer's tension long before the maidens attended. Their dance and minimal attire had the usual effect on the many noble guests. Who cared who was married? The girls were there for their entertainment. The expectation of such licentiousness was no longer considered a luxury as it was so anticipated on such occasions. Wine flowed copiously. Celer's guests were impressed and spoke enthusiastically of provincial achievements. Silanus, for all of his apprehensions, was totally at ease. Pleasant conversation became laughter and then delirious exchanges of most inordinate humour.

To pay tribute to his hosts, Celer paraded into the room various animals whose breed would constitute the main courses. Goats, sheep, ducks and a pig preceded the heifer. Then accompanied by six guards and secured with ropes, Elena was led into the room. The barely clad Christian-convert received the immediate scorn and ridicule of the mob. The false accusation asserted that she had been involved in a plot to murder Celer. Then to the amazement of the assembled guests, the Deputy Consul approached the woman, untied the ropes, dispersed the guards, and declared her to be free as an act of his benevolence for the citizens of Ephesus. The applause and salutations were immediate. Elena was then escorted by Muscipula to the Tyrannus Baths, there to be appropriately cleansed and with every opportunity to express her gratitude. Even Silanus was profoundly amazed.

Expressions of amazement continued until the meal. No one in recent years had ever witnessed such clemency. The accolades resounded with Celer ultimately informing the guests that it was Silanus' example that prompted such leniency. Thereafter the salutations honouring the Pro Consul continued intermittently for hours.

The meat in the main course was effectively seasoned with spices from all regions of the Empire. Celer made sure he mentioned the sources of these delicacies so as to appear to be totally in accord with Nero's plan for global commerce. Several Senators mentioned the lands beyond the Indian Ocean where the expensive salts, spices and silks were being obtained. Although such trade existed long before the current emperor, Nero's campaign had convinced Rome that this prosperity was due to solely his commercial prowess.

By the third hour, several of the important guests were taking young women to the side rooms that were specially designed for these occasions. Celer too obliged himself, having to relieve his anxiety.

This entire event had been designed to accommodate Agrippina's demand. The Emperor's Mother had Celer wrapped around her fist to do whatever she chose. After all, it was Celer's skill in alchemy and knowledge of un-edible substances that presented her son with the grandiose opportunity to become Emperor. Nero and Agrippina didn't feel they owed any gratitude to Celer. On the contrary, Celer had no alternative. He had to do what they wanted him to do and he was under their thumb to do it again. It was either obey, or be accused of murdering Emperor Claudius.

Helius attended the side room responding to Celer's request. A young wench had already departed having expected more and receiving nothing. Henceforth it was all business to Celer. Helius confirmed everything was already in place. The special tray was poisoned, that one would be offered to the Pro Consul alone. The potion would take its time so that no one could ever accuse any respectable person at the Prytaneion of any foul dead. "Thirty minutes maybe," Celer confirmed.

Celer remained alone in that enclave pondering the affairs of state, which to him meant controlling the factions. He knew enough about political philosophy to ascertain that good government meant far more than just defining truth and the benefit of an educated-elite. Letting his mind race away from the issues at hand, Celer considered the sects and how they had so little to offer the community. Each had its own agenda, and as such they were becoming a divisive force causing Celer to fear the prospect of revolts similar to those in Jerusalem. "Apollo, steer our cunning hearts!" he declared in his mind.

Darius entered the room with the obvious advice that nearly everyone in attendance was drunk. He announced that Burrus had already left to position himself near the baths. Their commitment and preparedness delighted Celer. All four legionnaires were in place with specific roles.

Celer returned to the main hall being quite at ease and ready to engage in further discussion. Several of those from the influential families were Greek and accordingly they expressed appreciation for Sophocles' play at the outdoor theatre. 'Seven Against Thebes' was the second in a trilogy of dramas involving 'Oedipus Rex' and 'Antigone'. The Deputy Consul employed these drams, as he did all Grecian tragedies, to gain support from the Greek community to the detriment of Hypatius. That Silanus had also viewed the performance was a benefit.

'Seven Against Thebes' was a moral tale about the extremes of human nature in a struggle for power. Pride was the issue with two brothers confronting each other for the throne. One brother was slain, and the other died a slow death, eventually rotting and then being consumed by animals. In Greek culture, if a corpse rots it can nevermore be united with the soul. Thus when Antigone found the partially consumed remains of her brother and buried him, she had committed a grievance crime. The consequences were immeasurable.

Silanus was grossly intoxicated approaching well past the fourth hour of the celebrations. Much to Celer's surprise, the Equestrian General suggested that they shortly leave for the baths and then sleep within the complex. Celer reacted quickly noting that the personal chariot had already been prepared for the Pro Consul. Following a hand signal, Helius approached Silanus with a tray of grapes, olives, quartered pomegranates, melon and the luxury of mandarins. Musicians once more accompanied the display that was always first offered to the guest of honour.

Silanus had nothing to fear that evening as every aspect was so exquisite. He still marvelled at Celer's decision to free the woman. This was an entire new philosophy within the Empire. His reservations about Nero's reign were being dismissed.

As expected, Marcus grabbed a mandarin first. Celer watched for any reaction. While doing so he told the others that they came from North Africa near Gibraltar. The Senators reacted to the advice recounting the tales of Augustus' triumphs in that region. Other platters were being presented to the other guests who were all equally satisfied. Olives were a delicacy for the Pro Consul. After several of those, he became queasy and leaned back on the couch. Celer sensed that reaction and immediately orchestrated the rest of his deed. Helius assisted Silanus from the couch. Others aided them directing the Pro Consul to the waiting chariot. Silanus stood there quite uncertain of his agility. His head was spinning. With two hands he grasped the top rim. Helius was already on aboard to steer the chariot. Darius then squeezed into position preventing the Silanus from falling to the side. Immediately they were racing down Curetes Street toward the baths.

Inside the Prytaneion, Celer grabbed the tray of poisoned goods and threw them into a fire bin in the back room. The evidence was gone. Any potential witnesses were too inebriated to talk sense. The victim was on his way to his funeral.

The Tyrannus Baths were a series of significant two storey structures. The total complex was about sixty meters by twenty-five meters. The privy walls were everywhere, all at right-angles creating several large enclosed baths for both men and women. Water temperature in three pools satisfied the preferences of all users. The entrance had two porticos, one straight ahead to the baths, and the other for change rooms. It was secluded and safe, except for anything unexpected; and that was always possible.

On route his stomach heaved. The uneven stones didn't help. The choking started. This rapidly became an uncontrolled hacking cough and then foaming preceded his vomit. Darius forced the Pro Consul to lean to the side to propel the excretion away from the racing chariot. Convulsions then followed in a delirious display of uncontrollable fury. Quickly he was grasping for air; but there was no relief.

By the time they arrived at the baths and turned right into the lane way Silanus was dead. They left him doubled over the carriage's rim. Hastily they departed the chariot with horses resting just off the road near sage brush. The steeds neighed almost right away as any animal would do when confronted with sudden uncertainty. Burrus rushed forward with enough cloths to wipe the chariot clean.

Inside the baths they hurriedly gathered with Muscipula. The four assailants celebrated the deed that would assure them appropriate promotion or reward. Everything looked normal: four Roman gentlemen enjoying the luxury of a warm water pool. This was Rome and they did what Rome wanted. There was no remorse.

Once Elena satisfied the quota of regular customers that she was compelled to do, Muscipula returned her promptly to the Prytaneion. The chariot was not as pristine as the Pro Consul's. However they were alive, and unknown to Elena he was not. The men's toga she was encouraged to wear flowed in the breeze. Every aspect about her captivity she deplored. Now she was free, and the world in spite of the dark of midnight was aglow. Celer was there waiting for her.

Celer welcomed Elena with flowing conversation concluding that the past was forgotten. She was elated with that sentiment. Muscipula's hand motion conveyed the deed was done. Celer tried to withhold his beaming expression. Inside they talked with their guests, many of whom were ready to pass out. As was the norm they would fall asleep on the cushions or in someone's lap. There was never the need to assume that guests would return home.

Inside the baths, having left the pool the three legionnaires exchanged high pitched laughter celebrating the good fortune that their nemesis was out of the way. Darius and Burrus dutifully spoke of Nero's contribution to their well-being and to the economic growth of the Empire. Speaking of the need for change seemed so natural, especially when they concluded that change had been good. No one spoke ill of Claudius or Silanus, but the unspoken message was abundantly clear. Their conversation took no more than thirty minutes, before Darius directed Helius to accompany him to a side room. This was precisely the cubicle where Muscipula led Elena upon their arrival three hours prior. Helius was at first puzzled about being sequestered; however Darius' smile eased any worry. Darius talked of the potential for Helius' promotion suggesting the reality rested with him. Helius asked about what else he had to do in order to accomplish this. Darius spoke in riddles without a direct answer. He was finding it difficult to talk in contrived circles about something that could never be. In an instant, before Helius could even turn, Burrus flashed into the room with his dagger drawn. In the same instant it was buried into the back of Helius' neck. Darius immediately covered the victim's mouth with a piece of Elena's discarded attire. Burrus stabbed again. Helius struggled to survive but there was no room and no strength to fight back. Burrus pulled his own blade and shoved it deep, repeating the blows into the lower abdomen. Within twenty seconds, Helius was dead. The tiny room remained silent. Towels wiped the blood-covered floor. Elena's prior attire, stained in blood, was prepared as false evidence.

Celer escorted Elena to a private room, extremely luxurious compared to her prior lodgings. There she was given the opportunity to sleep.

Elena had no idea how long she had closed her eyes. Suddenly they opened and the entire building was shocked into consciousness with the torrent of screams, "Treason! Treason! Silanus is dead!" Darius was certain he was heard throughout the complex. Other guards rushed in from the doorways. Celer dashed into the hall, acting surprised even though he knew this would all happen.

No one questioned how Celer and Darius were able to see the strange powder on Elena's toga. When her prior blood stain clothes were presented with news of Helius' death, the conclusion had been reached. She ran screaming, pleading her innocence; but she didn't get far.

"Sir, believe me?" Elena begged for understanding.

"Take her!" Darius instructed the guards.

"Noooo!" the pitiful woman cried, her tears drowning her face and then the floor; as they pulled her to her feet, ripped her clothes, gagged her, and then with leather straps bound her hands.

"Take her my friends, for your pleasure." Darius ordered the guards as if he himself was the director of the entire plan. "Keep these as evidence," Darius instructed while handing the blood stained garments to one of the guards.

"Today tell the people of our remorse and our valiant attempts to revive Rome's pearl!" Celer proclaimed to the remaining guests.

The screaming Christian woman was then dragged by four guards to the prison. Celer couldn't believe their good fortune. Not only was Silanus dead; but now they could blame the Christians for two deaths.

Chapter Thirty-Five

Eternal Rest

December, 54

The two sisters completed their rugged trek. Into cold winds blowing unceasingly they ventured up into a world of jagged crests and steep cliffs. High on Mount Pion they came to rest but only for that moment. The entire city was there before them: so many occupied in daily chores yet so disinterested in recent events. They peered down upon that valley between the Stadium and the Temple where fields lay barren in those weeks before the winter solstice. The main thoroughfare was busy as it always was; but no one left its levelled surface to enter the Gardenus Caelestis. Within that haven between monuments and among palm trees, a chaotic mass of rocks lay unattended.

Days after his sudden death, no one seemed to care. "Unforeseen health factors," the people were told. Celer made sure the word was spread quickly by his discordant band of wretches. Darius and Burrus knew more, albeit not better. A nightmare of hellish visionaries compelled Celer to act further. Soldiers could only be trusted when they are silenced. Whether that came from Rome or his own decisive thinking, he couldn't recall. However he knew that a sword once drawn is not always returned to its scabbard.

"She is there," Lachesis advised Clotho.

"On board," Clotho added.

"Where is he now?" Lachesis began their litany.

"Beneath the stars," Clotho's voice echoed into the valley.

"Beneath the earth!" Lachesis' shrill laughter bounced off the face of the cliff.

"What is to be done?" Clotho was being a trifle philosophical.

"Twixt grave and Styx," Lachesis declared.

"Where Hermes flies."

"Dead men's bones are Cerebus' prize." Lachesis continued her cynical appraisal.

"Charon wakes."

"And Hades quakes!" With Lachesis' final declaration thunder rolled across the mountain top.

Darius looked up to view the sudden rumble from the peak of the mountain. It had just been a sunny afternoon. The change made him quiet uneasy; but he remained committed to his task. He had been to Rome only once before. On this occasion, he was delivering a scroll prepared for a Patrician named Seneca. It was confirmation of the Pro Consul's death with information concerning the accused and affirmation that any chance of rebellion had been squashed. Darius felt sincere pride in being chosen for such a task. He had heard so much of Seneca, his importance in Rome especially his relationship with their Divine Emperor.

Six other passengers boarded the same vessel. Besides these there were eight rowers on deck and another eight below to assure the Deputy Consul that the scroll would be delivered in a most timely manner. The six passengers included five men. The woman was well refined in dress and manner. No one knew her. She did not speak. As the thunder on the mountain roared one last time, she looked to her sisters and smiled at their devilish intent.

In the evening the five male passengers retired with eight oarsmen. The second shift continued to propel the vessel onward away from the Achaian coast toward the Adriatic. "Perhaps three days," Darius had been told by the captain. He went to sleep satisfied with their progress.

– Ephesus Pure in Heart –

The woman chose not to sleep, indicating a preference to remain awake because of her fears. However she had no apprehension, just fiendish intent. The midnight fog had dissipated by the time the sun sparkled on the horizon. Only a few clouds dotted the sky ahead of them. The woman mysteriously was no longer on board. Atropos had kissed the squirming legionnaire's final delusion. Just before noon, the captain discovered Darius. He was dead.

If Atropos had not completed the deed, there were already on board a few retained to accomplish the same feat.

All on board blamed her suggesting she must have committed the deed and then drowned herself. Throughout the day, the captain defended his crew stating he noticed nothing untoward during the course of that night. There was no autopsy. There was no sign of frothing from the mouth to suggest any poison. The cause of death could not be identified. "Unseen health factors," he suggested.

****

Burrus galloped with his three guards, companion legionnaires commissioned by the Deputy Consul. The sixty-five mile journey to Sardis was expected to take more than a day. Centurions with their legions were always positioned at intervals along the route.

Repeatedly three hags appeared in the course of his journey. "Witches!" was his first impression. Seeing them a second time was an ominous warning. Then watching them later cross his path, made the entire trek threateningly foreboding. Burrus dug his heels into the steed, and it bolted down the road, head-long into a narrow valley bordered by a rugged incline on one side and a cliff on the other. As suddenly terrified as he was, Burrus knew that beyond that last hill a centurion was stationed. There he could find rest and relief.

Burrus and his three legionnaires pulled into camp in the late afternoon. It was already dark, with the sun setting early just before the winter solstice. Surprisingly he was greeted with mild anticipation. To a learned man that should have been a serious omen. However Burrus dismissed it as one Roman inconspicuously greeting another. The centurion allowed Burrus to do most of the talking. Burrus never spoke of his purpose, until one of his cohorts inadvertently mentioned Silanus' death. There was a sudden hush within the tent as many wondered aloud about the potential factors involving the Pro Consul's murder. The centurion's expression conveyed a keen interest, but his sympathy was limited.

"What will he do now?" Lachesis asked her sisters from the mountain peak overlooking the camp.

Atropos raised her arm, and immediately clouds began to gather.

Meanwhile, having retired to his own tent, the centurion read the scroll provided to him hours before.

> Men who murdered our illustrious Pro Consul Marcus Julius Silanus Torquatus will pass your way. They will carry this scroll. Do the will of our Divine Emperor. Do what Rome deems just.

Burrus and his companions had been provided with their own tent for lodging that night. By mid-day he expected to be seeing Deputy Consul Antonius in Sardis. He went to sleep proud of his achievements, honoured to be in the Roman Army, and pleased with his association with Celer. Burrus never woke to see the morning sun rise.

In his quarters, Celer celebrated the silence, not with lechery or drunkenness, but with a quiet nod and a confident smile.

Chapter Thirty-Six

Reaction and Apprehension

February, 55

The reaction to news of Silanus' death was immediate. The Romans were accusatory. The Greeks were apprehensive. The Jews feared, "Who is next?" They widened their distance not wishing be associated in any way with the sect that was accused of Silanus' murder. Trepidation enveloped the Christians. They didn't have to ask, "Who's next?"

The Greeks had always loathed the prospect any potential action by a disgruntled Roman Army. Now 'potential' became 'probable'. Being able to orchestrate the influence they possessed had been their means of survival. "Will Rome turn on us?" philosophers in the theatre pondered with no one certain of any answer.

Uncertainty also ruled the visitors. Perhaps these more than any others understood the consequences of a military force determined to enact revenge.

There was no time for any pity or remorse. The questions abounded and the fears quadrupled. When the absence of Burrus and

Darius were discovered, fears of a revolt were more than just whispered conjectures. "Did the Christians also murder the legionnaires?" That query was posed too many times until it became the accepted truth.

The Christians were confronted with the consequences of the accusation almost immediately. John experienced hasty mistrust of his entire message. Groups of Christians became silent worshippers. Their self-assuredness became caution. Friendships abruptly ended. In the market, sales by Christian merchants dropped dramatically. Both Susannah and Miriam could attest to that. In various venues, the opinions of Christians were not invited or totally dismissed. Though at no time in the general public were Christians ever loudly accused of being responsible, many feared the crime of association. Still, no one was able to identify the extent of any insurgence. The followers of Christ unjustly became tainted as rebels. However, to the Roman Army they had become just another enemy.

Roman violence was not immediate. Celer applauded himself as the new leader of the Prytaneion relishing the reality that such fears could cause. Fear: he always viewed it as his strongest weapon. Repeatedly since the murder he had thanked his gods for his good fortune of getting rid of all who were involved in the murder and then being able to accuse the minority sect. Elena, the girl, was raped repeatedly until Rome decided its pleasure was satisfied. Then abruptly the wench was slain.

Seneca, Nero's advisor and tutor, deplored the news. He knew enough about the Empire and the many factions to quickly ascertain the reliability of all information reaching the port of Ostia. The iters and Via Appia too were clogged with rumors. Silanus was dead and nothing could be done to bring him back. Sure there were other deaths, decisions made by Nero or his wife to secure his position as a divine god. However this one never made sense. The Christians had not murdered any Roman official before this. Why would they choose Silanus when he above all other Consuls and Governors was more than receptive to the needs of the cultural minorities? How could a woman have done it? Why would she? How did the Ephesian Legionnaire die onboard a vessel? The accused woman wasn't there. Then there was the vague story of another murder in a Roman camp? There were too many questions that had no reliable answers. Rome had too many other issues. The Empire did not need the murder of its Pro Consul in the Province of Asia.

Chapter Thirty-Seven

Fate and Determination

May, 55

The shaking started again in May. Everyone immediately feared the worse. The tremors felt deep, not a prolonged clutching force, but rather a series of quick jolts. Citizens ran into the streets grabbing whatever they could. Those essentials did not always include family members. Amid screams of panic, the earthquake continued for about one minute and then stopped.

Thirty years prior, two quakes in just six years devastated the city. However life continued after those and some buildings were reconstructed from the fallen rubble. Even the lot, where Miriam and Chiara provided for the orphans, had previously been covered with debris from a shattered temple. All along Curetes Street there were sections were damage remained very evident. Just when the city had restored itself to approximately its prior grand design, the shaking started once more.

"Justice!" was the Roman cry condemning the Christians for the Pro Consul's death. For the Greeks there was utmost apprehension for their Temple of Artemis. For the Jews still suffering from the allegations made against the Hebrews at Saturnalia, interruption of the Purim gatherings was not considered lightly.

During June there were no more tremors, just rivers of rainfall suddenly flooding the fields and plains. Miriam had experienced such torrential rain only once before in Syria – large incessant drops that could pierce thatched roofs. In the fields providing crops for the Ephesus and the Empire, the floods devastated the vegetation. Silt and debris flowed into the harbour complicating the congestion already created with centuries of excess silt.

Slaves died in the mines as rain-water flooded the underground passages.

Miriam had to move her orphans immediately from the base of the hill into her home for weeks while John was in Pergamum and Thyatira. Quickly, other accommodation had to be found among the available buildings that were left standing. The market for weeks lacked fresh produce; and those farmers who still had crops were susceptible to theft. From famine to flood, Ephesus was definitely not immune. Attributing blame was always the norm; but this time for the incessant rain the Romans could no longer accuse just the Christians.

Similarly Rome could not justify blaming any minority group for the additional tremors. They occurred two more times in the summer of 55AD, rocking the Anatolian peninsula, causing landslides and considerable damage especially in the remote mountainous areas.

Luke had left one week before the floods committing himself to the additional evangelization process in Troas. The areas of Lydia, Phrygia and Bithynia in northern Anatolia were also the focus of his efforts. He had reported such vitality in those small towns and villages after his second visit. Friendships had been established in regions that had never before been receptive to Ephesus. That animosity was the consequence of the three Mithridatic Wars when Rome attempted to seize the territory more than one hundred thirty years prior. Candidly, when Luke left for his first excursion to those areas not much was expected. Respect for Ephesus or anybody from the Province of Asia was extremely remote. Yet Luke was successful: the Grecian Jew who embraced Christianity. As a philosopher he engaged the learned. As a sympathetic caring person he attracted the peasants. As a doctor he was wanted by all. He spoke with conviction, with a positive tone conveying his absolute commitment to his beliefs. Orphans were not abandoned. Widows were sheltered with other families. The sick were cured not by physical medicine alone, but by his ability to work miracles. There was no hesitancy regarding Luke's position on any issue. His consistent approach was an allurement to many who wanted something better in their lives. Thus, it was a sad day when Luke left Ephesus as they knew it would be the last time that they would see him. However that was best for the growth of Christ's community. Luke had even talked of visiting the islands with the hope that in those city states there would be converts.

The last meeting involving John, Luke and Miriam had involved fundamental issues. The most essential item for affirmation was the definition of Christ's presence in the celebration of the Last Supper. Among the believers there was a growing misconception that the bread handed to the recipients was only a representation of Christ. John adamantly refuted that suggestion declaring that the bread once blessed in the celebration of the Lord's Supper actually became His Body, not just a representation. This creed was essential. However they prepared themselves that this might be hard for many to accept. The Greek community already used bread and wine in the offerings to their goddess Mithras. It was not unreasonable that these could also be offered to the Christian God. However the suggestion that the Bread and Wine became the actual Body and Blood of Christ caused many Greeks to reject the Christian beliefs. Yet, it had to be done; and it was better to be right than to presume a piece-meal belief was satisfactory.

At the same time that they were affirming the Presence of Christ in the celebration of the Lord's Supper, they were purposefully elevating the status of the celebrant as a Representative of Christ. Thus the concept of individual Sacraments was being expounded. The person leading the celebration was there by the Grace of the Holy Spirit. Aspects too of forgiveness and confession were considered along with the rite of baptism. Regarding forgiveness, the process remained one of general absolution. Concerning baptism, age and commitment were issues that required ongoing discussion. That last meeting among the three was memorable, and then sad with Luke's final departure.

The points raised in that conversation were then shared with Paul, Apollos and Bernardus. Aquila and Priscilla were also involved. There was quickly total agreement on the issues of the Eucharist and the Holy Spirit's Grace in Baptism and Forgiveness. In spite of the potential for Roman tyranny against the Christians when considering the accusations following Silanus' death, the leaders of the Christian community became more committed to defining and resolute in spreading the Faith. With the constant threat of tribulation, they obviously had nothing to lose and thus their commitment grew beyond any limits.

Luke took with him the scrolls and parchment he had completed. He had been for years preparing his story on the life of Christ based on information provided to him by Maryam, John, and Miriam. His historical knowledge of events, his discernment of the Torah and Psalms, and input from various officials provided additional insight. More importantly, as he repeatedly told John, there was the aura of the Holy Spirit's inspiration in his determination to provide Truth to the Faithful.

The rest of the parchment and scrolls, including John's writings, Miriam had secured in a metal box within the block enclosure. Thankfully it had been placed above a boulder adjacent to the granite slope in such fashion that streams from the hill top flowed to the sides. Within these was a copy of Paul's letter to the Galatians. Above all else, one of Miriam's most important roles was to continue to produce the parchment and then safeguard the finished work. In this she was resolute.

During the aftermath of the floods, the entire Christian community came together to assist those sorely affected by the torrential rains. They had become "de Actio Ecclesia".

Chapter Thirty-Eight

Journey to the Interior

September, 55

In the last hours of August, ten months into Nero's reign and just weeks after Paul left Ephesus for Macedonia, John began another visit to the communities in the interior. His first stop was Smyrna on the Aegean coast. To reach the community of believers in Smyrna, John had to travel east into the valley and then proceed north behind Mount Pion through a series of valleys for approximately eighty kilometers.

Smyrna was situated on the south bank of a large harbour. Mountains framed lush valleys to the east and south. This terrain assured productive industries in mining, agriculture and husbandry. The multi-cultural population was predominantly Greek, very similar to that of Ephesus. The philosophers and influential were keen on exploring new parameters in life, and accordingly there were a significant number of converts in the first years of evangelization.

After less than one week in Smyrna, John continued his trek heading eighty-five kilometers east to Sardis. With five villages on route, there were sufficient rest areas, and nourishment centers. Roman legionnaires were also there at intervals to provide safe passage.

No matter where John travelled in Anatolia, especially in the valleys, there were so many reminders of the reason why the Ephesians chose the images of bees, stags, and wild animals to adorn their coins four centuries prior. Wild life was plentiful. Orchards were alive with birds and honey bees. Deer or wild animals could be seen at least every five kilometers descending from the mountains or strolling out of caves, or taking advantage of fast flowing streams. Even if he did not have his attendants with him, John was never alone in the midst of God's creation.

In the ancient kingdom of Lydia, Sardis was the capital. Throughout the centuries its population remained predominantly Greek. Sardis was also recognized for a cultural achievement that elevated its significance above that of other cities. The Jewish citizens could trace their heritage directly to Noah. In the Book of Genesis, citizens of Lydia were referred to as 'Lud' because they were the offspring of Shem and the grand-children of Noah. The residents were receptive to minorities; but for the Romans they had little patience.

The Roman occupiers preferred to initially safeguard the coast once they had assumed control of the northern breadth of Anatolia. For about fifty years Sardis had become a trifle insignificant except for a Roman Legion stationed within the city. Once Pergamum, Troas, Smyrna, Ephesus, and Miletus were secure, Rome's interest in the interior increased. Sardis to Smyrna provided an essential route from the interior to the coast. The city commanded the fertile plain and agricultural production in the Hermus Valley. The Patricians of Rome could be well fed.

The production of crops was not Sardis' only commercial strength. The city was home to a multitude of manufacturers. Husbandry guaranteed meat and clothing. Sheep shearing produced wool and garments. A dyeing industry developed and became essential in the weaving of quality carpets.

The mountains provided mining. The rivers and streams, especially the Pactolus, assured the necessary flow of water to separate and wash precious metals. Engineering techniques were so advanced that gold and silver could be separated from the base rock in a process guaranteeing the purest metals. The production and sale of jewelry, necklaces, bracelets and charms inherently followed. Rome was so impressed that it granted to Sardis the right to issue valuable coins for the Empire, which then became a standard for commercial transactions.

Patrolled access along the route to Smyrna's harbour assured international sales and trade. Military protection also guaranteed commerce for the Anatolian interior. Mount Tmolus to the south and west along the route provided additional security. When the earthquake in 17AD destroyed most of the city, Sardis was rebuilt using the wealth of its own citizens. There were many in Sardis who could never be exposed to the concept of being poor.

Throughout Sardis, the traditional Roman and Grecian buildings provided the essential functions. The theatre, though not as huge as the outdoor auditorium in Ephesus, allowed John to use the venue for promoting the Faith. Lectures and debates involving members of the Hebrew Temple had achieved some success. However it was in this open-air environment, in the wonder of God's creation, that John achieved his converts. With everything in such wonderful order all around them, how could there not be a loving God who was so keenly interested in the life and opportunities of each person? Such philosophy focussing on universal love convinced many who cherished the process of philosophical debate to consider the benefits of Christianity.

Antonius greeted John in a friendly formal manner as if the disciple was a dignitary from a foreign land. During the trepidation of Nero's reign, such courtesies were afforded to so few. In John, Antonius saw a man committed to a cause of temporal and spiritual peace focussing on the importance of human life not the deification of man-made statues. In the Deputy Consul, John perceived a man troubled by his position and his empire and accordingly did what he could to ease that burden with light conversation and encouragement. Throughout his visit, John employed the benefit of example to encourage more believers.

After that, John continued his journey north to Thyatira, and then another eighty kilometers north-east to Pergamum. The entire venture was expected to exceed two months, with his ultimate desire to return to Ephesus before the rainy season in the late autumn.

Chapter Thirty-Nine

Search for a New Home

September, 55

Visiting Maryam's abandoned home became a necessity. Miriam had to seriously explore her options. Her present abode was not big enough. John moved into a room added to her dwelling. He stayed there on those rare occasions when he was in Ephesus. It was no more than just a large cubby hole. Her production of clothing and sandals, her cooking, the preparation of parchment and saving the scrolls had basically consumed the available space. Then there was also Anna who needed room, and the orphans who occasionally attended. Plus, there was the requirement of kitchen facilities. Ultimately, it was the fear of more torrential rain that could destroy all of their work prompted her to consider functional alternatives.

Realizing John would be away for at least another two weeks, based on his usual repertoire Miriam decided this was her time to act. They had talked about it before and she knew that whatever she decided would have his agreement. John was like that with her, absolutely wonderful. Miriam thought regularly about their relationship. There was nothing physical, except for the hugs. Occasionally they would kiss each other's forehead: a simple expression that they cherished the mind and soul of the other person. At the same time, Miriam envied any young women who had found marital bliss. She was never quiet about the occurrence of abuse within a family. Alexa often challenged Miriam about her life's decisions commenting on how wonderful her own life had been with Philemon. Their conversations reflecting on relationships would last for hours. Alexa admitted at one time that Miriam was the only person she could talk to about such issues, "As men still don't want to hear us." That honest assessment was a sad reflection on the continuing state of society. Before long every conversation turned into an exchange of humour allowing them to bury any anxiety within their smiles. Friendship was wonderful and they knew how to embrace it.

The laneway up the mountain passed four rows of dwellings. After that it widened turning first to the right and then to the left ascending the incline. At that level, still less than half-way to the top, several homes had been built. They were generally surrounded by paths allowing access in all directions. Only a few had the pristine lots allowing a general view of the city below Bulbul Mountain. However, most of everything tended to be obscured when the saw grass trees were in full foliage. Junipers provided most borders. There were also the tall palm trees, jasmine, and fruit tress – mainly oranges and lemons. Poppies, asters, buttercups, and colourful weeds grew everywhere except on the cultivated roadways.

Maryam's house had not been totally abandoned. Truants had obviously made themselves a livable arrangement although there was no sign that the fireplace was ever recently used. Cobwebs were many. A rat, or maybe it was just a mouse, scurried across the rear and out the back door. "Need a cat," Miriam stated the obvious. The cloths they brought were well used that morning cleaning the remaining furnishings. By mid afternoon they were feeling the warmth of the sun on the structure. That was always a benefit to stone block construction. Their conversation during the cleaning process was limited. Alexa could clearly read Miriam's mind. She was already committed to moving into those premises; not just for the room, but to preserve what she considered to be so sacred.

****

The regally dressed Roman walked onto the dock from the stately vessel. Everyone paid attention. However, no one at the harbour recognized him. By chariot he was rushed to the government buildings. Within the hour legionnaires were dispatched throughout the city to detain a select few residents. Philemon was one of the first. Bernardus realizing he could be next raced toward the mountain to alert Miriam and Philemon's spouse. Luke, Paul and Timothy had already left Ephesus or they too would have been confined. John, away from the city, had no knowledge of the day's events.

Philemon was not jailed, just sequestered to a room within the Prytaneion. Fearful and feeling threatened he had no idea what might happen next.

Chapter Forty

Not Just an Inquisition

September, 55

Lucius Annaeus Seneca immediately took control of events after the vessel docked. This was a Patrician of stately appearance, political in manner and determined to achieve his potential. Actually he had already accomplished that having been a confidant to Emperor Claudius and an advisor to Emperor Nero. Respecting Seneca was essential to receive the Emperor's approval.

Seneca grew up in wealth and affluence among the select few in Rome. Regardless, he was very much a pragmatist having great esteem for common sense. To this philosopher, the Empire was more important than the rich Patricians in Rome who were constantly striving for more power. In his thirty's, Seneca chastised his fellow Senators for their extravagance, particularly the over consumption of food in the city of Rome when many in the Empire were without basic nutrition. This sentiment was repeated often most notably throughout the decade of the 40's when famine and drought spread across the

Empire. Even into the next decade he espoused the same view without even incurring any disconsolate expressions from either Emperor.

Seneca was a respected writer having composed: Oedipus, Octavia, Phaedra, Meda and other works. These political commentaries were well received although being critical of the upper echelon.

Seneca, besides his propensity to criticize his peers, also had a penchant for satisfying his passions. That was not difficult to accomplish, for in Claudius' inner sphere alcohol and immorality were everywhere. The entire scene of debauchery gave Seneca ample opportunities to satisfy his personal needs. Ultimately he was caught having sex with Claudius' daughter. The young lady had also been Caligula's sister. The punishment clearly reflected Seneca's imperial authority as he was not put to death, but instead was exiled to Corsica. In 41AD he rested and imbibed while 'vacationing' in the manor and estate provided to him.

That exile lasted only eight years. In 49AD, at age fifty-three, he was appointed as one of two tutors to the twelve year old heir apparent Nero. Five years later when Nero assumed the laurel wreath, Seneca became an advisor and confidant reflecting the trust between him and his beloved Emperor. While Seneca was close to Nero, Nero was proficient. Everything and every act were intended to benefit the Empire.

Celer made the critical mistake thinking he could get rid of Silanus, Darius, Burrus and the Christian girl without further questions. Seneca had achieved his status, not by silence, but by diligent enquiry.

Seneca's plan was simple: to have Celer and Hypatius with him posing questions to those who could be involved or might have information relative to the murders. Seneca called them "murders", because there was no other logical explanation for the four deaths. He had heard enough rumors in Rome that Celer had been involved with Agrippina in concocting the poison that ended Claudius' reign. Could Celer have performed the same deed in Ephesus? Seneca knew the answer. The person who immediately grabbed control could never escape the condescending opinions of being the primary suspect. By having Celer as an inquisitor made the Deputy Consul susceptible to any public accusation as these sessions were held with total immunity. If he wanted, Seneca could even mask the citizen so as to provide for his or her security and safety. Seneca trusted no one, and that was the foundation of the process.

Celer was apprehensive from the moment he was warned of Seneca's attendance. No date was given, but the term 'immediate' made it very clear that it would occur soon and had a serious overtone. The acting Pro Consul suddenly became every one's friend. It took a significant amount of alcohol to change his mood and perception of his inferiors, but in a matter of days the transformation had taken place.

Hypatius knew too well that Celer was responsible for Silanus' death. He was ever fearful of Celer's brash and authoritative manner. Even when Marcus Silanus was alive, Celer basically ruled the province as he had control of the army. Hypatius, in that respect, never understood why Silanus had to die. Further, there was a more perplexing issue. Silanus was Pro Consul for seven years. His term would have been over in three years, and Celer would probably have been selected as the new Pro Consul. "Some people are just idiots," Hypatius concluded.

Philemon was questioned for less than an hour. The expanse of the Christian network throughout the province was identified but only in generalities. There was no reference to specific locations. Philemon affirmed that the adoration of Artemis was not permissible in their religion. When provided with the opportunity, he astutely mentioned care for the orphans and the support for major industries.

Others were then questioned. The most specific information they provided was their advice that they would meet together at someone's residence, not always the same location, to share a meal. When asked about opposition to certain charms and amulets, Bernardus' response summarized the Christian view, "We do not hold them in the same esteem." Such replies amused Seneca who appreciated the skill in the ambiguity.

Miriam did not have to wait long. Three legionnaires had accompanied her from her abode to the Prytaneion. She was petrified at first, but while waiting inside and noting how quick the inquisitors were, she took a more unruffled approach to the process.

The enquiry process took place in a hall, not the grand hall with Celer's throne chair. Miriam sensed the acting Pro Consul was rather uncomfortable in such mundane quarters. The walls of the room were covered in murals, painted by local residents. Miriam had been in the Prytaneion once before but never in that room. She was provided with a couch, but chose to stand for a while. The inquisitors sat on cushioned chairs behind a table. On the table a sheet of parchment with a stylus was provided for each person conducting the enquiry. The absence of resin drew the conclusion that not much would be written. A scroll with a ribbon was already prepared to make the entire process appear wholly diplomatic. Water was also provided; but there was no fourth cup.

"Do you continue to profess that our Caesar is not your God?" Seneca's question was direct.

Miriam's response was quick and loud causing Celer to add, "Are you saying Nero is not a god?"

Before Miriam could even ponder the question Seneca interjected, "She has answered that." Miriam smiled, proud that she had devoutly professed her faith.

Her expression was noted by Hypatius who continued with his questions pertinent to Jesus Christ. The Deputy Consul already knew the answers having been for these many years acquainted with several Christians living within the province. "Are you a Christian?"

"I tell you what I have already said. You know that I declare my belief in the Lord Jesus. That is why I am here."

"She holds us in contempt," Celer declared.

"We want to be very clear of your practices. No one is on trial here for your beliefs." Seneca provided the assurance countering Celer's tone. "But we want to know, to have it clear, what you mean by this profession. When you deny that Caesar is a god, are you setting yourself in opposition to Rome? Are you capable of murder?" The last comment stunned Miriam. The strained look on her face conveyed how much her mind was being wrenched. "Murder?"

"The girl was accused. Do you know her?" Seneca was more to the point.

"I did. I saw her at the market ... occasionally." Miriam tried to be calm.

"You work the market," Celer announced.

"I just said I did." Miriam's abrupt response was suitable to the inane comment.

"You have been heard to quarrel with legionnaires." Seneca was trying to get the inquiry back on focus.

"I understand these gentlemen are dead." Miriam's wry comment shocked Seneca.

"That is true," he surmised.

"But even the Roman galleys?" Hypatius added.

"The issue was not with the sailors, dock workers or your forces. I spoke then suggesting too many trees were being cut. Silt now fills the harbour making trade difficult. In time there will be no more passage for your cargo vessels or your galleys."

"Were those your words?" Celer's questions were now insulting her intelligence.

"You have the eyes of a mole and the ears of a fish." With her abrupt comment, Seneca adjourned the meeting for a few moments. The first hour had not achieved anything significant, that was not already known.

In a corner of the room, the Romans spoke forcefully, mainly Seneca telling Celer to not say another word. Perhaps it was his final statement in a rather definite voice that Miriam could hear. "Rome already knows enough about what happened here."

Regardless of Seneca's admonition, Celer continued with his questions. "To whom do you pay your tribute? Do send payment to Jerusalem?"

Her answer was simple, "Your soldiers attend weekly to grab the first coins from my table. You have records, no doubt"

"Who receives your profits?" Celer continued hoping to catch the woman with an inappropriate comment about funding some rebel group.

In reply, Miriam explained her finances, "For supplies and produce for resale, for care of orphans, and funds for those needing shelter."

"And your rent?" Seneca added.

"Of course," she smiled realizing by his expression that he was impressed.

Seneca stayed on the topic of the orphans. He had already challenged the Empire's standards on orphans and slavery especially the norm of automatically compelling orphans to become servants.

In response to several questions on the subject, she replied, "We provide shelter as you would do for your own children. There is nothing out of the ordinary. These are the offspring of dead parents, dead because Roman means severed parental care. These are the children lost in a war of cultures and displaced by edicts. We provide care. That's it!"

Seneca was satisfied with the response noting that in the way she presented her argument, However, Celer being himself was not finished. "For what purpose?"

Miriam was incredibly calm under the circumstances. It was to her benefit that two members of the panel let her speak candidly. "I help the orphans because I too was homeless. My body, even that, was no longer my own. I know what it's like to be forgotten. Therefore I choose to do what I can to help those who are alone. I have only one hope: to do God's will."

Celer again interrupted asking about the orphans once they become adults. In response Mirian added, "Are you asking if these children will become zealots? Do you ask if we train rebels? The answer is clearly, 'No!' You're being absurd!"

It was about mid afternoon when the light rain became a downpour. Hypatius was becoming concerned about flooding. The litany of Celer's innocuous questions had surpassed everyone's patience. Seneca took the reins to conclude the meeting on a lighter note with polite queries concerning Miriam's past. Too often the elite in Rome had viewed the entire Empire in generic terms. Seneca was more interested in the humanist aspect: the particular ingredients that make certain people excel. The woman in front of the panel was clearly not your norm.

Miriam provided courteous advice concerning her youth. "I never stopped being Hebrew. I still eat as a Jewish woman eats. I think, I feel, I love life as much as any woman. Being Hebrew has not shamed me. It has allowed me to sense God more than I ever could if I were Greek or Roman. I am proud of my heritage. I find courage in my God."

"It's about your God then?" Seneca had to ask.

"What else is there to live for? We're all going to die."

The Roman statesman smiled. He had met his match. He then questioned Miriam about the resurrection as this was at the heart of the dispute for many Patricians.

"And what of Caesar?" Celer demanded an answer.

– Ephesus Pure in Heart –

Miriam stared at the acting Pro Consul then shook her head with an expression that would have insulted a prudent person's self esteem. However, Celer was not about to elevate his pride to the level of the hoi polloi. "Nero's not a god. If Caesar be your god, then your last god, Claudius, is dead. God cannot die!"

With that Celer had completed his enquiry. Seneca spoke up as the senior spokesman advising he has his information, and that he planned to sail in the morning. He then handed Celer a scroll while Miriam sat on the couch leaning forward.

Celer read the document slowly. It was the conclusion of the enquiry process – already completed before the panel even met – stating that the cause of Marcus Silanus' death was ill health, specifically 'an unknown health condition'.

Hypatius and Celer left first. Celer took his chariot to the Harbour Baths to celebrate. Hypatius departed in the rain to visit a Senator. Seneca then spoke briefly with Miriam: a philosophical discussion involving a stoic who was genuinely exploring other beliefs. Miriam enjoyed the exchange, thinking it was rather foreign to Roman culture to have Nero's advisor seem to respect a Christian woman's opinion.

When it came time for the evening meal, Miriam left in the pouring rain: getting drenched, but her mind was washed clean of Roman insensitivities.

Chapter Forty-One

Searching for Sense

October, 55

> Blessed are you when people curse you and persecute you, and tell evil lies against you for My Name's sake. Be happy and be glad for your reward is great in heaven. (Matthew 5:11)

The words, though not yet recorded by Matthew, resounded in her mind. Like so many others she had actually heard the Lord speak those words on that mountain.

Miriam had been the peacemaker. She humbly did what she could do to spread the Word. "Why?" she still asked herself. Trembling like a kitten chased by wild dogs, she had left the session. Miriam would never have called it a meeting, as there was never any intent by two of the tribunal to ever consider anything she said as having trifle importance. Miriam felt completely abused. They had raped her mind, and ripped out her heart. Everything their community accomplished seemed in peril. Nero didn't have to proclaim his edict. Celer spoke for the Emperor regarding conditions that were to exist in his province.

She prayed that John was safe. He should be back within the week, maybe sooner if he heard the news. That John had even heard of the enquiries was very remote, as the Romans had surrounded the entire region with a wall of silence. The Christians were able to continue their celebration of liturgy and the practice of their faith, but amidst fear. Miriam knew too well, as she had experienced time and again, that undefined rules of oppression were the most to be feared. She had heard it said about Celer that he used fear to dominate others. Miriam had witnessed that herself in the extreme.

Within her home she sat there crying like a lost child. Shivering she tried to compose herself. "Be strong," she pathetically instructed her mind; but sense had disappeared. Her face covered her hands, her palms wet with tears. Nothing would stop them.

The morning sun rose on the timid creature who had fallen asleep on cluttered cushions. She turned slightly realizing this had not been a dream. Her mind cringed trying to compose an iota of logic. She had to do something; but, what? Exhaustion was a benefit. Though there were voices outside and even a knock at her door, her being was closed to any interruption.

In the early afternoon, she awoke with a start realizing that she should have been at the market that morning. It was just another worry for a woman had clearly spread herself too thin. Closing her eyes once more, she let herself mull her options.

Did she stay here, or move up the mountain to Maryam's house, or move into the valley near Clement's farm? What was expected of her? Evangelizing? Probably not, there were enough. Taking care of orphans? Definitely. And, widows? Possibly. The market? She had no choice. Papyrus? That was a 'must'. Clothes and shoes? She loved to continue.

Realizing how much John and the others needed her parchment; there was no option in that regard. That was clearly the case too in terms of preserving the finished documents. The market was a necessity for the basics in life, making clothes and baked goods necessary. It didn't take long for Miriam to realize she had prepared her niche and was not in a position to just walk away.

The alternatives became basically two: this house or Maryam's abode.

If she chose Maryam's house that would fulfil her dream of residing in the same dwelling where the Lord's Mother once called home; except there was the issue of accessibility. If John was spending days at her residence in the expanded section, he did so mainly because of its proximity to the main streets. To move farther away would not be to his benefit. The present residence provided preservation facilities for the scrolls and parchment. There was her garden. Further up the hill, Miriam was not absolutely certain about security arrangements or growing facilities. Then there was the inescapable factor: her age. Miriam was almost fifty. Bones were becoming fragile, and joints were aching regularly. Change was always good, but change has to be submissive to reason.

Ultimately, she decided to stay in her home, and provide Maryam's house for widows to help the cause being developed by Chiara and Clement. In the next days, before John's arrival, Susannah attended regularly. Miriam renewed her baking activities. One afternoon she even trekked to the marsh to pick more papyrus, getting herself muddy in the swamp, to gather the long stems. They were essential for sandals and straps. "Get yourself moving, old lady!" she smiled to herself.

By the time John returned, everything was near normal. In the next days and weeks she disclosed aspects of the enquiry. His expression declared his worry compelling John instinctively to recall Christ's words at the Passover Meal,

If the world hates you, know that it hated Me before you.

Those initial concerns became praise to the extent he even changed his mind and promised to take Miriam on his next mission north to Smyrna and Pergamum.

Chapter Forty-Two

From Troas to Jerusalem

September 56

After leaving Ephesus in 55AD, Paul sailed to Macedonia, south to Athens and then around the Achaian peninsula to Corinth. Macedonia was territory across the northern perimeter of Achaia stretching from the Aegean Sea in the east to the Adriatic Sea in the west. On the west coast, Corinth was the dominant center in terms of culture and commerce. At Corinth, Paul stayed with Timothy during the winter of 55AD. During this time, Paul composed his letter of instruction to the Romans.

Before the spring of 56AD, Paul left Timothy in Corinth planning to return to Antioch in Syria. That route took him east to the coastal ports in Achaia, where he stayed for less than three months. After receiving warnings that the Hebrew leaders in Jerusalem were intending to arrest him, Paul journeyed north to the cities in Macedonia. Thessalonica and Philippi in particular drew his attention. Throughout this journey from Corinth, many disciples accompanied him with fervent desire to spread the Word.

Across the top of the Aegean Sea, Paul travelled from Philippi near the border of Thrace to Troas in northern Anatolia. There he met Luke. In all of these venues, the number of followers increased with vibrant commitment to the Holy Spirit. This was especially true in Troas where Luke had devoted himself to their spiritual awareness and growth with considerable success.

Both Paul and Luke were thoroughly trilingual in Greek, Hebrew and Latin. In Troas, they found themselves able to have a reasonable effect on the lives of its residents. Although the believers still constituted a relatively small portion of the population, the influence of example was becoming a more effective tool in the evangelization process. Paul's visit drew the attention of many followers to the extent that the first evening dissertation lasted right through the night till the morning sunrise. During that evening, a young man who had died after falling from an open window was restored to life. Miracles continued throughout the missionary journeys as examples of the power and authority of the Holy Spirit. When Paul left Troas, Luke accompanied him.

They sailed from there south among the islands in the Aegean to Miletus, avoiding Ephesus directly. From Miletus, Paul sent his letter to the believers in Ephesus urging them to avoid idolatry and embrace the Spirit.

Paul did not have a vessel of his own, and always relied upon the ships in port for his transportation to the next harbour. His skills as a tent maker were definitely beneficial when repairs to sails were required. This trade made Paul a valuable asset on any voyage.

From Miletus, they sailed to Rhodes, and then to Patara in Lycia on the southern coast of Anatolia. After their next voyage took them near the coast of Cyprus, they landed at Tyre.

It was at Tyre that believers again warned Paul of the perils if he chose to visit Jerusalem. Still committed to returning there, Paul boarded a cargo ship and continued his voyage: first to Alexandria and then back north to Caesarea in Palestine. In that city, there were many devout believers who preached the Good News. Several of these repeated the warnings to Paul not to visit Jerusalem.

At that time Felix was Procurator of Judaea. His animosity toward the Christian sect matched Herod Agrippa's tyranny. In fact it could safely be said that from the time of Herod Agrippa in 37AD to Festus in 62AD, every legal attempt was being pursued to destroy all memory of Christ. The Pharisees easily followed suit feeling they had been disgraced by Christ. The Saducees were totally opposed to the concept of resurrection making Christ anathema to their beliefs. Inciting the ire of the Hebrews in Palestine and Syria was not a difficult task for any leader of the Jewish people trying to save his job.

The warnings continued. These ultimately compelled Paul to respond to his friends declaring his utmost faith.

> What are you doing with warnings like these, trying to dispel my heart? I am ready to not only to be tied up and imprisoned in Jerusalem, but to even die there for the sake of our Lord Jesus. (Acts 21:13)

Paul arrived with Luke in Jerusalem, and stayed at the residence of a family who had committed itself to Christ very early in the evangelization process. Using that as a base, Paul attended the Temple regularly to talk with Jewish believers. He even participated in the Jewish Sabbath ritual. To those who questioned Christianity being available to the Greeks, Paul responded that they were co-heirs to the redemption of Christ. In every meeting and during every debate he espoused the necessity of faith in Christ Jesus and being open to the power and influence of the Holy Spirit.

Luke meanwhile was completing his version of the life of Jesus Christ using all of the available information he had learned from his cherished association with Maryam, Miriam, and John.

Chapter Forty-Three

Pen to Papyrus

January, 57

By the Roman year of the Consulship of Caesar and Piso in 57AD, Christianity had spread across the northern peninsulas of the Mediterranean to Gaul. Along the breadth of northern Africa, communities were established. With pride and determination, eagerness for God's Kingdom could not be restrained. In spite of fears, persecution and death, zeal for the Resurrected Christ blossomed throughout the polytheistic lands.

By 57AD Paul had composed seven letters to the communities in Philippi, Thessalonica, Galatia, Corinth and Rome. The first of these, the Letter to the Philippians, was written in Antioch of Syria about 49AD following his first missionary journey. From Ephesus, Paul sent his letters across Anatolia to the Galatians, and across the Aegean Sea to Corinth. Then during his second and third missionary journeys while stationed in Corinth, Paul directed letters to Thessalonica, and composed his instruction and appeal to the Romans.

During that same year, Peter wrote the first of his epistles while he was in Corinth. His letter was addressed to several communities of Anatolia including the provinces and districts of Asia, Galatia, Cappadocia, Pontus, and Bithynia. That he should have considered it necessary to have included so many distinct regions affirms the extent of his missionary endeavours after leaving Antioch of Syria. Before the end of 57AD, Peter left Corinth to extend his missionary work into the heart of iniquity and malevolence that was the city of Rome.

Meanwhile already in Rome, Matthew had completed his affirmation of Christ as the Anointed One, the Lord and Savior, the eminent Teacher, and the one and only path to salvation. Although historians continue to conjecture when it was written, the recording of the Good News story was definitely completed between Claudius' decree against the Jews and Nero's Great Fire. In fact there is no reference to Nero. Matthew keenly witnessed Christ's miracles throughout the three years of His public life. The Sermon on the Mount captured the hearts of early Christians. As a friend of the Romans being their tax collector, Matthew still had some respect within the urban community. The evangelist had access to papyrus as same was plentiful among the philosophers, writers, artists and manufacturers. Matthew was able to safely ship the documents to other communities prior to the restrictions in place in 52AD. More than likely, Matthew's Gospel had been completed about 50AD for the Romans throughout the Empire to discern the importance of Christ in their lives.

Scripture was bringing God's word to the communities, reassuring many converts who had sacrificed so much in their lives to join the fledgling Ecclesia.

Chapter Forty-Four

Be Not Afraid

July, 58

If dates were important to Paul, he would have been celebrating his fiftieth birthday in that summer of 58AD. However his age never deterred him from total commitment to the Resurrected Christ. In Jerusalem his evangelical message focussed on Christ being the fulfillment of the Messianic Promise, and on the necessity of the Spirit. The Pharisees believed in the resurrection after death and in angels and spirits. The Saducees were opposed to these beliefs proclaiming: there was no resurrection and no angels. The Spirit of God was anathema to them. As he himself was a Pharisee, Paul ventured that he could achieve some support from their ranks. If the Pharisees believed in spirits and angels, then the concept of the Holy Spirit would not be that remote. There was hope in his heart when Paul spoke in the Temple.

That Christ considered the Gentiles to be co-heirs in the right to redemption, that proclamation incited the anger of many devout Jews. Paul even invited the Gentiles to participate in prayer in that most sacred shrine. The opposition of the Jews became radically elevated when Jews from the Province of Asia, who were in Jerusalem at the time and who had already heard Paul, objected to the presence of Gentiles and Paul's teaching relative to them being co-heirs. They accused Paul of denouncing the Law of Moses, which was basically a charge of blasphemy that deserved death.

During the ensuing riot, Paul was grabbed, and then beaten. Roman legionnaires had to immediately intervene to prevent his death. Then the Roman Commander instead of freeing the victim decided to appease the mob by placing Paul in chains and leading him away to the inner court. Before the Romans could haul him away, Paul repeatedly declared his innocence, and demanded to speak once again to his accusers in Hebrew. This astounded the Commander as he had thought Paul was the Greek rebel whom they had been seeking relative to a previous riot.

Paul took that opportunity to declare his kinship with the Jewish community, starting with details of his religious development and his life as a Pharisee.

> I am a Jew born in Tarsus of Cilicia, but brought up here in Jerusalem as a student of Rabbi Gamaliel. I received strict instruction in the Law of our ancestors and was just as dedicated to God as are all of you who are here today. I persecuted to the death the people who followed the Way. I arrested men and women and threw them into prison. The High Priest and His Counsel can attest that I am telling the truth. I received from them letters written to fellow Jews in Damascus. So I went there to arrest these people and bring them back in chains to Jerusalem to be punished.

To the audience that was the satisfying part. Paul then provided details of his conversion.

> As I was travelling and coming near to Damascus, about midday a bright light from the sky flashed suddenly around me. I fell to the ground and heard a voice saying to me, "Saul, Saul, why do you persecute me?' (Acts 22:3)

Paul attempted to continue with his story; but the Jews would no longer tolerate the abuse. Any attempt at any accord ended the instant Paul disclosed that his mission was to bring the Good News to the Gentiles. At that moment the mob vociferously reacted, openly declaring their intention to kill him.

To appease the mob, in the same manner Pilate used with Jesus, the Commander ordered that Paul be taken to the inner court and flogged. That plan was immediately stopped when Paul declared himself also to be a Roman by birth. The chains were immediately removed and Paul was provided with lodgings fitting a Roman.

The next morning, the Commander squirming for a resolution insisted that Paul once more speak with the Jewish people, but this time the discussion should involve High Priest Ananias, and his Counsel.

Immediately Paul spoke of salvation in Christ Jesus. Without pause the High Priest ordered that Paul be struck. Rather than fighting back or even turning the other cheek, Paul demanded that the High Priest tell the others on what authority he was acting. The answer would have been a simple one; except Paul blurted out that he was a Pharisee. A High Priest could not exact punishment on a Pharisee. With the momentary silence, Paul continued

> I am on trial because of the hope that I have that the dead will rise to life. (Acts 23:6)

This was one of the most astute statements that could have ever been made under those circumstances. First he had successfully challenged the authority of the High Priest, and now he was tearing the Counsel apart. The Counsel was composed of Pharisees and Saducees. Because Paul had asserted that "the dead will rise"; a melee instantly developed between the Pharisees believing in after-life and the Saducees denying the after-life. The Doctors of Law, who were mainly Pharisees, intervened to decide the issue.

> We can find nothing wrong with this man. Perhaps a spirit or angel did speak to him. (Acts 23:9)

The Romans then pulled Paul away from the mob, providing him with lodging safe within the barracks.

– Ephesus Pure in Heart –

That night Christ appeared to Paul with words of gratitude and direction.

> Don't be afraid. You have been a witness to me here in Jerusalem. You must also do the same in Rome. (Act 23:11)

Chapter Forty-Five

Journey to Rome

September, 59

Forty members of the Jewish congregation, best described as zealots, remained committed to ending Paul's interference in their beliefs. Even though the disciple was still within Roman custody, they plotted. Their plan was to entice the Roman commander to let Paul once more speak to the Jewish Counsel. On his way to the Temple, they would murder him.

When the news of this audacious plot was heard by Paul's nephew, he notified the Romans. Accordingly, the commander sent Paul from Jerusalem to Caesarea with an armed escort. In Caesarea, Paul fell under the protection of Procurator Felix. Because Paul had not yet been charged, and there were no accusers present, the procurator kept Paul secure in the governor's headquarters.

Within the week, High Priest Ananias with his lawyer and five members of the Council arrived in Caesarea presenting formal charges and asking for the death sentence. The Jewish lawyer accused Paul of starting riots, and defiling their Temple. Paul refuted those charges, reminding them that he arrived in Jerusalem to worship in the Temple and offer sacrifice.

> I worship the God of our ancestors by following the Way that they say is false. I believe in everything written in the Law of Moses and the books of the prophets. I have the same hope in God that these have: that all people both the good and the bad will rise from death. (Acts 24:14)

Felix stayed the charges waiting for further evidence from the Roman commander who was still in Jerusalem.

Paul was again questioned by the procurator in the presence of the procurator's Jewish spouse. After Paul witnessed to the Lord Jesus, Felix sent Paul to jail with significant restrictions. He did this because his term as procurator was coming to an end, and he did not want to leave any outstanding monumental concern for his successor, Festus.

Procurator Festus, having been informed of the situation, left Caesarea and travelled to Jerusalem to address the Hebrew grievances. After spending almost two weeks in the company of the High Priest and his Counsel, Festus returned to Caesarea to conclude the problem Paul had created. Answering his accusers and the specific charges Paul declared that he had done nothing to violate any Jewish Law, and appealed, as a Roman could, to the Emperor.

Festus had no intention of disturbing or frustrating Nero. Accordingly he delayed referring the matter to Rome. Instead he chose to meet with the puppet leader, the designated King of Judaea. Their initial meeting generated another opportunity for Paul to declare his faith. After hearing a summary of Paul's life and his conversion; the King concluded:

> This man has done nothing for which he should die or be put in prison. He could have been released if he had not appealed to the Emperor. (Acts 26:32)

Paul and other prisoners were then placed on board a Roman vessel for their voyage to Rome. The vessel docked at Sidon, then sailed past Cyprus to the port of Myra. There they were transferred to another vessel destined for the Italian peninsula. A storm during the voyage drove them past Crete and off course causing the vessel to hit a sandbar near Malta. Paul and the other survivors remained on that island for three months until another vessel originally from Alexandria could take them to their destination.

Peter was already there having completed his own missionary journey from Antioch to cities and towns in eastern Anatolia, and then to Corinth. In 57AD after assisting in the growth of the Christian community in Corinth, Peter completed the voyage to his final destination: Rome. Mark had joined Peter during the missionary work in Anatolia, and was temporarily with Peter when they arrived in Rome.

In March of 60AD, after a journey of seven months, Paul finally arrived in Rome. Throughout the entire period when Paul was in Jerusalem, then Caesarea and on that voyage, Luke was with him: providing company and recording Paul's missionary endeavours.

The Christians greeted Paul outside of Rome following his arrival. Even though he was still restricted in some of his activities due to the presence of the Roman guard, Paul was able at their request to speak with the Jewish leaders of Rome. Without any reservation he declared his absolute faith in the Lord Jesus asserting that His Kingdom was at hand. Paul's speech once more repeated all of the aspects of his life, his conversion and his mission stressing that the redemption is available to the Gentiles as well as the Jews. As a philosopher, a Roman, a Jew, and as a missionary devoted to the principle of life after death, Paul continued to preach, perform miracles, and witness the growth of the Christian faith in the capital of an empire John was calling Babylon.

Chapter Forty-Six

Condicio Apis

October, 63

He who has a mind to understand, let him understand. Be cautious. The devil can give birth to a passion that has no equal. That which is born from evil is contrary to human nature. That is why I say to you: Be of good courage. If in life you are discouraged seek first the Kingdom of God. Behold God's creation in all its wonder. He who has ears to hear, let him hear. When the Blessed One had said this, He greeted them saying, Peace be with you. Receive my peace unto yourselves. Beware that no one leads you astray saying: Behold here he is, or lo there! For the Son of Man is within you. Follow Him! Those who seek Him will find Him. Go then and preach the gospel of the Kingdom. Do not lay down any rules beyond those I appointed you, and do not declare a law, like the lawgivers, lest you become burdened by your own folly. When He had said this, He departed. (Gospel According to Mary)

With that Miriam completed the fourth chapter of her narrative on the life of Christ. She intended in the days to come to record the rest of her story, particularly the events and meetings with the Apostles following the Ascension.

After that session with Seneca, where Celer didn't have his way, Miriam, having discovered the tension of testifying about the Lord, became determined to do more. If she was going to encourage others, she knew she first had to have completed similar tasks. There were too many occasions in all aspects of life where giving instructions had become easier than actually doing the work.

To accommodate all aspects of her endeavours, Miriam restricted her time at the market to two or three days per week. She found she could sell just as much and earn the same amount by selling the same amount of produce on fewer days. Age was catching up with her, and arthritis was not abetting. Still, perseverance ruled.

The start of the seventh decade witnessed growth in the care of orphans and widows. Chiara and Clement were doing their best. The program was also receiving support from non Christians, perceiving the benefits in both the means and the end result.

Care for the disadvantaged was also addressed in many attempts throughout the region. Support was significant at times, but there remained so much reluctance to associate with the ill, the diseased, the lame or the blind. The cruel perception that nearly everything in life was either totally good or totally bad remained a tragic hurdle. The world of superlative extremes provided little opportunity for compassion. Her struggle then became having people, especially the philosophers, realize that there was an entire realm of compromise and opportunity between the two poles. Blindness was not contagious. Being lame was not always caused by disease.

However Miriam had to accept some of their reservations. Polio and tuberculosis existed. They did not have formal names. More often than not, the victim was accused of bearing the sins of his parents. Then there were the sexual transmitted diseases. Miriam never ventured to explore why the mortality rate in certain districts was higher than in the farming communities. If she did, she would have identified the consequences of immorality in a Roman world.

That entire issue had become the focus of many of her discussions with Bernardus, Philemon, Aquila, Apollos and John. Miriam believed strongly that there were consequences to any evil act, even trivial issues. The effects of sin were not just spiritual. Any evil act directed the perpetrator in two directions: to either seek forgiveness or to complicate the fault. Such further culpability included: deceit, anger, rage, violence, abuse, divorce, theft, greed, gluttony, jealousy, immorality, prison or potentially murder. She had seen too much of it in her life. In that regard the concept of a realm after death that was somewhere between heaven and hell prompted further discussion.

The issue of baptism was on more than one occasion discussed in terms of the appropriate age to baptise a person. Susannah's query with respect to children who were suffering terminal ailments received many thoughtful comments with the pledge to revisit the issue.

During those nine years since the death of the Pro Consul, the Christian community in the Province of Asia had grown by almost forty percent. The difficulty with numbers once again, was that no one was actually keeping count, and the new converts with increasing fears of Roman oppression were not always ready to overtly declare their conversion. Christianity in some areas, in order to avoid tyranny, was becoming a silent vogue.

During that same time, Miriam's involvement in the evangelization process had expanded. She was now with John and others visiting Miletus and Smyrna: both sixty mile journeys. Charitable example was a key ingredient in the conversion process. Philemon was regularly on such trips. Occasionally Alexa accompanied him.

John's excursions started including the islands. Many of these had been independent states before the Romans arrived. Nothing changed significantly after Rome's intervention with respect to government, sentiment or philosophy. There remained in the islands demonstrable animosity to new tenets such that Christianity. However, Patmos was amazingly different. This island encompassed approximately forty-five square miles. Its sheer cliffs provided a foreboding image to any approaching vessel. The only harbour allowed docking for shallow-hull boats. Commerce was predominantly fishing contributing to significant exports. A few areas were suitable for crops, but produce was grown for their own sustenance. In that particular venue, John discovered a receptive population. Fisherman could relate to his experience and skills. Farmers considered carefully the many parables concerning vines, figs, trees, and seeds.

John continued to experience his mystic sessions. After the fourth occasion, Miriam was firm in her belief that these experiences were heavenly inspired. She insisted John stay that night to record the revelations. It was indeed a marvellous adventure to read such verse. However, sooner or later, preferably sooner, John would have to assemble the parchments in a logical order and ultimately conclude his instruction pertinent to the many angelic and horrific apparitions. This entire process drove Miriam to gather from their marsh or receive from Alexandria as much papyrus as possible. Now that Mark was in Egypt, they had a reliable means to obtain the quality product.

Using Maryam's former house to store these completed parchments was essential. The climate had changed slightly in those years with cooler winds sweeping the peninsula. Humidity could destroy parchment; but Maryam's house with the stone construction and ventilation provided secure storage away from oppressive heat.

Timothy was so central to the process of communication. From Paul and Peter, he had arranged delivery of their letters. Documents were then copied for the various Christian communities.

Nearly all of the leaders in the Christian community accepted the reality they could never safely return to Jerusalem. Similarly Antioch in Syria was questionable. Although there remained in Antioch a sizeable ecclesia, the city was home to the King of the Judaeans, and was a center for the procurator's administration of Roman justice. The Jewish Counsel in Jerusalem remained committed to annihilating the Christian presence. As long as that sentiment ruled Palestine, Antioch could never be wholly safe.

Still, it seemed the animosity toward the Christians in Syria might be abating. News from the Indian sub-continent arrived by means of traders who reported on a fellow named Thomas. The experience of Simon and Jude were recounted by others who had visited Armenia. That province was embroiled in an ongoing war with Rome at the time. There was no certainty about any aspect of life in those years.

Early in the Roman year of the Consulship of Marius & Afinius, 62 AD, Pompeii was levelled by a massive earthquake. Nearly every villa, mansion or palace was destroyed. Roads heaved. The supply of fresh water was obliterated. The harbour and monuments were razed by the violent occurrence. A tsunami was reported affecting various islands, with the vibration crossing the Adriatic Sea toward Corinth. In Rome, the anger of the deities was on rampage. Even though rebuilding was started very quickly, not all of the villas were considered essential in the future of the city. More could happen at any time.

The cyclical droughts and famines returned between 60AD and 63AD. However, with the increasing prominence of Ephesus within the Empire, enough food was made available there to sustain its population.

Illness and death from uncertain causes became prevalent in late 62AD. As to how far this spread no one kept records. Recurring plagues were normal, however no one every kept track. Death was inevitable and at times it came quicker for some than for others. If the historians were mathematicians, they would have noted that as commerce and shipping increased the suddenness of incurable diseases was magnified. No one blamed trade or cargo from ports on the Black Sea for the spread of infectious disease at that time.

Following the death of Marcus Silanus the expectation was one of Roman abuse and tyranny. However, for reasons unknown, Celer never completed the expected purge. Seneca remained true to the Emperor and the citizens of the Empire prompting the development of far reaching policies by his written works and position as advisor to Nero. With so much progress everywhere within the Empire, there was no need for abuse and retribution in any segregated area. Judaea however was urging Rome towards the precipice of militant action to control the rebel factions. However during the last eight years in Ephesus, also called Apis - the City of the Bee, there was unusual and unexpected civic pride.

Tress had been planted and the city beautified. Plans for more monuments and temples invigorated many residents wanting employment. In some trades, the hours of labour for slaves and servants were reduced. Highways to Ephesus from the interior were upgraded. Aqueducts were completed. Dredging of the harbour was restarted. Conditions in the theatre and stadium were improved. Trade and commerce increased once more. A significant portion of the omnipresent Roman Army had been dispatched to Armenia.

Other legions were sent to Palestine. Still others joined the naval force protecting the Mare Nostrum.

Celer sat in his office in a late afternoon of October, 63AD. The Roman vessel had without warning arrived with a messenger and a scroll from the Emperor himself. Celer's presence was being demanded in Rome to prepare plans for a revolving ceiling in a palace that Nero was planning to build. Celer responded hastily while the messenger waited, leaving behind the Province of Asia, to employ his rarely used engineering skills to please his Emperor.

Chapter Forty-Seven

Burning of Rome

July, 64

It took Nero five years to realize he didn't have absolute control of the Roman Empire. During that time, he was dominated by Agrippina, his mother. After all, Nero basically owed his position to her cunning style and murderous rampage. The Empire became a sullied world of intrigue where nothing was certain except taxation and death; and Agrippina controlled both.

Nero put a stop to that in March, 59AD when he had Agrippina murdered. Britannicus and Marcus Silanus were already dead. Nero didn't have to fear his family or any pretender to the throne. He was now solely in charge of his own realm. After all he was a divine god. Divinity had allowed Nero to engage in a continuous murderous spree, securing his position of absolute prominence. That which he deplored so much in his mother, he became.

Gods do not live in dung heaps. During the prior centuries the city of Rome had declined into a state of total disrepair. The entire city within the seven hills was a contrast of wealth and poverty, of affluence and dire servitude, of magnificence and rotting structures, of flowing rivers and cess pools. Marble lasts longer than wood. That tenet prompted the use of stone, block and marble in the construction of buildings for the elite that were to last for eons. However, such structures were never intended for the Plebeians; and the common people were still the majority of the population. They lived mainly in one storey wooden structures. Their shops and factories were also made of soft woods creating buildings with a multitude of limitations. Their tables were floor boards, and their beds covered straw. Renovations were delayed or denied in the decades of Anno Domini as timber was required to build ships for war and cargo, and to reinforce the docks and existing vessels. Improvements for the inferior class were out of the question. Wooden shops and dwellings were left to rot.

With rivers being so essential for commerce, sustenance and sewage, most cities were established on water ways that inherently meant swamps and low lying areas in their proximity. Malaria and disease were the consequence. Recurring plagues and illness had their own agenda. Ponds became cisterns. Roads crumbled into ditches. Culverts overflowed flooding properties. With all of the difficulties inherent in an old city, so many improvements had to be done, but funds for such endeavours did not exist. However, if a new palace for the Emperor was being considered, then funds would always be available for that project.

While Plebeian living standards deteriorated, new Patrician monuments and structures were overwhelmingly illustrious. Sections of the city were being enhanced beyond reasonable expectation. But regardless of how magnificent these new buildings were; there still remained degrees of affluence among the influential. No one could be better than the emperor, and no one's building could surpass Nero's Palace. In 64AD his palace was not the most distinguished or ornate edifice within the city. The Emperor was determined to change that.

He presented his plan to the Roman Senate to level one third of the city of Rome and erect in that same area a series of palaces, gardens with marble boulevards and monuments. The entire complex he called 'the Neropolis'. Nero wanted a city in his name commensurate with his divine status. Anything less was idolatry. Nero demanded an artistic capital that very much matched his interest and ability in all sectors of the arts. Nero didn't get approval for this version of heaven, causing a brick wall to be built between the Senate and their Emperor.

Regardless of his divinity, Nero was not able to control the climate. By early July of that year, the Lo Scirocco Winds were sweeping across the Italian peninsula depositing a blanket heat wave with no opportunity to avoid the extreme arid conditions. Wood frame buildings rapidly became a tinder box. To escape the offensive conditions, Nero and his select advisors left the city for his palace in Antium on the Tyrrhenian coast. He was leaving behind a palace structure of immense size in need of repairs. His plan had been thwarted; but he never surrendered his dream palace of gold and marble: Domus Aurea.

The fire started in the dark early hours of July 19, 64AD, in shops where flammable goods were normally stored near the Circus Maximus. The Circus Maximus was one of the most prestigious and magnificent structures in Rome, renowned for chariot races and athletic games. This was constructed less than a quarter kilometer from the Tiber River in the Twelfth District. The terminus of the Via Appia was to its east. Nero's existing palace was about three hundred meters to the north. In every direction, monuments divided the horizon. Fire was not unusual in Rome. Subsequent to this there were other fires also causing significant damage. However these flames were different.

If this was tried as an arson case in any later generation, Nero would have been found guilty. He had the means as he controlled a city buried in intrigue with limited services. He had already declared his intention to rid the city of the buildings in the districts that were damaged in the fire. He was the one to profit from the fire with the construction of his House of Gold. He was the judge deciding responsibility to the extent he could and would never accuse himself.

The dry timber with bales of hay and flammable goods sent the flames flying high into the night air. The Lo Sciorocco breeze carried the sparks to the east and north into surrounding structures and districts. The farther away from the Tiber the fire spread; the more out-of-control it became.

Nero returned to the city only when the fire had consumed his Gardens of Maecenas on the Esquiline Hill that were adjacent to his palace. The Emperor's palace soon became a charred remnant. Nero feigned support for the Plebeians by various acts of superficial charity providing temporary accommodations in remote areas of the city not destroyed by the flames. Eventually ten of the city's fourteen districts were either totally destroyed or damaged beyond the state of repair. The first part of his plan went to perfection.

The second part was attributing blame. Nero was an artist, a writer, and a musician. He acted, played musical instruments and composed. He admired dramatic works and symphonic ensembles. Nero had little time and definitely no patience for philosophers who generally promulgated theories, ideas and commentaries that were not always in accord with Nero's perception of his deified self. Christians were philosophers. This preacher Peter was both a Christian and a philosopher. Paul was becoming philosophically obnoxious to many in Rome as he was forever espousing the virtues of a Jew the Romans had crucified. The Christian community in Rome before July, 64AD was the smallest religious sect. They basically could not defend themselves except in words, and had only their teaching to safeguard their faith. They were vulnerable. They were dispensable. Who else could be responsible for a fire that destroyed almost seventy percent of Rome?

Tacitus, the noted Roman Senator and historian, reported on events following the fire regarding cause and consequence:

> To stop the rumour that he had set Rome on fire, Emperor Nero falsely charged persons who are commonly called Christians. Chrestus, the founder of their sect, was put to death by Pontius Pilate, Procurator of Judaea, during the reign of Tiberius. Pernicious superstition arose claiming he was alive. This was repressed for a time, then broke it again, not only in Judaea where the mischief originated, but in the city of Rome also. All things horrible, and disgraceful events flowed from all quarters based on that common belief. Accordingly, first they who confessed to be Christians were arrested. Based on their information, a vast multitude was convicted, not so much for burning the city but because they hated the human race.

Tacitus proceeded then to describe the horrific deaths and agony.

Within two months following the fire, Nero started the construction of his Domus Aurea. That magnificent palace would take four years to complete. Celer, from the Province of Asia, was once again called to Rome because of his engineering ability to work on the revolving ceiling. Boulevards were widened. Pillars, monuments and Nero's statue were constructed to celebrate the rebirth of the city. These events coincided with the celebrations of the tenth anniversary of Nero's reign.

On the very day of Nero's jubilee, October 13, 64AD, Peter having been identified as leader of the Christian community was crucified. Torturing Christians by horrific means in public displays became Roman entertainment. Faith in the Risen Christ was suddenly demanding a lot more than just an agreement to be baptised.

Chapter Forty-Eight

Flames of Persecution

August, 64

John stormed into the stadium screaming from his heart, demanding that the murderous exhibition be immediately stopped. Almost on cue, the jeering mob drowned the voice they considered so pathetic.

A Christian lay dead on the stadium dirt, having dragged himself to the far end to escape the raging dogs. A streak of blood followed him on the sandy surface till his last gasp. His anguish had been terrifyingly loud, filling the valley with the torment that Christians were forced to experience. The Romans had no more room for crucifixions and not enough courts to try the religious criminals. The bloodbath in the stadia throughout the Empire was the norm to eradicate the vermin. Wild Boars, untamed lions, hungry tigers, starving wolves, or vicious dogs delighted the Roman citizens committed to their divine emperor. Some venues employed the sport of butchery by trained gladiators. The Christians had no defense. Even if in the remotest possibility they survived, they would then be declared guilty of witchcraft.

John screamed even louder. The Christians who were present for sympathy and prayers remained relatively quiet else the mob would turn on them too. The Apostle repeated his cry denouncing the slaughter, becoming a vile joke to the mob. Those around him rebuked him with their raised fists and laughter. When he continued to beg for reason, the mob's frustration became anger. After minutes of taunting him, Roman legionnaires surrounded John forcing him away from the display of tyranny.

The guards knew who he was. Nearly everyone in Ephesus recognized him as the leader of that Christian sect. To the Christians he was their Bishop. To the Roman officials, regardless of any sentiments, John was known as a prudent and sensible individual prone to take the middle road when pursuing peace between factions. However this was Nero's realm where the extreme was the norm, and anyone challenging his wish or design was guilty of treason and sedition.

John was hauled away first to the gymnasium complex adjacent to the Harbour Baths. There, Muscipula sat as the judge. All around the dining hall, guards were positioned as if providing security for the weak link in Roman authority. Within the room, Patricians viewed Muscipula's manner and decisions. They had a keen interest in everything that was decided. The Province of Asia was still very much considered a Senate responsibility, and their families all had members in the Senate.

Celer had risked much to award the former jailer this position, only because most of Celer's trusted friends were now gone. The memory of Marcus Silanus over the course of ten years had not disappeared. There remained a sentiment wishing for the peace and accord attributed to Silanus' rule. Perhaps all of these events mellowed Celer in his role as acting Pro Consul. He was now in charge of the general peace within the province while doing the will of the Emperor to avoid the interference of the Emperor.

John was not mistreated even on route to the gymnasium. In the facility he was provided a chair and opportunity for any beverage. Conversation was civil. The judge obviously felt uncomfortable, stammering as he was known to do. The elite Patricians were not impressed. Just less than an hour after his arrival, John was being dispatched to the Prytaneion to meet Celer. John had witnessed a similar series of events thirty-seven years before when Christ was being taken from one building to another to be judged and finally passed to the procurator for the final decision. John had prepared himself for these moments.

****

News of the fire horrified the residents of Ephesus. Such devastation was truly unbelievable. Although the majority of citizens had never seen Rome, all of the officials had at one time either lived or visited there. They all talked of the grandeur that was no more. In the same sentence with sentiments similar to those of their Emperor, the Christians were blamed. Then the devastating stories of torture and death circulated giving reason to accomplish the same level of tyranny everywhere. Peter's crucifixion dug a hole in John's heart.

Christians reacted quickly. Some who were simply renting mundane abodes moved elsewhere. Others fled to one of the many islands. The majority stayed momentarily burying their faith so as to at least guarantee same for future generations. Mark's description of the final days was seriously considered. Were they approaching that time when Christ would re-appear? It was that belief that bound these to the Christian ideals. Care of the orphans moved away from existing locations. Many social services moved far from the city core into the valleys.

The first persecution tore at the fabric of their religion the hardest. The death was not a spectacle, but rather a quick blow, a dead body and a message to all Christians who denied the emperor's divinity. Once started, Celer realized how much delight the troops gained by such murderous displays, and how little control he had of events.

Many Christians debated within their families with due consideration given to all alternatives. By the end of the first week, it had been confirmed that such tyranny was not happening within predominantly Greek cities. There upon an exodus to the interior started spreading the Faith to the small towns where tolerance and cooperation generated commitment to the needs and life of the community.

– Ephesus Pure in Heart –

Miriam moved up to Maryam's house. Just that extra distance gave her assurance. Philemon and Bernardus devoted themselves to helping John in the core. Apollos and Aquila directed their efforts into the valleys. Eighteen to twenty hour days were their commitment to the Faith: celebrating liturgy or providing reassurance.

By that early afternoon of Dies Veneris seven Christians had died in the stadium.

****

Celer displayed his disgust for John and the Christians once John stood before him. The acting Pro Consul was himself disgruntled because for these last ten years he had never been formally awarded the position. There was no other family in all of Rome who could trace itself back to the days of Romulus and Remus. It was at that time that the Celer family was the guardians of the founders of Rome.

This man standing before him was just a Christian. Celer thought John would have excelled as a Roman if he ever chose to buy his citizenship. However this man, some called a 'Metropolitan', was so inanely determined to follow the precepts of a human Romans had crucified. Really nothing more could be done for him.

One of the guards approached Celer carrying a silver pitcher and bowl, believing the acting Pro Consul would just wash his hands at this first opportunity and hand the Christian to them for the next round of games in the stadium. "A pathetic lot," he told Celer.

"You would tell me he's only good for Rome's fancy." Celer's retort surprised the worried Apostle.

"Just entertainment," the guard said before leaving.

The bowl and pitcher sat on the table to Celer's side. "Don't worry," he told John.

"Get me the Quaestor," Celer called to the guard by the door. He was referring to the incompetent Muscipula. Everyone seemed to have an opinion about Celer promoting the former jailer. But silence was golden among the Roman soldiers. Living in silence was better than dying with your mouth open.

"Hades would have been my choice," Celer coldly told John. John was anxious but not suffering trepidation. As John did not respond, Celer exclaimed further to insult the Christian, "If only Cumanis had completed his task!" He was referring to the procurator who about fifteen years prior had crucified monotheistic believers in Palestine. Still there was silence. "Nero glories in our stadium," the acting Pro Consul asserted.

"Just stone slabs without life." John's cold declaration annoyed Celer.

"You know I have the right...." Celer stopped abruptly thinking John would immediately blurt a comment interrupting him. However that did not happen.

"You killed that Christian woman yesterday and her husband today." John's accusation was very clear.

"You think so." Celer abruptly changed his tone asking one of the guards to bring two chairs and place them at the table. Then the acting Pro Consul directed John to have a seat with him. It was oak furniture, laminated, quite impressive. The chairs were padded.

Celer sat across from John. A hand signal told the guards to leave. They were surprised, but they left. In the same moment Celer reached into the pouch of his tunic. He then placed the object on the table. "Tell me about this."

John stared at the cross. He recognized it was one manufactured by Christian labourers in Ephesus. He had been shown the design and finished product for circulation among the believers. They were prohibited from using lead or heavy metal. Instead they used a very thin metal fibre buried in terra cotta that was then laminated. The finished product was a small cross about thirty millimeters by thirty millimeters. On the back a pin was often attached so that the charm could be worn on outer clothing. John explained the manufacture and purpose, concluding with the comment, "Instead of Artemis." That was shrewd as Celer obviously would have had no affection for the Greek goddess.

Their exchange continued. John was candidly surprised by the entire tone and demeanour of the acting Pro Consul bearing in mind the slaughter he just witnessed.

"What else do you plan?" The question was rather abrupt compared to the prior conciliatory tone.

John had no answer.

****

– Ephesus Pure in Heart –

Muscipula did not respond hastily to Celer's demand for his attendance. He leaned back on a couch in one of the rooms of the gymnasium complex with three members of his own entourage. Muscipula could never be accused of not taking advantage of a situation.

Agnete was a servant girl born of Greek parents, on an island in the Aegean she could not remember. The ludicrous judge believed she was Christian. That was reason enough for him to have his way with the woman.

"Has she confessed?" Muscipula questioned.

"Like a spider she sits spawning her vice." The advice was what he expected.

"What do you have to say, harlot?"

The girl, maybe seventeen years old, stared at him.

"Tramp, speak to me!" Muscipula demanded. Before she could even contemplate an answer, he struck her face. The girl spit blood in his direction.

"Do you know I have the power to save your life?" This was a common Roman threat.

Agnete just stared at him. The guards were amused by the exchange. Muscipula then tore her clothes, and taking a remnant of her attire, he blindfolded her.

"Play me the fool, will you?" Muscipula derisively laughed taking advantage of her inability to defend herself. "Get me her friends! Bring me anyone who has known her. They will honour Caesar or die!"

His comrades left leaving the innocent girl with the lecher. For several minutes he stared at the whimpering teenager; then abruptly dragged her to his private quarters.

****

Bernardus completed the voyage and return to the harbour without any issues. The boat captained was a Christian, well known to Bernardus and Philemon. On the island John had already met several residents who endeared themselves to Christ's message. Above all else, they shared the importance of preserving the Word. Equally important, they hated Celer and despised anything Roman.

– Ephesus Pure in Heart –

The bundles he carried would have caused any legionnaire or Roman sailor to question the contents and purpose. However with this captain such enquiries did not take place. He had handled the shipment of grain and other food products for many of the Patricians before this, earning their respect for his uncanny method of obtaining taxes and profits on goods delivered to the city of Rome. No food delivered to Rome was ever taxable; however his tales about the cost of additional irrigation during droughts earned him a thankful stipend.

Bernardus' cargo was precious. These were the parchments of letters from the disciples, John's own incomplete writings, and two narratives on Christ's life. Similar documents had already been delivered to Corinth, Alexandria and Syria. With tragic events in these last weeks, action regarding the sacred writings was required immediately.

In a cave facing east the documents were stored. The venue prevented the papyrus from being damaged by cold damp winds from the north, or the dry heat blowing north from Africa, and the prevailing moist winds and storms from the west. In that location they were protected from human adversarial elements by those committed to the Faith.

****

Was it Celer's age that made him mellow? The entire conversation was an unending wave of troughs and crests of an ever changing temperament. They continued well beyond normal hours for dining ultimately concluding that John had two alternatives: death or exile. Celer vowed he could not stop Nero, if the Emperor was not satisfied with developments in the province.

Eventually the acting Pro Consul agreed to the proposal that: if John were to be exiled, then he would have at least two weeks to bid farewell, that there would be no more Christians tortured or put to death in the stadium, and there would be no Christian homes torched.

Celer rose from the table and called to one of his advisors. A minute later those two were quietly talking. John didn't hear a word. Then as they were ending the conversation Celer spoke out loud, "Tell everyone no more Christian deaths. The Julian Games are concluded!"

– Ephesus Pure in Heart –

The Julian Games were established in honour of Julius Caesar. The difficulty with these games was that by July everyone had attended some sort of festival every week for the last eight months, and as Julius Caesar was starting to suffer ill-repute; the purpose and frivolity of those games had lost their purpose.

A scribe attended and prepared a scroll for the Emperor telling him that Ephesus has completed the celebration of the Julian Games, and will continue to be mindful of the Emperor's desire to promote the arts. In particular, Celer mentioned renovations to the outdoor theatre, the Emperor's monument and various plays that would definitely draw the Emperor's admiration. It was strange, John pondered, that a grandiose statue of Nero could save Christian lives.

The realization of what he was saying and terms of the agreements were slowly completing the trek from John's lips through his mind to his heart. He would be giving up so much to preserve the Christian community and end the terror of Nero's purge.

Chapter Forty-Nine

Final Farewell

October, 64

The expected seasonal brisk winds had yet to blow on that damp October morn. Miriam stood there on the dock begging that this day did not have to come. Two weeks ago John told her. He said it was his only way to maintain the peace. "For the growth of the Ecclesia," he reassured her. However her mind was far from understanding the sense.

The meeting with Celer had affirmed that times were uncertain. Candidly there were few Romans John could trust. At the top of that list, there was Celer. Being astute was John's virtue. Having both eyes fixed on the future was the Bishop's attribute. "If Celer is in Nero's pouch, he won't be here long," John suggested to Miriam. Being mindful that the Province of Asia was still basically the protectorate and jurisdiction of the Senators and that the Pro Consul was only appointed with the consent of the Senators, John explored all of the possibilities. If Celer returned to Rome, then the Senators probably would take over the rule of the province without a Pro Consul, using the legions for support. The Senators would not want another emperor's appointee. Furthermore, the Senators and Nero were becoming totally abhorred with one another to the extent there were repeated rumours of plots to rid Rome of Nero's presence.

Subsequently, John worked on his relationship with the Senators in the province endearing them to the social activities of the Christians, and affirming the Christian interest in trade and agriculture. Within those two weeks, John had met with every Senator in Ephesus: gaining their pledge. The foundation of the Christian movement in Anatolia was becoming a furnished main floor.

The vessel bounced against the dock, buffeted by the waves driven by the current. The captain was trying to be professional in his demeanour. He had a job to do, but would prefer not having to do it. Bernardus was on board viewing the final greetings on the dock. He had during the night arranged for extensive supplies to be brought on board. Bernardus felt good about himself. He had never tired of all of the requests, of the many long days and endless months, of being the best to everyone. The term 'multi-tasking' appropriately described his daily chores.

Two legionnaires also waited on the dock, not near the vessel, to report that it left at the appropriate time. Celer wasn't there. He was to be leaving for Rome by the end of the month.

"This is not the end," John reassured Philemon.

The Greek gentleman mentioned a general perception of many Christians, "They believe it is. They expect Christ to appear any moment."

John had always challenged that view as it tended to limit enthusiasm for spreading the Good News. There was no virtue in just waiting for any event to happen.

> God's kingdom is not limited to this generation. His promise to Abraham was not just for Isaac and his family alone. They worry too much over matters about which we all have no control. What purpose was there in Mark writing to the Greeks: Concerning that day and hour no one knows, not the angels, nor the Son, but only the Father?

The final conversation with Philemon continued dwelling on the subject of leadership of the community, the work of the deacons, and the ministers preaching and celebrating the Rite of the Last Supper. In that Philemon had been keenly involved in many of the journeys and discussions made him a valuable continuing asset in the growth of the religious community.

"Eternal happiness awaits us." With that final salutation John concluded his farewell to Alexa and Philemon. They left heading along the dock towards the north.

Susannah was waiting in the distance with the children having already bid farewell.

"Your smile?" John tried smiling himself to overcome Miriam's mournful expression. "Please?" he continued not getting the reaction he wanted. He just shook his head with a grin as Miriam tried to evoke a smile.

"I never want to forget," she whimpered.

"You won't," he assured her.

"I'll never let myself. You will write," she offered.

"I had better or you'll drag me off the island." His quip caused a smile.

"Resins should be enough." Miriam tried any topic to avoid saying good-bye.

"To be burned, just like you taught me."

"Do you have...?"

"Peace, Miriam. The supplies are stored." John's assurance was kindly received.

He then spoke of their garden, the produce in the valley and Clement's farm. The sincere hope was that talking about anything else would lighten her burden.

"What will you do without me?" she finally quipped.

John couldn't escape being honest. "What we do now, we'll do more. We are like two doves released to do more than just sit on the same perch."

"I'll miss your kind words." Miriam was ready to cry.

"Be a face of confidence."

"There you go again," she said about to shed tears. Miriam appeared angelic in her cream coloured toga that she wore only on special occasions.

John tried words of reason.

> Be certain that others understand. I believe it was Seneca that demanded I be exiled. Celer would have had me dead. However, do not talk openly in those terms. Remain at odds with Rome, not at war. Be the lynx you always claim to be, then be watchful like the house cat. Fear not, Miriam, you are never alone.

"Must this really happen?" she continued.
"Will you be the one to redesign God's will?"
"Must I be?" she pitifully questioned.

John had to state it clearly. "Your choice. I leave, we live. I have your heart, your mind and your prayers....now, yesterday and tomorrow. Nothing has changed. Nothing will change."

With that they sincerely hugged not willing to ease from each other's arms.

It took longer for Miriam to dry the tears. "Your verse, I'll miss it too. Never forget how you intrigued Luke."

"How?"

"Describing us as feathers on an eagle's wing. There's too much in that head of yours. Promise me again?"

He promised, "You have my word. I'm sure you'll be taunting Bernardus to deliver you more parchment."

"Anna wanted to be here."

"I said good-bye to her. She is a lovely person." John added his commentary on the many respectful families and friends in their community. That seemed for a while to dispel any tears.

"This is hard for an old woman." Miriam gave up keeping the tears inside. "Everything we've done..." she whimpered.

"Will be remembered by some and forgotten by many."

"Have you no tears?" Miriam wondered.

John's reply was absolute honesty.

> Only those I keep inside. I will cry. I'll miss you. I will miss your smile. I'll miss your enthusiasm ... and your frustration with everything I did.

He chuckled at her reaction.

One of the guards approached them with a reminder to board shortly.

Miriam broke their momentary silence.

> Your words the other night. Thought a lot about that. What does one say? You convinced me to stay so long ago when I wanted to run. I'll always think of you as the young man who knew no fears, jumping in with every reassurance that the ground was always at his feet and the angels about his head. Will they ever remember us?

"Children eat and have shelter. There they wait for you, more than just footnotes in a Roman tale."

The guard repeated his request.

"Would that I had your mind to write the future, your strength to assure others, and your love to open my arms and let free the most cherished person in my life?" Miriam's statement was total admiration.

"The tide demands us," the guard spoke for the third time.

John could not delay in repaying the compliment.

> You will always be remembered by the many forgotten on the streets, by children who are lost and alone, and by women bound in licentious servitude. History will record that you ministered to the Lord's meals, that you renounced your past, and that you were the one whom the Lord chose to announce the greatest news God could ever proclaim: He is risen.

The guard demanded their attention once more. Miriam instantly prompted John in the other direction, clutching his right hand between hers.

"John, you've shown me my heart." She was about to explode inside.

"I couldn't have had a better friend." John's words preceded their long embrace. Their minds were wrapped around each other's hearts. Her tears flowed upon his cheeks. Not a word was whispered till he looked once more into her eyes and reached up to dry her tears. He was sixty, and she was fifty-eight. Their life-long friendship was coming to an end and neither in that moment was ready to accept God's will. Tears flooded her cheeks, washing his palms.

"Does this mean we're married?" Her delightful wry humour touched his heart once more creating a broad smile to hide his tears. The simplicity of marriage had always been her topic. Now as they were parting she chose humour once more to lighten the moment. John had always thought she had several personalities wrapped within the one mind. Miriam had proven once again that she'd be an enigma for any Greek philosopher.

"Time has been precious." His words ended their embrace. This time he was wiping his own eyes as he perceived the honesty of the woman's soul.

The guard stepped forward the final time placing his hand on John's shoulder. "Come sir.

We must go."

John's words were the final expression of lasting friendship to the sobbing woman. "Peace Miriam. When we meet again, it'll be forever." With a final kiss, they said good-bye.

His footsteps were heavy as he boarded the craft. Miriam from the dock watched his every move. John was wearing the new sandals and cloak she gave him yesterday. Bernardus and the captain greeted John with words of support. Once the ropes were loosened the boat eased away from the port into the harbour; then it turned in tight formation to begin the one hundred kilometer voyage. "He's in good hands," she sighed knowing it was too late to regret the inevitable.

Susannah's control of the orphans was limited at the best of times. They were always overly active, though surprisingly polite and mature considering the family trauma they had witnessed. Three girls led the others running towards Miriam. "Varten! Varten avia!" they called begging the woman's attention. Miriam turned with her arms wide open to embrace the children. She was right at home.

Chapter Fifty

Bishop Timothy

February, 65

From between the bars in the two square foot opening, the frail prisoner reached, painstakingly extending his right hand. With his thumb he imprinted the sign of the cross on the visitor's forehead. It was for both a solemn moment. The jailors discounted the event having seen this visitor many times before. On occasion, they had even allowed him to bring and remove parchment. There was never any objection to the resin. Their prisoner was well known, infamous in terms of Roman ideology, and cherished by the remaining Christians who had not yet been tortured. Timothy blessed himself and then together with the prisoner repeated their version of the Lord's Prayer. Greek was the norm used for discussions in the Roman cells knowing the guards would never understand.

With Peter's death and then John's exile, immediate steps had to be taken by the most revered in Rome's Christian community to replace the pillar of the ecclesia in Ephesus. Timothy who had been Paul's confidant and messenger was the most trustworthy. As a disciple and evangelizer he had accomplished much in southern Anatolia, Achaia, and Corinth. Timothy was reliable and absolutely committed to the Lord Jesus. Timothy left Rome in early 65AD, having been anointed with Paul's blessing as the Bishop of Ephesus and realizing that he would never see Paul alive again.

****

Senate control of the Province of Asia restored relative accord among the various factions and in all facets of government. In those first months without John, the Christians were not apt to stress any differences. By early November, Celer had departed for Rome. Hypatius was accepted, not as Pro Consul, but as one with limited capacity who had always been sincere in his attempts to monitor certain affairs within the province. The Saturnalia Festivities took place as was the norm during December. Trade and commerce continued to expand. Educational institutions flourished. Roads were being repaired. Construction of the aqueducts created employment. Nero's monuments were being built. The brutal massacres in the stadium had stopped. Hope was routine, while military manoeuvres were limited. The energy in the region had blossomed with the sense that intrigue was definitely buried in the past. The stoics were satisfied.

****

However, events in Rome should never have given anyone anywhere within the Empire any hope of any guarantee of peace and stability. Following the fire, Nero orchestrated the rebuilding of Rome in grandiose style without the support of the Senators. His unilateral decisions on many issues annoyed the Senate. The incredible expenditure was outrageous. His Domus Aurea was the epitome of extravagance.

Then there was Nero's realm of tyranny. By 65AD the Emperor had gotten rid of every possible claimant to his throne. He even then went searching for the most remote individuals who might make a ridiculous assertion. Soranus, a very distant relation, was erroneously accused of witchcraft for which the punishment was death.

Instrumental in that accusatory process was Nero's friend, Celer. The Emperor's web of intrigue had become a mesh of deceit.

Nero continued to murder Christians without provocation in the Circus Maximus. Being gored by wild animals, or being butchered by gladiators: this was his brand of entertainment. Pouring oil over the victims and then setting them on fire was not out of the question.

However, his tyranny was not limited to the Christian sect. Nero had developed a phobia to the degree it became total insecurity. Anyone who may have said anything to even displease any person devoted to the Emperor would be guilty of sedition. The penalty was death, loss of property, and slavery for the victim's family members. Fear ruled the city of Rome.

When the Senators complained, Nero immediately declared and employed reprisals against the Senators: increasing taxes, limiting food and produce, reducing land use, and restricting meetings. If the Senators did meet, Nero was there to monitor and accuse.

Ultimately the plot to murder Nero became more than just a vague wish. The Senators and Patricians found in Gaius Piso, a General who was committed to the Empire at the cost of the Emperor. The entire plan which also included a program for succession became derailed when one of the lesser conspirators leaked the information to the Praetorian Guard who alerted the Emperor. Immediately retribution flared throughout the Empire. Seneca, who for many years had trained and advised Nero, was accused of being one of the culprits. He was forced to commit suicide in 66AD, or be beaten to death.

****

Meanwhile in the regions of the Empire embroiled in conflict, Roman Generals were amassing troops and had established enough military might to assert their own claim to be Emperor. Nero lacked the ability to control Galba, Otho, Vitellius or Vespasian. The credibility of their perceived claims attacked Nero's vulnerability.

****

In Jerusalem the zealots directed the persuasion of the Jewish people demanding an end to Roman rule. Statues of Roman Emperors had no place in the Holy City especially within the Temple. Taxation rules had changed. Claudius' leniency toward the Jews was forgotten. Daily sustenance was jeopardized with the insistence that Rome and other regions be fed first. Revised trade routes had compromised commerce in Palestine. Recurring drought and famine were cause for mob revolt. The Hebrew faith itself was in jeopardy with increasing demands for Emperor Worship. Audacity amplified. Procurator Felix had more than a decade before ordered coins to be issued during the reign of Claudius, with the reverse side having the image of a cross. The horizontal beam represented Britannicus and the vertical bar represented Nero. That any currency still existed denoting Britannicus, whom Nero had murdered, was an insult to Nero's divinity. Yet the coins were still in circulation. The rebellious action of thieves and rogues interfered with the flow of some goods. Roman roads in Palestine were no longer safe. Calm was abandoned and the Hebrews revolted. Rome was quick to react.

Christians fled Jerusalem going east beyond the Jordan River to Pella in the region of Peraea near the Dead Sea. There, generations later their scrolls would be discovered preserved by time in abandoned caves.

****

Suicide became the escape process in the latter years of the seventh decade. In 68AD having been chastised by the Senate and abandoned by the Patricians, Nero faced the consequences that no one of any true importance in Rome considered him to be a divine being. He was just a tyrant who applauded murder and torture, and who considered it beneficial to spend vast sums on him-self. The Senators and People of Rome applauded Nero's decision to end his own life.

Following Nero's death, Celer was one of many who lacked supportive friendships within Rome. He was charged with perjury following those false accusations against Soranus. Even though he was never convicted, suicide appeared to him at that time to be the best personal result.

****

While the Roman world focused on the city of Rome, Christianity was spreading throughout the Empire. Actually it was the debauchery in Rome that prompted many in the Mediterranean region to realize Christian tenets were more desirable than Roman tyranny. Christianity gave people a viable alternative.

Paul was beheaded in 65AD during Nero's purge of conspirators and all opposing elements within the city. The Emperor's disgust for Christians had been equal to his discomfort with philosophers, and his need for vengeance.

Following Paul's martyrdom, Linus was appointed to be the Bishop of Rome in 67AD. Linus, born in Tuscany in 10AD, had been ordained by Paul. He was committed to priestly and social service administering to the many spiritual and temporal needs of the burdened Christian community. Linus remained Pope until his death in 76AD.

The Evangelists, John and Luke, were busy composing and completing their narratives on the life of Christ. John finished his text about 70AD. Luke concluded his gospel passages about five years later. These texts, together with Mark's and Matthew's earlier narratives, became so instrumental in providing assurance, hope and direction to the Christian communities. Others too completed details of Christ's life, Miriam was one of these. Christianity gave the terms 'love' and 'sacrifice' new and endearing meanings.

About five years after completing his gospel, Luke finished recording the details of the spread of Christianity following the ascension. Thereafter John recounted all of his heavenly apparitions and his visions of hell. The text of his Revelations was copied innumerable times sharing same with every community searching to be washed clean in the blood of the Lamb. John's letters too were dearly read for they proclaimed the universal tenet: God is Love.

****

That aspect of 'Love' Miriam never brushed aside or took for granted. She remained diligent to the social needs of the ecclesia: with orphans and widows, for shelter and nourishment, for the right to worship in the liturgy and beliefs that truly brought people closer to

Christ, to the Son of God whom she had met when they were both on the road to Jerusalem.

Miriam met with John on occasions after he was first exiled. However such meetings were never disclosed so as to keep the Romans at bay. On one occasion, about 70AD, John handed to her his completed version of the life and goodness of Christ. Immediately it was being copied for other centers of Christianity.

Miriam smiled with an incredibly happy expression throughout her reading of the text. Time and time again, John declared his belief in the Son of God. He constantly stressed the Son's relationship with the Father, focused on redemption and forgiveness, identified the importance of sacrifice, and affirmed the role of the Spirit. She noted, at first puzzled, that his gospel on the Feast of the Passover never mentioned the rite involving bread and wine. He chose instead to record Christ's last instruction and His prayer for all people. John's narrative was a universal appeal for peace, redemption and eternal bliss in Christ Jesus.

****

Timothy was Bishop of Ephesus during trying times. Senators controlling affairs in the province lessoned frustrations. However without the leadership of one dynamic presence, ambiguity became more of an anxiety. The influence of the Greeks increased while Rome's dominance was waning. Trade with Thrace, Achaia, Macedonia, Corinth and Germanic territories was expanded. Atropos was again delighted. Greek deities had regained prominence over their Roman counterparts. In 97AD, thirty-two years after he was appointed, Timothy the Bishop of Ephesus was murdered by Greek sympathizers because the Bishop refused to worship Artemis.

John died a few years later - alone. Miriam was not there, having already passed to Eternity. Everyone who spent precious moments beneath the cross sharing Christ's agony did not die a painful death. They lived an eventful life, not free from torment, but always aware of the bliss awaiting them. Their works did not die with them. Miriam's orphans continued to receive care in the hills that surrounded Ephesus, away from any tyranny that ebbed and flowed with an Emperor's propensity for cruelty.

– Ephesus Pure in Heart –

In 313AD, all of their work, sacrifices and efforts were crowned with the Edict of Milan. Christianity flourished as the official religion and philosophy of the Roman Empire. Nero looked on from hell while Atropos was buried in Grecian lore.

More than five hundred years later, Miriam's grave was discovered in those hills. You can never decide your death, but you can always celebrate the life you decide to live.

– Ephesus Pure in Heart –

SOURCES

Anatoloia News	Beads Produced in Anatolia, Ankara Turkey. May 2010
Angelo, Jack	The Healing Wisdom of Mary Magdalene, Bear & Company, 2015. ISBN: 13-9781591431992
Asch, Sholem	The Apostle, Pocket Books, New York. 1943.
Bacon, Melanie	Mary and the Goddess of Ephesus, Create Space Independent Publishing, ISBN: 13-9781450558372
Barclay, William	Letters to the Seven Churches, Westminster John Knox Press, Louisville. 2001 ISBN: 10-0664223869
Banks, E.J.	Sardis, International Standard Bible Encyclopedia, Wm. B. Eerdmans Publishing, Grand Rapids. 1939
Bargman, Dale	Paul's Travels, On Line. 2014
Batchelor, Doug	At Jesus' Feet: The Gospel According to Mary Magdalene, Amazing Facts Publishing. 2000 ISBN: 13-9780828015899

Bible Gateway	All the Women of the Bible: Mary Magdalene, Christianbooks.com. 2015
Bledsoe, Sharon	Mary Magdalene: The Lost Diary, Fair Havens Press. Australia. 2011 ASIN: B006K1PR5Q
Bonechi, Casa	Ephesus, Travel & Holiday Guides, Firenze, Italy. ISBN: 13-9788880295914
Bourgeault, Cynthia	The Meaning of Mary Magdalene, Discovering the Woman at the Heart of Christianity, Shambhala Publications, Boulder, Colorado. 2010 ISBN:13-9781590304952
Bouquet, A.C.	Everyday Life in New Testament Times, B.T.Batsford, London. 1953. ISBN-13: 978-068414833
Breen, A.C.	Acts of the Apostles, Robert Appleton Company, New York. 1907
Brownrigg, Ronald	Who's who in the New Testament, Holt Rinehart, New York. 1971. ISBN 13-9780415260367
Burstein, Dan et al	Secrets of Mary Magdalene, CDS Books, Australia. 2006 ISBN: 10-1593152051
Bunson, Matthew	Encyclopedia of the Roman Empire, Facts on File, New York. 1994 ISBN: 0816045623
Butler, Rev. Alban	Butler's Lives of the Saints, Sarto Books, New York. 1982.
Carrington, Phillip	The Early Christian Church, Cambridge University Press. 1957 ISBN: 13-9780521164616
Carroll, James	Who was Mary Magdalene? Smithsonian Magazine, 2006

Clark, Rev. Rufus	Life Scenes of the Messiah, John J. Jewett & Company, Cleveland, 1855.
Coulson, John	The Saints, Hawthorne Books, New York. 1958.
Devellier Donegan	Roman Empire in the First Century, Devillier Donegan Enterprises, On Line. 2006
Dumper, Michael	Cities of the Middle East, ABC-CLIO, California. 2006 ISBN 13-978156079195
Duruy, Victor	History of Rome and the Roman People, University of Toronto Press.1883
Falkener, Edward	Ephesus and the Temple of Diana, Kessinger Publishing, Montana. 2003 ISBN: 13-9780766178335
Freely, John	The Aegean Coast of Turkey. Milet Publishing, London. 1999 ISBN: 10-139789754130713
Gantz, Timothy	Early Greek Myth: A Guide to Literary and Artistic Sources, Johns Hopkins University Press, 1996 ISBN: 13-9780801853609
Garnsey, Peter	Trade in the Ancient Economy, University of California Press, Berkley. 1983 ISBN 13-9780520048032
George, Margaret	Mary called Magdalene, Penguin Books, New York. 2002 ISBN: 13-9780670030965
Gibbon, Edward	The Decline and Fall of the Roman Empire, Harper & Brothers, New York. 1836
Gilles, John	History of Ancient Greece, Thomas Wardle, New York. 1835

Goldsworthy, Adrian	The Roman Army at War 100BC to AD200, Clarendon Press, Oxford. 1996 ISBN: 10- 0198150903
Hadas, Moses	Stoic Philosophy of Seneca, W.W.Norton Inc., New York. 1981 ISBN: 13-9780393004595
Hamilton, Edith	Mythology, Little, Brown & Co., Boston. 1942 ISBN: 13-9780316341141
Haskins, Susan	Mary Magdalene, Myth and Metaphor, Harcourt Trader Publishers. 1994 ISBN: 13-9780151577651
Haskins, Susan	Mary Magdalene, The Essential History, Vintage Books, London. 2005 ISBN: 13-9781845950040
Henry, William	Mary Magdalene the Illuminator, Adventure Unlimited Press. Kempton, Illinois. 2006 ISBN: 13-9781931882637
Higgs, Liz Curtis	Unveiling Mary Magdalene, Doubleday Religious Plumbing New York. 2004 ISBN: 13-9781400070213
Hionides, Harry	Collins Pocket Greek Dictionary, William Collins & Sons Ltd., London, 1977 ISBN:13-9780008135898
Holy Bible	Benziger Brothers, Inc. New York. 1961
Hooper, Richard	The Crucifixion of Mary Magdalene, Sanctuary Publishing, London, 2008 ISBN: 13-9780974699547
Jirku, Anton	The World of the Bible, Weidenfeld & Nicolson, London. 1967 ASIN: B0000CO3PD
Johnson, Sherman	Early Christianity in Asia, Journal of Biblical Literature. Atlanta. 1958
Just, Rev. Felix SJ	Paul's Associates & Co-Workers, Internet, 2013

Kepler, Thomas	Interpreter's Dictionary of the Bible, Abingdon Press, Nashville, Tennessee. 1962. ISBN: 13-9780687192687
Keskin, Naci	Ephesus, Istanbul, 2000 ISBN: 13-9757559989
Kidd, A.D.	Latin - English Dictionary, Saphrograph Corp., New York. 1969
King, Karen	The Gospel of Mary of Magdala, Polebridge Press, California. 2003 ISBN: 13-9780944344583
Kraybill, Nelson	Imperial Cult and Commerce, Sheffield Academic Press, Sheffield. 1996 ISBN: 13-9781850756163
Kusadasi Guide	Aegean Region, Kusadasi Guide On Line, 2015.
Laale, Hans W.	Ephesus Abbreviated History, West Bow Press, Bloomington, Indiana. 2011 ISBN: 13-978144971619
Lardner, Nathaniel	Works of Nathaniel Lardner, Thomas Hamilton, London. 1815
Lefkowitz, Mary	Women's Life in Greece and Rome, John Hopkins University Press, Baltimore. 1982 ISBN: 0801883091
Mainse, Reynold	Day One Ephesus, Mainse Media Group, On Line. 2012
Margoliouth, J.	Ecclesiastical History of John, Bishop of Ephesus, BiblioBazaar, South Carolina 2009 ISBN: 13-9781110450862
Mathews, Mark	Riches, Poverty and the Faithful, Cambridge University Press, New York. 2013. ISBN: 13-9781107018501
Maydell, Karl	Ephesus Bible Study Commentary, Outskirts Press, Colorado. 2010 ISBN: 13-9781432757809

Meyer, Marvin	The Nag Hammadi Scriptures, Harper One, New York. 2009 ISBN: 13-9780061626005
Mitchell, Stephen.	Anatolia. Oxford University Press, New York. 1995 ISBN: 13-9780198150305
Morrison, Martha	Judaism, Facts on File Inc. New York. 2002. ISBN: 13-9780816047666
Morton, H.V.	Women of the Bible, Dodd Mead, Australia. 1956 ASIN: B0007DS38Q.
National Geographic	Everyday Life in Bible Times, National Geographic Society, Washington. 1967
Onen, U	Ephesus, The Way It Was, Izmir, Turkey. 1985 ASIN: B001MSOR9O
Palmer, Douglas	Great Archeological Discoveries, China, 2005 ISBN: 13-9781592287185
Perowne, Stewart	Roman Mythology, Peter Bedrick Books, New York. 1988.
Plummer, Alfred	Epistles of St. John, Cambridge University Press, Cambridge. 1886. ISBN: 13- 9780521043214
Powell, John	The Mystery: Biography and Destiny of Mary Magdalene, Steiner Books. 2008 ISBN: 13-9781584200581
Rhyman, Joseph	Atlas of the Biblical World, Greenwich House, New York. 1982.
Roberts, Mark Rev.	Reflections on Christ, Church and Culture, Patheos.com, Online. 2007
Salmon, E.T.	A History of the Roman World 30BC to 138AD, Methuen & Company, London. 1968. ISBN:13-9780415045049
Jane Schaberg,	The Resurrection of Mary Magdalene, Continuum International Publishing Group, New York. 2002 ISBN: 10-82641645-4

Schulte, Carl	Mary's House in Ephesus, Tan Books, North Carolina. 2011 ISBN: 13-9780895558701
Smith, William	Dictionary of Greek and Roman Antiquities, Little Brown, Boston. 1859
Smitha, Frank	Macrohistory and World Timeline, Internet. 2003
Snyder, Howard	Radical Renewal, Cambridge University Press, Cambridge. 1961 ISBN: 13-1597523283
Starbird, Margaret	Woman with the Alabaster Jar, Bear & Company, Vermont. 1993 ISBN: 13-9781879181038
Swanson, Gail	The Heart of Love: Mary Magdalene Speaks, Lightning Source. 2000 ISBN: 13-97809774657501
Tacitus, Cornelius	Annals of Imperial Rome. Random House, New York. Reprinted 1942.
Tellbe, Mikael	Christ-Believers in Ephesus, Mohn Siebeck Tubingen, Germany. 2009. ISBN: 13-978316150048
Trebilco, Paul	Early Christians in Ephesus, William Eerdsmans Publishing, Michigan. 2007 ISBN: 13-9780802807694
Trebilco, Paul	Jewish Communities in Asia Minor, Cambridge University Press, Cambridge. 1991 ISBN: 13-9780521401208
Van Tilborg, Sjef	Reading John in Ephesus. E.J. Brill, Netherlands. 1996 ISBN: 10- 9004105301
Weigle, Marta	Spiders and Spinsters: Women and Mythology. Sunstone Press. 2007 ISBN: 13-9780865345874
Wikipedia	Various articles

Willcock, Malcolm	A companion to the Iliad, University of Chicago Press, Chicago. 1976 ISBN: *10*-0226898555.
Youngman, Bernard	The Lands and Peoples of the Living Bible, Hawthorne Books Inc., New York. 1959.
Front Cover:	*A Laminated Terra-Cotta Cross from an excavation site in the Roman Province of Asia. Property of History Alive*

Printed in the United States
By Bookmasters